BELINDA BLAKE AND
THE SNAKE IN THE GRASS

I stroked the glossy top of a nearby rhododendron leaf, glancing around. The carriage house was bordered by a small grassy plot, surrounded by well-kept flowerbeds that backed up to an old stone wall. Although the house secretary had told me I didn't have to weed my flowerbeds, I had an itch to do just that. Flower gardening was a passion I'd developed as a teen in Upstate New York, where I had acres to experiment with color groupings and flowerbed styles. But today I'd have to settle for yanking those nuisance blackberry sprouts the gardeners had missed.

I ducked inside to grab my work gloves, then set about pulling the lemony-green, thorny weeds up from the roots. I had worked my way halfway down the bed when I noticed something tucked into the thick boxwood hedge that ran along the stone wall. The red sole on the heel gave me pause. Could it really be a Louboutin? And only one of them? Maybe some of these nouveau riche youth had wild parties outside and didn't even notice when they lost such an expensive shoe. How very Gatsby.

I snickered. I wouldn't know the difference between a nouveau riche and an established gent in this town. It hadn't taken me long to realize that even though my family was well-respected in Larches Corner, New York, no one cared who I was in Greenwich, Connecticut.

I grabbed for the patent leather heel, but it took only a split second for me to realize it was connected to something else. A tan foot.

And the foot was connected to a sleek, tan leg.

I dropped the heel like it was on fire, then stumbled backward onto the stone patio. I couldn't make sense of what had just happened.

There was a body lying in my flowerbed.

Belinda Blake and

the Snake in the Grass

Heather Day Gilbert

LYRICAL UNDERGROUND
Kensington Publishing Corp.
www.kensingtonbooks.com

To the extent that the image or images on the cover of this book depict a person or persons, such person or persons are merely models, and are not intended to portray any character or characters featured in the book.

LYRICAL UNDERGROUND BOOKS are published by

Kensington Publishing Corp.
119 West 40th Street
New York, NY 10018

Copyright © 2019 by Heather Day Gilbert

All rights reserved. No part of this book may be reproduced in any form or by any means without the prior written consent of the Publisher, excepting brief quotes used in reviews.

All Kensington titles, imprints, and distributed lines are available at special quantity discounts for bulk purchases for sales promotion, premiums, fund-raising, educational, or institutional use.

Special book excerpts or customized printings can also be created to fit specific needs. For details, write or phone the office of the Kensington Sales Manager: Kensington Publishing Corp., 119 West 40th Street, New York, NY 10018. Attn. Sales Department. Phone: 1-800-221-2647.

Lyrical Underground and Lyrical Underground logo Reg. US Pat. & TM Off.

First Electronic Edition: June 2019
ISBN-13: 978-1-5161-0881-7 (ebook)
ISBN-10: 1-5161-0881-7 (ebook)

First Print Edition: June 2019
ISBN-13: 978-1-5161-0884-8
ISBN-10: 1-5161-0884-1

Printed in the United States of America

To my dad, who concocted the original Belinda, Katrina, and Blitz stories to keep us entertained on long car trips. The characters are all grown up now, but I hope they still carry some of the whimsy of your stories with them.

Chapter 1

The first time I saw Stone Carrington the fifth, I had a snake wrapped around my neck.

Now granted, he acted as if it was something he saw every day, a girl with unwanted snakeskin accents in her curly blonde hair.

"Pet-sitting," I explained, trying to extricate myself from the ball python I had agreed to "walk" for his owner. "They're supposedly a relatively mild breed," I continued.

"I should hope so." He dipped his tennis visor in a fake bow. Unfortunately, he had emerged from the tennis courts at the exact moment the snake had started climbing me like a tree. "Stone Carrington. And you are?"

"Belinda Blake." I felt the need to over-explain, one of my persistent habits. "I'm your new tenant. In the carriage house. It's lovely, by the way." The snake had stopped wriggling, so I walked a bit faster toward my small house. Why had I chosen to walk up the main drive for another gape at the Carringtons' mansion?

Stone gave me a once-over as the snake moved again. I was sure my ripped jeans, worn Crocs, and gamer T-shirt didn't impress, but I was yanked from my self-conscious musings as the python slithered over my shoulder and disappeared down my shirt. I launched into the dance of death, jerking about like Elaine from *Seinfeld*.

"Here, let me help," Stone said, making an arguably decent attempt to extricate the wriggling creature from my shirt by wrapping both hands around its tail.

The snake gave a low hiss and slid down further.

"Never mind," I said hastily, pulling my shirt up and throwing modesty to the wind so I could see the snake's beady eyes. "Grab its head! We have to grab it!"

Stone was a bit too hesitant as he obliged, and the snake lunged at him. "It can sense our fear! Just call animal control or something!" I shouted. The snake's patience was probably exhausted and soon he would start nibbling on me.

Stone did as I said, pulling an expensive-looking cell phone from his white shorts, which must've been a bit chilly in November. Still, the shorts managed to show off his naturally tan legs.

The snake continued his horrifying quest to cozy up somewhere on my torso until one of the older gardeners approached us. "Pardon my intrusion, but you are having trouble, no?"

"Yes. Could you help get this thing off me?"

The swarthy-skinned man began to tell a story with his hands. "When I was a boy, I spent many hours playing with snakes. You have to sort of sneak up on them and"—here he grabbed the snake by the head, tugging gently until it loosened its grip on my shoulders—"you grab their neck, like so." He held it aloft, triumphant.

"Thank you, Jacques." Stone slipped his phone back into his pocket and crossed his arms, probably hoping Jacques wouldn't hand him the snake.

"Let's get him back in the cage," I suggested.

"Perfect," Stone said. Relief showed in his aqua eyes.

I led them into my house, which was still full of half-unpacked boxes. I hadn't even unrolled my favorite, albeit threadbare Indian rug. It would add a nice touch to the wide-plank pine floors.

The snake's cage was more like an oversized fish tank and the top was tricky to open, but it didn't take long for Jacques to transfer the willing captive into his preferred bed.

"Thank you so much," I said. "Are you around often?" I wanted to send him a thank you card.

"Most days I am, mademoiselle."

I found Jacques's French accent charming and I dusted off some of my high school French. "*Merci beaucoup* for your help today."

Jacques extended a rough hand and I placed mine in it. He lifted my hand to his lips for a brief kiss. *"Enchanté."* Giving me a wide smile, he strode back to his work.

Stone seemed a bit shell-shocked, watching the snake winding his way into a ball. "You really are a pet-sitter? For snakes?"

I nodded. "And other animals. I try to be flexible—it pulls in a different clientele than your average dog or cat sitter, though they're on my roster, too."

"Greenwich clients?" He pushed his visor up to see me better, which shoved his dark bangs into an artless puff that was adorable.

Although Greenwich, Connecticut, had its share of wealthy pet owners, I'd already built up my business in Manhattan. "So far, my jobs have been in the city, but I do plan to start advertising locally."

Stone nodded seriously. "Word of mouth is likely the best advertisement. I'm happy to put in a good word for you with my friends. Just give me the go-ahead—you can call up to the house and ask for Stone." He paused. "Well, you'll need to ask for Stone the fifth, otherwise they'll connect you with my father."

I maintained a straight face. Stone the fifth. I didn't have to guess what a boon Stone the fifth's word of mouth would likely be. He was doubtless well-connected in Greenwich, with a name like that and a mansion like the one behind my carriage house.

I walked him outside, grinning. "Sure. If nothing else, you can see I'm really hands-on with my clients."

He raised an eyebrow. "How long are you on duty with the snake? And why aren't you watching him at his own home if you're sitting him?"

"I agreed to take him for outings," I muttered.

"Outings?"

"I mentioned I had moved to Greenwich and his owner thought that would be an excellent way for..." I struggled to remember the snake's name. "For *Rasputin* here to enjoy life, with nice long walks in the sunlight and extended sleepovers in Greenwich."

Stone laughed. "You're kidding me."

"No, he really did believe it would be therapeutic for this aging reptile, like a spa day."

"Actually, I meant you're kidding me that someone named his snake after a sadistic maniac like Rasputin."

"Takes all kinds," I said, trying to tamp down a full-on grin.

"Okay, well, I was on my way to a match, but I hope I'll see you around again. You're quite an interesting tenant, Belinda Blake. Enjoy your new home."

I waved. "I'm sure we'll run into each other."

He nodded before loping off in an elegant, tennis player way.

After walking inside and giving Rasputin a major scolding through the Plexiglas, I brewed myself a third cup of coffee before deciding I could use more sunlight. Ever since I'd moved to Greenwich, I'd had a hankering to be outside. It was a nice switch from my previous studio apartment in Manhattan.

I'd tried to maximize my small yard space by setting up a cheap red bistro table on the stone pavers on the back side of the house. It did bring a sort of international flair to my humble new abode. Anticipating a warm cup of coffee and time to wind down from the snake incident, I threw on a lightweight hoodie and walked around to the back patio.

I dusted off the metal chair and sat down. Taking a long drink of creamy coffee, I found my thoughts returning to Stone Carrington the fifth. The initial impressions I got from him were: wealthy but humble, friendly but cautious, and handsome but not obsessed with his looks.

All this added up to one conclusion. Stone was some kind of delicious enigma. It was strangely comforting to run into a wealthy person with nuance.

I stroked the glossy top of a nearby rhododendron leaf, glancing around. The carriage house was bordered by a small grassy plot, surrounded by well-kept flowerbeds that backed up to an old stone wall. Although the house secretary had told me I didn't have to weed my flowerbeds, I had an itch to do just that. Flower gardening was a passion I'd developed as a teen in Upstate New York, where I had acres to experiment with color groupings and flowerbed styles. But today I'd have to settle for yanking those nuisance blackberry sprouts the gardeners had missed.

I ducked inside to grab my work gloves, then set about pulling the lemony-green, thorny weeds up from the roots. I had worked my way halfway down the bed when I noticed something tucked into the thick boxwood hedge that ran along the stone wall. The red sole on the heel gave me pause. Could it really be a Louboutin? And only one of them? Maybe some of these nouveau riche youth had wild parties outside and didn't even notice when they lost such an expensive shoe. How very Gatsby.

I snickered. I wouldn't know the difference between a nouveau riche and an established gent in this town. It hadn't taken me long to realize that even though my family was well-respected in Larches Corner, New York, no one cared who I was in Greenwich, Connecticut.

I grabbed for the patent leather heel, but it took only a split-second for me to realize it was connected to something else. A tan foot.

And the foot was connected to a sleek, tan leg.

I dropped the heel like it was on fire, then stumbled backward onto the stone patio. I couldn't make sense of what had just happened.

There was a body lying in my flowerbed.

Struggling to my feet, I didn't take time to clear my head. I ran, willy-nilly, toward the manor house. I needed to let my wealthy landlords know there was a dead body in my back yard.

Chapter 2

The first person I saw was Jacques, who was driving a lawnmower directly up an incline that made me hold my breath for his safety. He appeared to be chopping and bagging the few leaves that had dared fall onto the sweeping Carrington lawn overnight. The Frenchman seemed to be quite fearless, just what I needed in this unbelievable situation.

I positioned myself directly in his path, waving my arms like a lunatic. The moment he caught sight of me, he geared down.

"There's a dead woman in my flowerbed," I shouted, gesturing to my carriage house.

"A what?" He turned off the mower and walked my way.

"A dead woman. What do we do?" My heart was pounding.

"*Sacré bleu!*" He grabbed my arm. "Who was it?"

"I have no idea. I didn't look at her face. I didn't know the...protocol... for finding a dead body outside my rental house."

Jacques took off his work gloves and shoved them in the pocket of his navy coveralls. "I will tell Mrs. Lewis and she can call the police. Perhaps you should come in with me."

Mrs. Lewis. I had forgotten the name of the house secretary, a thin, older woman with the brisk air of someone who never veered from schedule.

Today might be a bit of a shock for her.

As for me, I felt a little under-terrified. But my ability to distance myself from gruesome situations was a habit I'd perfected as I'd helped my dad with his veterinary procedures. I was able to maintain a relatively decent level of detachment unless something horrible was touching me, like a snake that wrapped its way into my hair and clothing.

Jacques led me around to a flagstone patio behind the mansion. Fountains burbled and birds chirped politely from the hedges. It really was an idyllic place, save for the dead body over in my yard.

We walked onto a fully furnished, covered porch that spanned a considerable length. Jacques pushed open a charming red Dutch door that gave onto a kitchen gleaming with steel and granite. By the time we'd made our way through five or six impeccably decorated sitting rooms, I was thoroughly lost.

Jacques took an abrupt turn into a smaller room where Mrs. Lewis sat at an antique desk, pecking at an ancient computer keyboard.

"There has been an incident," he said.

Jacques struck me as a master of calm and understatement.

I waited as he explained to Mrs. Lewis, who in turn shot several dubious looks my way. Even I had to admit it seemed strange that this body showed up at the exact time I was moving into my rental house.

Without getting my side of the story, Mrs. Lewis first called Security, then the police. Did most families in Greenwich retain their own security forces?

Her task finished, she finally walked over to me, her dainty kitten heels clicking on the dark wood floor. "Thank you so much for bringing this to our attention."

"Of course," I said, rather bemused. She'd chosen an odd turn of phrase under the circumstances. I couldn't think of one good reason I'd keep a dead body a secret.

"I will notify Mr. and Mrs. Carrington and I will let the police know you were the first on the scene. They *did* advise us not to touch anything..." Her voice drifted off as she scrutinized my casual attire. For the second time today, I felt underdressed at my own new home.

"Of course," I repeated. I couldn't seem to come up with anything else to say.

* * * *

Jacques stayed behind to help Mrs. Lewis as she broke the news to the family, so I had to find my own way out of the labyrinth of rooms in the manor house. By the time I got back to my own place, both Security and the police had descended on the crime scene.

I sat at the bistro table and gave my statement while keeping a curious eye on the corpse. When the officer left me to help pull the body out, I was shocked at how young the woman appeared—I had pictured a middle-aged,

Botoxed housewife of Greenwich. This girl couldn't be far from my own age of twenty-six. She wore a chic miniskirt, flowing periwinkle blouse, and long gold necklace.

As they wheeled the gurney past me, I caught a closer glimpse of the body, which hadn't been zipped up yet. The woman was a bottle blonde—easy to spot since I'm a natural blonde. Her highlights were perfectly placed and well-maintained. Not cheap.

It also looked like her face was mottled—more like spotted. Either she'd had some kind of contagious disease, or all the blood vessels had burst. And given the raised red welts around her neck, it seemed pretty clear she must have been strangled.

As they cordoned off the flowerbed with police tape, my attention shifted to the security guard who had pulled up a seat next to me. The man was built like a bear, but his skin had paled and he looked like he was about to be sick.

"Do you want to come inside and get a glass of water?" I offered.

He shook his head, his eyes following the mystery woman as they zipped the body bag and loaded her into an ambulance. There would be no screaming sirens, no flashing lights for her today.

The shaky security guard spoke up. "I need to get back to the house. If you happen to remember anything else, my name's Val."

"Thanks."

As he stood, he nearly knocked the tiny bistro chair over before hurrying toward my driveway. I heard an engine rev, then he ground the small truck into gear and took off down my gravel drive. Maybe he felt more nauseated than he'd let on.

I walked back to my front door, watching to make sure Val made it back okay. But to my surprise, he didn't head to the manor house. Instead, his blue and white security vehicle made a sharp turn and he whipped into a parking space right next to the tennis courts.

* * * *

That night, as I crushed garlic for my penne arrabiata, I put my dad on speakerphone.

"How's the snake?" he asked.

"Doing okay, but he had a kind of rough day, so he's still curled up in his clay flowerpot. I'm going to keep him here tonight, then take him back to the city tomorrow."

"Makes sense. Don't forget to keep his water bowl full to provide a little extra humidity in the tank. You might want to mist the interior once in a while with a water bottle, too. And be sure to flip on that heat mat you told me about. How long have you been watching him?"

"A few days. His owner will be back next weekend, after Thanksgiving."

"So you'll be feeding him." Dad was subtly reminding me that snake food doesn't come neatly packaged in a can.

"I plan to give it a try when I get back to the apartment. Nothing like handling some frozen rats." I shivered, wishing I'd come up with a different career for myself. But this job paid the bills, when combined with my video game review articles. Not to mention, it allowed me to function as my gloriously introverted self. *Most* days.

"Hang on—your mom wants to talk."

I heard the front porch door slam, and I imagined a breeze blowing my way from Larches Corner. Mom was probably sitting in her favorite yellow Adirondack chair, smelling like the juba oil she'd worn since I was small.

My crunchy, organic mom had no greater dream than to get off-grid someday. She actively worked at it, too, much to my dad's dismay. Her latest attempt was to install a composting toilet, which Dad categorically refused to use, for fear the waste would somehow wind up fertilizing our tomato plants.

"Sweet girl," Mom said. "How are you? All settled in?"

Mom's alto voice unleashed the emotions I'd reined in tight throughout the day. I found myself spilling the entire story of the dead woman in the flowerbed, even though I knew what would happen—I'd rouse the Mama Bear.

Sure enough, Mom launched into a diatribe. "What kind of owners let a girl die on their grounds? Do you think they covered it up? Are they strange?"

I intuited her next question before she asked it.

"Should I come down there?" What was insinuated but not spoken was: *"And kick some butt?"*

I had to put on a show of confidence, no matter how fake it was. "No, Mom. I'll be okay. I love the space in this carriage house, compared to that studio I had to share in the city. My career is thriving and the clients are lining up. I need to stick this out."

Mom sighed. I heard ice clinking. She was probably drinking homemade lemonade, or maybe unsweetened iced tea. "Well, honey, you know you're welcome to visit anytime. Are you still coming in for Thanksgiving?"

"I wouldn't miss it. I'll head in next Tuesday." My stomach growled loudly at the sight of the bowl of pasta I'd mixed up. I sprinkled a liberal dose of parmesan on it as I said my goodbye to Mom.

I queued up the next episode of *Burn Notice*, which I had been binge watching for months. I hadn't taken more than three bites when I heard a bang on my front door.

Had someone thrown something at my house? I walked toward the picture window, throwing a glance at the snake on my way. He was lounging on top of his flowerpot, flicking his tongue at me as if I'd invaded his territory.

Another rap sounded and I peered out the window. I had no curtains up yet, so whoever was out there would have an unobstructed view of my face.

Stone Carrington the fifth stood on my step, as yet unaware of my inquisitive stare. He'd changed to pants and a button-down shirt and his hair was perfectly tousled. He would have looked exactly like a model in a Ralph Lauren ad, if it hadn't been for the tight line of his lips and the serious look in his eyes.

Stone Carrington was worried, and I wondered why.

Chapter 3

I held off on opening the door, taking a couple more bites of pasta first. Far be it from me to deprive myself of sustenance just to chit-chat with the rich guy next door.

Or so I told myself.

Wiping at my sauce-spattered mouth with a napkin, I stepped to the heavy wood door. I turned the ancient knob and opened the door, just a crack.

"Could I help you?" I asked curtly.

Stone nodded, angling his face so he could see more of me through the mostly-closed door. "I'd like to talk. Is this a good time?"

There was no really polite way to say it, so I was honest. The penne was delectable, and it wouldn't be warm for long. "I'm actually eating now."

"Oh, I see. Sorry."

My resolve caved when I met his dejected gaze. "It's okay—come on in. I'll finish my supper and we can talk."

Stone stepped in, sliding his leather shoes off just inside the door. His socks were a bright turquoise and purple argyle.

He focused on the snake, which was also focusing on him. "How does one ever get used to a creature like that, I wonder?"

"Beats me. I'm going to have to bathe the thing at some point, too. Not something I'm looking forward to."

I gestured toward my shabby couch, with all the aplomb of one offering a chair in the Oval Office. "Have a seat."

He sat and looked at the TV screen. "Michael Westen and Fiona. I love that show."

I hid my surprise. "I'm nearly on the last season."

"That one was tough to watch at first."

I stood at the kitchen counter, taking a few bites of my now-lukewarm pasta and watching Stone closely. I had a hard time reading him.

"Would you like some coffee? I have decaf," I offered.

"No, thank you." He hesitated, then plunged in. "I need you to tell me all you know about the dead woman. Did you see much?" He wasn't going to play me for a fool. "I figured your security dude told you all about it. I saw him head over to the tennis courts."

He nodded, unfazed by my observation. "He did tell me what he saw. Val tells me everything."

I couldn't offer information I had no business sharing. "Why do you care so much?"

"Because I knew her, and her name will be plastered all over the news soon. I need to understand what happened to her."

He wasn't telling me everything, I was sure. I took a wild stab. "Why do you *need* to understand what happened? Had she been at some kind of party, maybe in your house? She was dressed for a date." I cringed, realizing I'd just divulged more than I'd planned to.

He noticed my irritation. "To answer your question, yes, she was in our house last night. Every Monday night I have a billiards party, inviting over a few close friends to play pool. Margo Fenton was an old family friend, and it wasn't the first time she'd attended." He swallowed. "I guess it will be the last, though. Val recognized her immediately, because she'd acted nervous last night when he opened the gates for her."

I swallowed the pasta I'd forgotten was in my mouth. "So why didn't Val tell the police he recognized her?"

"Val wasn't sure what to do—he's loyal to me. He's been our head of Security for years." He leaned back into the couch, and some of his tension seemed to dissipate. "Don't worry—I'll call the police station when I leave you, fill them in on the details of that night."

"So why are you here again?"

He leaned toward me. "Val wasn't sure how she died, but I'd like to know, so I can help my family prepare for the inevitable media coverage. I thought maybe you'd heard or noticed something when you found her, or maybe when you were talking with the police."

I rinsed my bowl before walking over and dropping onto the opposite end of my blue velour couch. Stone's legs were long and lean and didn't fit neatly under my coffee table, like mine did. Although, truth be told, I usually had my feet propped *on* the coffee table as I played video games.

Pink light filtered through my wide back window. I glanced out at a sunset that had enveloped the flowerbed of doom in a golden light.

Stone's full attention was on me, and it was a hard thing to resist. His bright eyes had an undeniable smolder factor, even though he wasn't flirting.

He possessed a quiet power that wasn't showy and didn't stem from his wealth. It was the power of honesty, I thought. He had been up-front with me, so I would return the courtesy so his family could be prepared for the front-page headlines.

"It looked like she'd been strangled, if you want my non-professional opinion," I said. "She was wearing a long necklace, but I'm not sure if someone could've used that to choke her without breaking it."

Pain wrenched his features, making it obvious he'd truly cared about Margo. "I guess that means nearly anyone who was here last night could've done it."

Luckily, I'd been snake-sitting in Manhattan, so I knew I wouldn't be a suspect. I wondered just how wild Stone's pool-playing parties got. "Was she drunk, do you think?"

He shook his head. "Margo wasn't a heavy drinker. She'd probably only had a couple of beers, although, honestly, I wasn't paying much attention."

He didn't elaborate as to what he'd been paying attention to, but I wondered if it was another woman.

Rasputin rubbed his thick body against the Plexiglas, then slithered back into his flowerpot, as if he had seen enough of humans for one day.

Stone seemed to snap out of his thoughts. "Okay. Thanks for the information. I'm going to call the police station and fill them in on the billiards party. You want me to call you back if they tell me anything new?"

"That would be great. Also, would you mind letting the cops know I won't be around for the next couple of days? I have to take Rasputin back to his place in Manhattan, and I'll be there for a day or two to take care of snake-y things." Things I was trying hard not to think about.

"Sure thing." Stone slid into his shoes. When he placed a hand on my arm, my attention was immediately riveted to his long, slim fingers. "Wait—I have an idea. I'm going into the city tomorrow night. I have a friend there who came over for billiards, and he might have a better idea about what Margo did after the party. Maybe we could meet for a meal, say around six, then we could visit my friend and you could be another set of ears when I ask him some questions?"

He removed his hand and I let myself meet his eyes. The introvert in me screamed that it would be a better use of my time to stay in tomorrow night and play my advanced-release, single player adventure game, but the foodie in me knew that wherever Stone Carrington the fifth decided to dine, it would be worth every penny. Plus, this billiards friend might unwittingly shed more light on Stone, whom I found quite intriguing.

"Just let me know where," I said.

Chapter 4

The snake's cage was far from portable, and once the taxi driver pulled to a complete stop in my driveway the next morning, it was obvious he wasn't going to make allowances for my unusual passenger. Especially since Rasputin was sliding around in plain view, drawing attention to his black-and-gold coils.

The driver vehemently shook his head. "No, miss. I cannot drive with that creature in my car. You leave it in your house, then I will be glad to drive you."

"But I'm taking him to his home. The snake has to come."

He nodded. "I understand."

I breathed a sigh of relief, hauling the cage higher...only to watch the taxi whip away, leaving me stranded.

The Greenwich train station was within walking distance—a *long* walk—but I had no idea what their regulations were about transporting pets. Besides, Rasputin would doubtless cause a mass exodus from any car we chose to sit in. While it was true I'd hired a private car to drive me from Manhattan to Greenwich, I'd kept a blanket over the cage. I should've thought of that before calling for a taxi.

I trudged back to the house, plopping the cage down on the front step and muttering at the snake. "Why couldn't you just stay all curled up in the flowerpot? You're such a show-off." I fumbled with my keys.

"I hope you're not talking to me." Stone's voice drifted my way. He was striding toward me, tennis racket slung over one shoulder.

"Just trying to get back to the city." I twisted the key in the lock. "It turns out that some taxis aren't snake-friendly."

Stone jogged closer. "That's no biggie. Just call up to the house and Mrs. Lewis will send a car. It's no problem—our driver, Red, is ex-Army, so I guarantee he can handle a pet snake."

"Wow! Thanks. I can pay, of course."

"This one's on the house. You can make it up to me by showing up tonight at six. I've booked us a table at The White Peony, on the Upper East Side."

I hid my surprise as he mentioned one of the most raved-about restaurants in the city, although I should've guessed he'd get us in there. I didn't even own the caliber of clothing I'd need to darken The White Peony's door.

I feigned nonchalance. "I'll be there. Now I'd better call Mrs. Lewis."

Stone grinned and sauntered back to his tennis court. Ten minutes later, a black car wheeled around and I settled the snake cage onto the leather seat. It was only as we pulled out that I registered that Stone's appearance was remarkably well-timed. Had he been watching me?

* * * *

Red turned out to be the talkative type, regaling me with war stories as we drove along I-95. By the time he dropped me off at the Upper West Side apartment where the snake lived, my stress levels seemed to have dropped.

Rasputin's not-so-humble abode was in a lovely section of town—an older, ten-story white apartment building with a view of the Hudson River. As I mounted the wide steps to the building, the doorman recognized me and swung the door open with a flourish. I noticed he didn't offer to carry the snake cage, though.

"Mr. Foley still out?" he asked. "Where'd he go this time—Chicago?"

It never ceased to amaze me that tenants trusted doormen with their personal information. When I'd lived with a roomie over on the Lower West Side, we hadn't told anyone about our comings and goings. But we hadn't had doormen.

Doormen functioned as a built-in security system, so of course they needed to know if residents took extended trips or had other people looking in on their animals. I shrugged off my tendency to play my cards close to the vest.

"Yes, Chicago. He's out until next weekend. In the meantime, it'll just be the snake and me."

I walked across the cool marble floors, jostling the snake's heavy cage in the process. I pushed the button on an elevator I'd already discovered moved slower than the Upstate snow melts in March. A woman in red, shiny heels joined me right before the door slid closed, and I was instantly reminded of the Louboutins Margo had worn.

I surveyed the quiet, tall woman whose manicured fingernail tapped at her blingy cell phone. A tiny Chanel bag dangled from a chain on her shoulder, and she wore a fitted blue velvet jacket. Gold jewelry adorned her ears, wrists, fingers, neck, and quite possibly her belly button and toes, as well. She was so engrossed in her compelling phone scrolling, she hadn't even noticed the snake that shifted in the cage at her feet.

Had Margo Fenton been like her, I wondered? Wearing fashionable, but completely uncomfortable shoes to show off her wealth? Keeping her cell handy so she could avoid talking to the plebes on the street?

The woman glanced over at me and I realized she wasn't as young as I'd initially assumed. Although there wasn't a wrinkle on her face, her neck and hands gave away that she was somewhere in her fifties—around my mom's age. I contrasted her fake appearance with my mom's happy crow's feet, her sun-freckled cheeks, and the white hairs dotting her blonde, ponytailed mane.

Funny how unglamorous the glamorous were, up close.

I grabbed the cage as the elevator finally jerked to a halt. The woman's sharp intake of breath told me she'd finally noticed Rasputin, although maybe it was just my Crocs.

As I struggled to unlock the door to 8B, I had to admit that I needed to up my fashion game if I was going to hang out with the likes of Stone Carrington the fifth. And I only knew one person who had any serious fashion sense.

I went inside and called my sister, Katrina.

Chapter 5

Katrina picked up on the first ring. "What's going on? I have a client showing up in five."

My big sister was a psychologist in Albany, and her job oozed importance. After all, she helped people straighten out their lives.

I didn't waste her time. "I need to find a rich-looking outfit to go out to eat at a really swanky place. Where could I find something fast? I'm on the Upper West Side right now."

Katrina rattled off names and addresses of several upscale consignment shops. Her memory was like a steel trap—unlike my own swirly-twirly memories of things that had no relevance whatsoever. And that wasn't the only way Katrina was my direct opposite.

Although we both had curly hair, hers was long and brunette while mine was bobbed and blonde. While my skin was tanned and freckled like Mom's, hers was porcelain white. Katrina was the responsible one, the one my parents called first when major life upheavals occurred. She had made good on her college degree and had added a Master's on top of it.

Meanwhile, I spent my time pet-sitting exotic animals and playing video games.

"What's the big occasion?" she asked.

"There's this guy in the manor house, and he's asked me to dinner." I decided to leave off the bit about the dead body I'd found in my yard.

"Guy in the manor house." She dropped her voice to a near-purr. "Sounds rich. Literally." She groaned. "Oh, sis, I have to go. They're buzzing my next one in. See you at Thanksgiving?"

"Sure thing. I hope you're bringing some of your homemade rolls."

As I hung up, I brushed away any pangs of homesickness so I could focus on the job at hand.

Rasputin's owner, Reginald Foley, had typed up a neat list of bullet points explaining the proper care and feeding of his ball python. My limited internet research had showed that Reginald was quite unusual in his snake handling methods. Most snake owners didn't take their snakes outside or bathe them every other week, but Reginald swore it kept Rasputin happy, and I'd agreed to do those things while he was away.

Which meant today had to be a bath day for the snake. Reginald would make his weekly call tonight, and he wouldn't be happy if Rasputin hadn't gotten squeaky clean yet.

Of course, this *would* fall on a day I had a date with an unbelievably good-looking man who was far above my station in life. A day when I really should shop for an outfit that would make me look like I fit in with the Greenwich socialite crowd. A day when I needed to wash my wayward curls.

Still, it had to be done. Since it was already three in the afternoon, I needed fortification before attempting the snake's bath. I tapped at cabinets until I located the fridge, which had been cleverly disguised with faux-cabinet doors. I pulled out salami, sliced Swiss, Dijon mustard, and pickles, then slapped them on a deli roll on the counter. I felt a bit shady digging around in someone else's kitchen, but Reginald had instructed me to help myself to the food. He had even stocked his fridge and cabinets according to the food preferences I'd specified in my application form.

There were some definite perks to pet-sitting for the wealthy.

I sank onto a pale blue French armchair and watched Rasputin as I ate. Sometimes, the snake's slow movements were more interesting to me than TV. By the time I finished my sandwich, he had draped himself over his water bowl, so I decided to get the bath going. I could probably slip him in and out before he knew what was happening.

I walked down to the oversized bathroom, finding the warm water dispenser Reginald had described. It actually poured non-chlorinated water into the tub at just the right temperature for Rasputin's bath. No muss, no fuss.

I hoped.

After prepping the snake's larger cage so I could slide him right into it after he had freshened up, I returned to his transportable cage to retrieve him for a bath. Predictably, he flipped into a ball, but not before I got my hands around his middle. He seemed fairly calm as we walked down the hall.

In the bathroom, I tried to gently transfer him to the tub, but he refused to let go of me. I leaned in closer and plopped him into the water with a little splash. He froze for a moment, then began darting from one end of the tub to the other using extended, S-shaped movements. I leaned back, hoping he wouldn't slither right up and out onto the pale wood floor, but he seemed to calm down and relax into the water's warmth.

My phone rang, so I dried my hands and slid the phone from my pocket. It was Stone.

"Yes?" I hoped I didn't sound snippy, but I was sort of preoccupied.

"Sorry to bother you again, but I wanted to let you know that I moved our reservation up by an hour, if that's okay? My friend Dietrich said we could swing by tonight, but he's heading out around nine for some party, so we'd have to get down there earlier than I thought."

I swallowed my apprehension, hoping I'd have time to find something to wear. "Sure. No problem."

"Will see you out front, then. Red already knows where to pick you up."

"Okay, thanks." My face flushed as I thought about spending one-on-one time with Stone at a fancy restaurant, and I was glad he couldn't see me.

I hung up and turned to set the phone on the sink. When I spun back around, there was no snake in the tub.

Something dark moved above me, and I snapped my gaze upward. Rasputin had somehow curled himself around the shower rod, and none too loosely. His tongue flicked out once, twice—like a warning. I'd read that snakes used their tongues to test the air temperature, but I still felt threatened.

I adopted the firm tone I'd used when kenneling fractious dogs at my dad's office. "Come on, big guy. You're all done here. Let's get you back in your comfy cage." I didn't want to come at the snake head-on, but there was no way to sneak up on him. Reginald had told me ball pythons rarely bite, but I had my doubts.

With my left hand, I snapped my fingers in front of him, then clamped my right hand over his back. I stopped snapping and grabbed him behind his head, like Jacques had shown me. The snake surprised me by loosening his coils and turning remarkably docile, so I could easily pull him from the shower rod. Once he was securely in-hand, I raced directly up the hall and deposited him in his larger cage. As if relieved, he slid right into his hiding place, which was a large plastic stone with a hole cut out of it. I figured I wouldn't see him until tomorrow, which was more than fine with me.

I took stock of my appearance and glanced at the clock. I had time to shower, but there certainly wouldn't be enough time for a shopping excursion. I ran into the guest room and rummaged wildly in my backpack, finally retrieving a bell-sleeved floral maxi dress from Anthropologie I'd shoved in at the last minute. It looked second-hand, because it was, and it was crumpled. Since I had no idea where Reginald hid his ironing board, I would just hang the dress up in the guest bathroom while I showered and hope for the best.

As for shoes, I'd packed Doc Martens, Converse tennies, and Crocs. There was just no fancying any of those up. The clock was still ticking and I knew it would take a while to tame my curls, so I made a decision.

I would probably be the first chick to ever show up at The White Peony in Doc Martens, but hopefully the maxi dress was long enough to hide them. At the very least, I'd have clean hair.

Chapter 6

When Red's black car pulled up early at four-forty, I had to race to put on my finishing touches. I quick-scrunched molding wax into my curls, added a final coat of mascara, and threw my wallet into a beat-up hobo purse with zero swag factor.

Rasputin was still tucked into the hole in his rock, but when I stepped toward the cage, he poked his head out. Maybe he was hungry, but his feeding day wasn't until tomorrow. Besides, I didn't particularly want to handle a frozen rat at the moment.

He looked at me with a snake-stare that was predictably soulless, but there was some new hint of recognition in those golden eyes. Or maybe I was imagining things.

As I strode out of the apartment, a different doorman stood sentinel at the front entrance. He was younger, maybe my age, and he looked me up and down twice, restoring my hopes that I had achieved some level of attractiveness. I beamed down at Stone, who was waiting for me on the sidewalk.

However, when I hit the next to last step, I tripped on my own lug soles and took a none-too-graceful tumble. Stone lurched forward in a vain attempt to catch me, but predictably, I landed on my hands and knees, directly in front of his soft, caramel color loafers.

He kneeled and extended both hands, carefully helping me to my feet. His brow furrowed in genuine concern. "Are you okay?"

Nodding self-consciously, I pulled my hands from his and gingerly brushed my palms together, to rid them of the dirt from the sidewalk. He produced a clean tissue to aid the process, and my cheeks burned with embarrassment. Although my knees and palms were a little scraped up, the thing that had sustained the most injury was my one remaining sliver of pride. "I'm fine. Just a klutz, that's all."

I hoped against hope he hadn't noticed my Doc Martens, but he motioned to the black boot tips protruding from under my dress. "Nice shoes. I guarantee Dietrich will love them."

I nodded, appreciating Stone's attempt to set me at ease.

Taking my hand, Stone helped me up and led me across the wide sidewalk to the car. Red gave me a generous wink, holding the car door open for me. As Stone walked around to the other door, Red whispered, "You look stunning this evening."

Stone started filling me in the moment I slid into the leather seat next to him. "My mom called Mrs. Fenton today, to offer condolences and to ask when the funeral would be. She said Margo's mom was totally beside herself, sobbing into the phone about how she couldn't believe someone would want to kill her daughter. It was gruesome."

I didn't think "gruesome" was the right word for a mother's grief, but I stayed silent. As I thought about Mrs. Fenton's grief, an unsettled feeling wrapped around me, just like Rasputin's coils.

Stone continued. "I honestly can't fathom it, either. Margo was really good-natured. She was the kind of woman you wanted to hang out with, because she never took things too seriously. She could laugh at herself. You don't find that quality often in the circles I run in."

I figured not.

"Actually, something about you kind of reminds me of her, Belinda." His hand briefly covered my own and he gave a light squeeze, sending an unexpected tingle up my arm. He smiled, effectively lightening the mood. "Why don't we *carpe diem* the heck out of this evening? This place has the best grilled quail I've ever tasted. And it might be old-school, but I also love their cassoulet."

My mouth watered just thinking of the pork-laden dish. Stone was truly a man after my own, bacon-loving heart.

Red deposited us by the entrance of The White Peony with time to spare. The red lacquer door itself was a work of art, and it featured a carved alabaster peony as its focal point.

The hostess showed us to a private dining nook, thus proving my suspicions that Stone Carrington the fifth was both a recognized and valued patron. I situated myself on the velvet L-shaped couch, inhaling the scent of fresh peonies that sat on the marble tabletop. How expensive would peonies be this time of year?

Stone slid in next to me, his thigh bumping my own. All coherent thoughts I might have had were utterly derailed. He smiled and his eyes, blue as Caribbean waters, focused on mine expectantly.

I needed to say something. Anything.

"Posh place," I managed.

"Isn't it? It's my mom's fave." He glanced over the menu, which was entirely in French. "Now let's order something delicious."

* * * *

I had finished my spring salad and polished off the first heavenly bite of cassoulet when Stone circled back around to our information-gathering mission.

"Dietrich Myers is a bit of an odd bird," he said. "He and Margo dated for years when he lived in Greenwich, and honestly, I never understood what she saw in him. He was the stalker type—always watching her every move and acting creepy when she did anything without him. She finally dumped him a few years ago, but I think he's still ticked about it."

"So how do we question him?" I asked.

"Well, he was at my billiards party Monday night, so I figure I'll just mention that and poke around to see if he knows anything."

"What do I do? Isn't he going to wonder why I'm there?"

Stone gave a short laugh. "I came up with a cover story that's guaranteed to soften him up. He's an artist, and artists love to have their egos stroked, right? So I'll introduce you as a painter wannabe and say you've been impressed with his style."

I frowned. "I took oil painting in high school, but I remember next to nothing about it. What kind of art does he do?"

"Weird art. Oils, I think. It's probably abstract, if that's still the correct term." He snorted. "Another perfect description is 'art you'd never willingly hang on your wall'."

Although it was true that I was at my best when flying by the seat of my pants, it would be a stretch to pretend to be an artist. I couldn't even remember the terminology.

Stone seemed to sense my misgivings and his voice deepened, taking on a near-seductive tone. "I promise I'll be right there to change the subject if he gets too inquisitive. Please don't back out on me now, Belinda. I've been looking forward to this evening with you so much." He leaned in close when I didn't respond, his expression cajoling as he covered my hand with his again. "Come on. Seize the day with me."

I had the distinct impression Stone was playing me, but some lonely part of me didn't mind being played.

"I'll do it," I said.

* * * *

Red dropped us off in a hipster section of Brooklyn called Williamsburg. Along Dietrich's street, we passed eclectic diners, indie art galleries, and secondhand boutiques. Dietrich's apartment building was a sleekly repurposed factory that was so large, it basically anchored the street corner.

Dietrich buzzed us in, and we paused in the entry room to gape at the wall-to-wall windows that overlooked the East River. The room gave you the impression you were floating in a spaceship, with its light wood floors, white walls, and spectacular view.

This was not the home of a starving artist, that was for dead sure.

We walked up to the second floor. Stone knocked at a thick metal door with an oversized number one painted on it, and Dietrich swung it open, greeting us with a smile and a waft of citrusy cologne. If I could've conjured up an artist stereotype in my head, he would have ticked every box. Dark goatee, check. Black turtleneck even when it was unusually mild outside, check. Slim cigarette dangling from his lips, check. The only thing he wasn't sporting was a beret.

"Stone, how delightful of you to visit. And who is this charming muse you brought with you?" Even his voice had a hint of international flair.

"Belinda Blake," I answered, before Stone could rush to explain.

Dietrich scrutinized my face, and I felt he was memorizing every detail of it. He must've liked what he saw, because he said, "You remind me of this one Klimt painting—the subject also has blonde hair, and she looks equal parts naive and knowing, like you. There are butterflies and purple and white morning glories climbing up her body." He nodded, as though agreeing with himself. "Striking, just as you are."

"Thank you." I made a mental note to scour the internet for that painting and see if he really meant that as a compliment. Thankfully, I had always been fond of Klimt.

Stone was suddenly staring at me like I had dropped in from outer space.

Dietrich gave Stone a weak slap on the arm, simultaneously taking a deep puff of his cigarette. "Wake up, my good man! Is this the first time you've really *looked* at our Belinda?"

While I appreciated the inclusivity of Dietrich's "our Belinda," it was quite apparent that Stone hadn't actually considered me part of his crowd yet.

Stone cleared his throat. "Very funny. What're you working on now?" He was launching into the "soften Dietrich up" portion of our visit.

As predicted, Dietrich was more than happy to oblige. The artist motioned us over to a semicircle of canvases. He had propped an oversized canvas on an easel, and we turned to take it in.

It only took me a moment to determine that I'd rather *not* take in that particular painting. Hideous excrement colors cavorted with blazing reds and oranges around a curvy, elongated purple blob in the center of the painting. The bottom half had yet to be painted, so I stared at that portion of white canvas and feigned a pensive look.

"And what does this portray?" Stone asked. I had to give him credit because he treated this as an inspirational piece of art. He didn't even crack a grin.

Dietrich frowned and clutched a hand to his chest, as if Stone's question had mortally wounded him. "Don't you see it? I thought of all my paintings, this would be the one you'd feel most deeply."

Stone's brow creased. He rubbed a hand through his bangs. He squinted closer at the painting and must've seen something he recognized in that swirling, psychedelic mess.

"Is this...Margo?"

Dietrich squealed and gave an excited jump. "It is. You must have recognized that the aubergine color represents the evil that overtook her in the end. Now, compare it to this one."

Dietrich gestured to a finished painting on the floor, this one done in more soothing blue and green tones. A squatty, curvy yellow blob seemed to be melting off the side of the canvas. Dietrich began to explain. "This was a nude I painted just last year—also Margo. I couldn't believe she finally agreed to pose for me, but then again, it's been years since our breakup."

He said "breakup" as if it were a mutual thing, but according to Stone, it wasn't. This man was obviously still hung up on Margo Fenton, even if she was dead.

"Speaking of Margo," Stone said, "what happened that night? One minute she was shooting pool, the next she was nowhere to be found—didn't even say goodbye. Do you think she left with the killer?"

Dietrich sank into a white couch shaped like a kidney bean. He gave Stone a long, measured look. "I have asked myself that a thousand times. I don't remember anyone else leaving, do you?"

Stone shook his head. "There were only six of us that night. Sophie and Jet weren't paying attention to anything, wrapped around each other as usual. I figured Frannie'd had an argument with Margo, since she'd plopped into that corner armchair and buried herself in booze. You and I were shooting pool. Lani was the only other person to come in, when she brought our appetizers and refreshed the ice at the bar."

"Lani," Dietrich murmured dreamily. "Your in-house Hawaiian kitchen goddess."

"She's fifty and has kids your age," Stone snapped. "You always romanticize things. Come on, can't you think of anything out of the ordinary that night? I have racked my brain and I sure can't. Or some clue as to who would've wanted to strangle her? Who's she dating now?"

Dietrich bristled. "That's not something she shared with me. I was no longer in her inner circle of friends, I suppose." He glanced at his paintings. "Still, I was content to paint her occasionally and try to capture her beauty for generations to come. Do you think I should send her family a painting, in memoriam? Maybe the one I'm working on now?"

Stone shot me a look and I lowered my head, unable to meet those dancing blue eyes. I was about to lose it. Thank goodness we'd never gotten around to feigning that I had an artistic interest in Dietrich's paintings.

"I think I'd wait until things settle down for the Fentons," Stone managed.

Dietrich nodded vigorously, jumping to his feet. "How about a glass of Prosecco? I have a little left. Adele hasn't picked up my groceries yet, so I regret to say the cupboard's a bit bare."

Stone glanced at his phone. "We should be going. Red just texted that he's pulling in down the block, and you know how parking is around here. By the way, did you know Margo's funeral is going to be tomorrow? The police said they would finish the autopsy today, so the Fentons can get things wrapped up before Thanksgiving. Will you be there?"

Dietrich shrugged. "Probably not. I don't believe in funerals. I mean, why mourn people who were going to die sooner or later anyway? I prefer to celebrate lives through my paintings." He tenderly stroked the edge of the partially-finished painting, then added in an almost reverent tone, "True artwork lives forever."

Unless it's destroyed by floods, fire, or worse. I squashed my cynical thought.

Stone and I said goodbye and slowly walked down the metal stairs from the second floor to the main landing with all the windows. Without speaking, we both stopped to gaze out at the green-gray river. The sun had set and city lights were flickering to life all around us.

"Do you think he's telling the truth?" I finally asked.

"I don't know why he wouldn't," Stone replied, seemingly mesmerized by the water.

"Well, he'd lie if he strangled her," I said.

Stone turned and gave me a thoughtful look. "Do you really think he did? He's shorter than Margo was. And probably not half as strong."

"Hate can fuel people, too."

"I guess so." He linked his arm in mine, leading me to the main door. Out on the well-lit sidewalk, the temperature had dropped, and I gave an inadvertent shiver. Stone noticed, and without a word, he took off his blazer and helped me slide it on. I reveled in its warmth and the masculine scent that lingered in the wool.

He offered me his arm again, and I tucked mine in his. He gave a sigh and said, "I dread going to the funeral."

I didn't offer to accompany him, because I was already booked for a ball python feeding tomorrow. Besides, I hadn't known Margo, save for my discovery of her body in my flowerbed.

"It'll be okay," I said. "Her family will be glad you're there."

But part of me wondered if they would, since Margo probably took her last breath on the Carringtons' estate.

Chapter 7

Katrina called bright and early the next day. "Tell me all about your date with Mister Manor House."

I groaned. "It wasn't really a date. And I didn't have time to go shopping, so I wore that floral maxi dress."

She gave a prolonged *hmm*. "What shoes did you wear with it?"

My sister knew me well.

"Doc Martens," I practically whispered.

Katrina took a few moments to ream me out for my shoe choice, declaring that no matter where I traveled, I should always pack a pair of leather heels. Then she gave me mental whiplash by launching into a lecture about how I needed to keep my pepper spray on me at all times. Apparently Mom had told her that I'd turned up a dead body outside my carriage house.

"You should've *told* me, sis! I've met a few psychopaths in my sessions, and I've seen how they think. I mean, what if this was a serial killer?"

"Thanks for that uplifting thought. I'm sure I'll sleep really well once I get back to my new place."

She huffed. "You really need to be careful, Belinda. I know you've done some dangerous things in your time, like parachuting and mountain climbing and going on that African safari, but this is different."

"Those things were hardly dangerous. And I doubt this is, either. I like my new little house and there's no way I'd consider moving again so soon. Do you know how hard it is to land an old stone carriage house like this, much less in *Greenwich*?"

"Doesn't matter where you live if someone's out to kill you," Katrina said sagely.

"How's Tyler?" I asked, changing the subject. Katrina usually loved talking about her obstetrician husband—either deriding him or extolling him, depending on her mood.

"You would not *believe* the size of the TV he just bought," she started. And I was off the hook, just like that.

* * * *

Rasputin didn't waste any time slithering out to greet me when I walked into the living room, proving without a doubt he was hungry. I went into the kitchen to retrieve the thawed, smelly rat I'd set out the night before.

Using the metal calipers Reginald had showed me, I grabbed the rat's flaccid neck and practically ran toward Rasputin's cage. I opened it and dangled the corpse in front of Rasputin, but he stayed curled in the corner, acting all casual about catching his dinner.

I realized that might be the key—he had to feel like he was *catching* something alive. I wriggled the rat in front of him and he started sliding my way. Rejecting the impulse to drop the rat and slam the cage shut, I wriggled the rodent harder and the next thing I knew, Rasputin had grabbed and flipped it into his golden, squeezing coils, constricting it. I gently tugged the calipers free and shut the cage so he could eat in peace.

There's a first time for everything, my grandma was fond of saying. But I hoped this was the last time my exotic pet-sitting career demanded I handle a floppy, thawed-out rat. Sure, I was partially awed to see a constrictor in action, but the larger part of me was convinced I'd die if Rasputin decided to give my neck a squeeze like that on our next "walk."

I thoroughly cleaned the calipers, countertop, and everything else the rat had touched. Then I retrieved the latest video game I needed to review and popped it in the game system in my room. Reginald had agreed to let me use it while I stayed over, so I could work both jobs at once.

The game was off to a slow start—it was a *Tomb Raider* wannabe, but the main character's storyline was nowhere near as engaging as Lara Croft's. In fact, I didn't care if I ran this animated chick right off the beautifully detailed cliff.

My mind was elsewhere. Had Dietrich been telling the whole truth? Why would Margo have allowed him to paint her nude (although unrecognizable as such), *after* their breakup had occurred? What if they'd gotten back together and they hadn't told anyone yet, and then what if, in a particularly stalkery moment, Dietrich had decided to kill her so her soul could live forever in his paintings or something?

I took a sip of my lime carbonated water. I was letting my imagination run away with me. Dietrich had seemed completely harmless. This wasn't some warped, real-life version of *The Picture of Dorian Gray*. Dietrich had loved Margo for a long time, according to both him and Stone. She'd dumped him. He had been sad, but most likely he hadn't taken a notion to exact revenge several years later.

No, Dietrich didn't fit the strangler persona.

I glanced out the window. It was another sunny November day in Manhattan, so it was probably sunny in Greenwich, too. It seemed almost profane that Margo Fenton would be laid to rest on such a cheery, cloudless day.

I jerked at my controller, now fully engaged in the game as several armored Samurai charged me. At this point in the game, all I had was a long sword, but it would have to do.

For the next two hours, I focused on the game. Then I flipped it off and took copious notes on everything from the main character's clothing to the nearly invisible pixelation on her skin. I evaluated the soundtrack, the likelihood I'd want to replay the game, and I compared it to other games of the same style. I'd taken numerous computer classes in college—mostly for fun—but they had come in handy with my freelance review gig.

When my stomach growled, I realized I was starving. The thought and *smell* of heading into the rat-thawing kitchen revolted me, so I phoned the local deli and ordered a turkey grinder. Tossing my pajamas to the side (a favorite perk of working from home), I threw on a long sleeved T and jeans, socks and Crocs, and headed out.

Fall was the one time Manhattan really tickled my fancy. Some crisp afternoons you could see the moon, smiling down on the city from a brilliant blue sky. It was a reminder that nature existed all around us, even if it felt like most of the Big Apple was manmade. Today I enjoyed some friendly banter with the deli cashier, took my grinder to a bench in the park, and sat under the trees to eat it. Truth be told, I missed home. The leaves had long since fallen there, but the air would hold that unmistakable tang of winter and the clear night skies would be spangled with stars.

My phone rang and I glanced at it. Stone.

I cut the pleasantries. "How was the funeral?"

He groaned. "Gruesome."

Gruesome seemed to be a favorite word of his. "How so?"

"Her parents were a mess. I mean, literally. I think Adam Fenton was wearing his college rugby shirt, and Ava Fenton looked like she hadn't washed her hair in days. I know none of that can be helped—they were grieving—but someone should've stepped in and helped them look a little more presentable for their own daughter's funeral. After today, my mom has determined to help Ava join the land of the living. She's visiting her tomorrow—along with a stylist she booked for the occasion to touch up Ava's roots, which Mom said were atrocious."

"Your mom's a regular saint," I said.

He missed my irony. "She does what she can. Hey, there was one weird thing, though. Frannie Rutherford has been best friends with Margo forever. I knew they'd had a fight of some kind before my last billiards party, but she didn't even show for the funeral today. I would've thought she'd let bygones be bygones at this point, you know?"

"That is odd." Although I appreciated the way he was including me in his ruminations on Margo's death, I wondered why he was sharing this with me. I didn't even know Frannie.

He went on to explain. "Anyway, I called her up and asked if I could swing by tomorrow." He paused, and I felt a knot of trepidation in my gut, almost like I knew what was coming. "Actually, I have a huge favor to ask, Belinda. I sort of asked if *we* could swing by."

"But I don't even know her, Stone," I shook my head, although he couldn't even see me.

"Well, about that." He cleared his throat, and his voice took on that persuasive tone I found myself bending for a little too easily. "She sort of inferred that you were my new girlfriend."

I laughed out loud, not sure whether to be angry, offended, or flattered. A homeless man plopped down beside me and I scooted over to give him space. "So you mean you want me to act like your girlfriend?"

"I wasn't saying that." I thought I could hear a smile behind his words. "You can either act that way or shoot down the notion; whatever you want. I could see how it would be advantageous, though. That way she wouldn't figure out you're tagging along for a covert interrogation mission."

"So that's what we're calling it?" Since our relationship had thus far been platonic, outside the few electrifying touches and glances Stone had given me, I agreed to go with him. "Fine, I'll do it."

"Thanks, Belinda." In a softer voice, he added, "Or should I call you *sweetie*?"

I nearly choked on a bite of sandwich and the homeless man shot me an inquisitive look. I swallowed and tried to play it cool, staring at the leaves rattling on the trees. "You're a funny guy," I deflected, though I couldn't help wondering what it would be like to be Stone's actual love interest.

"Anyway, trust me, I'm great girlfriend material." I gasped, wishing I hadn't let that tidbit pop out of my mouth.

Stone laughed. "I'll just bet you are. Hey, are you heading back to the carriage house anytime soon?"

Relieved at the change in subject, I said, "I do need to get back to my place to type up an article I'm submitting. I'll bring Rasputin along and stick around a little while. He's pretty sedate, now that he just ate a huge rat."

Stone made a fake gagging noise. "That's too much information for me. Anyway, are you going to need a snake-friendly ride? I could send Red to pick you up."

"Actually, I'd love that, if it wasn't too much trouble. I think I'll head back tomorrow, if that works for Red."

"Sounds like a plan. Maybe Red could pick you up around eight in the morning? Then I'll have him swing by your place later, around one, so we can visit Frannie."

I felt lame, accepting free rides from the young laird of the manor, but I told myself I was repaying him by bringing my interviewing prowess to the table. After all, I was helping him uncover someone who'd murdered his friend, right on his property. Besides, he was the generous kind of wealthy guy who probably thought nothing of sending his chauffeur out on pickup errands.

"Sure. I'll be ready."

I hung up and polished off the last few bites of my sandwich. Although I'd considered offering it to the homeless man, he was curled up at the far end of the bench and seemed to be ignoring me.

I dug around in my purse and pulled out a five-dollar bill, which was the grand sum of my cash. "Excuse me," I said, pushing the bill his way. "For you."

As the man roused and grabbed for it, his bleary, alcohol-reddened eyes clamped on mine. He didn't even say thank you, but I hadn't expected it.

That was another huge difference between me and my sister. I was always stopping to give money to the homeless, and she always told me not to. "You know they're just going to waste it on alcohol or drugs, BB," she'd say, using my initials as a pet name to soften me.

I didn't really care how the homeless spent it. All I knew was that I had a little money and they didn't, and I couldn't walk on by and do nothing.

I felt the same way about Margo's death. I'd found her, so it seemed I should go one step further and search for the one who'd viciously strangled her. For her family's sake, and for my own peace of mind as I tried to settle in at the carriage house.

Chapter 8

Rasputin's stomach was clearly distended when I picked him up to switch him to the smaller cage for our trip, so I figured he was still digesting his meal. I was amazed that snakes could go a week or two without food—some even went months during the breeding season, I'd read online.

I doubted poor old Rasputin would be breeding anytime soon. Reginald had mentioned the snake was already twenty-one years old, which was getting up there for a ball python.

He managed to slide into his flowerpot, hiding his head but leaving his tail hanging out. I misted his cage with water to make sure he had some humidity, since the air was dry and chilly this morning. Glancing out my front window, I wasn't surprised to see Red waiting for me—a full fifteen minutes early. I scurried around, making sure things were tidied up, then I grabbed the snake crate and my backpack, locked up, and went to meet Red.

* * * *

Red continued to solidify his easy friendship with me by sharing about some of the undercover ops he'd participated in over the years. By the time we reached the carriage house, I wondered if Red wasn't the *original* Michael Westen.

I unlocked my door, inhaling the homey smell of my cinnamon plug-in freshener. I set Rasputin down and turned on my coffee machine, then headed over to boot up my desktop computer.

My gaze skimmed over the living room, stopping on something white that lay on the floor just behind the front door. I must've stepped right over it when I walked in.

It was an envelope with my name written on it.

I rushed over and started to reach for it, but serious misgivings stopped me. I turned and went to the bathroom, returning with a pair of cleaning gloves. Maybe I was being paranoid, but the image of Margo Fenton's lifeless body lying in the flowerbed right outside my window flashed like a red warning light through my mind. While it was entirely possible this was a welcome note or some other legitimate form of correspondence, there was also the distinct possibility it wasn't.

The outside envelope was addressed to "Belinda" in a blocky print. I retrieved a knife to slit the top, then pulled out the crinkly paper that was shoved inside. This was no welcome note. It read:

If you're smart, you'll let Margo Fenton rest in peace.

My hand trembled as I slid the paper back into the envelope. It wasn't an out-and-out threat, but there was some implied malice accompanying those cryptic words and that carefully disguised block print.

I hesitated. Should I tell Stone, or should I call the cops? Val had asked me to let him know if anything else turned up, but that was before Stone and I became confidants. I might as well tell Stone first, then we could hash out our next step. He would be by soon to pick me up for Frannie's.

* * * *

I wasn't sure what to wear for this afternoon's meeting. Stone had said we'd be visiting Frannie at her parents' home. I really needed to take fashion notes the next time I went into downtown Greenwich. When I'd last visited the Rag and Bone store on Main Street, native shoppers seemed to sport a plethora of crisp white Brooks Brothers shirts, expensive accessories, and straight, blonde hair.

At least my hair could fit in—when I straightened it.

I did happen to be wearing a white shirt, but it was a *Star Wars* T-shirt.

My mom would tell me to embrace myself and to stop trying to be someone I wasn't. That seemed as good a philosophy as any. So instead of changing my shirt, I left it on and upped the quirky ante by pulling on my Doc Martens.

I could almost hear Mom's approval in my head. "Why fit in when you can stand out?" she'd say.

There was a brief knock on my door and I realized Stone and Red were waiting for me. I checked on Rasputin—his tail still drooped out of his flowerpot and he had barely moved. I shoved my bathroom gloves and note into my purse. I could explain on the way to Frannie's.

Stone greeted me at the door and gave me an appreciative glance. "Nice shirt," he said. He seemed very relaxed and a little sloshed, to boot.

"Thanks," I said.

Stone opened my car door, waving me in with a flourish. He leaned in as I sat down. "So how was your Manhattan sleepover with the snake?" He smiled, showing two rows of beautifully aligned teeth.

"Amusing...hey, you know what else was amusing? Giving said snake a bath. You ever tried that, Richie Rich?"

Stone laughed—a deep, pleasant sound—and closed the door.

Red gave a low chuckle from the front seat. I'd gone and done it again—blurted the first thought that popped into my head. I really needed to be a little more circumspect.

Stone opened his door and slid in next to me. He grinned. "So, Belinda, why don't you just say what you *really* think of me?"

I gave an enigmatic smile, because if I did share my current train of thought, I'd have to say how tantalizing Stone smelled—like tobacco and leather.

He slipped lower in his seat, letting his legs sprawl out. We sat in companionable silence.

After a few minutes, Red veered off a road and I could see the sound come into view.

"We're almost there," Stone straightened a bit in the seat. "Let me brief you on Frannie. Her full name is Frances Rutherford, but she never answers to that. Since she knows me, I'll probably lead the conversation as much as possible, but if you want to ask something, go ahead. Just phrase it carefully, because she's a little touchy about any insinuation that she's not pulling her own weight—even though she's not. She's been living with her parents since high school and although she's puttered around with sales jobs, she hasn't stuck with anything more than two months."

A little like Dietrich, living off the parents. I glanced at the man next to me, whose clothing, bearing, and hair screamed *luxe*. Did Stone himself have a job?

My musings were cut short when Red announced, "Here we are." I hadn't even had time to mention my mysterious note, but that would have to wait until our trip home.

I looked up at a sprawling, Tudor-style mansion. It had at least four floors and numerous side gables. It backed right up to the sound, and as soon as I stepped out of the car, I could hear the water gently lapping at the shoreline.

A tall, redheaded sylph in a fluttery dress pranced down the driveway like it was a catwalk. The oversized straw hat she wore dipped over her eyes, so I couldn't make out much of her face.

"Stone, darling. It's simply been too long." She extended a hand, as if he should kiss it.

Instead of obliging, Stone took her hand and gave it an unimpassioned pat. "Frannie, I saw you on Monday."

She shrugged and turned her attention toward me, actually pushing her hat brim up a few inches in order to better scrutinize my appearance.

"And this must be...Brunhilda?" she asked, with a totally straight face.

I couldn't stop myself. I snorted. "Actually, I'm Belinda," I said. "Stone, what on earth did you tell her about me?" I gave his arm a playful squeeze, kicking off our dating farce.

Frannie's eyes slid over to Stone, then back to me. Her condescending manner transformed into an uninhibited, flaming jealousy that matched her vibrant hair.

Frannie Rutherford was not someone to be trifled with, and here we were, trifling with her. I was ready to confess our ruse on the spot, but Stone had picked up the baton and he was charging along with it.

"Belinda just moved here," he said, making it sound like I'd swung into town and picked up my very own Greenwich manor house. "She'll be a great addition to our billiards parties, don't you think?"

Frannie tried to hide her frown. "Of course, darling," she said, her tone flippant, even as her eyes continued to size me up. She slipped an arm through Stone's and turned him away from me. "Come. Let's go have some piña coladas under the cabana." She glanced over her shoulder at me as she power-strode up the drive, practically dragging Stone along with her. "Or are you more of a strawberry daiquiri girl?"

"Virgin strawberry daiquiri for me, please." I didn't care how that made me look. Somebody had to stay sober at this beach party.

Stone shot me a questioning look, but kept silent and let Frannie lead him away. I tagged along on their heels, hoping Stone didn't choose anything too high-powered, since he still seemed a little tipsy from whatever he'd imbibed this morning.

"Of course," Frannie said. As we approached a huge beach cabana, Frannie barked out drink orders to a guy who was conveniently manning the outdoor bar. We settled into cushy lounge chairs and Frannie shoved her hat up a bit more. Then she burst into tears.

"I hated to miss her funeral," she wailed.

Stone seemed mildly impressed by this outburst. I observed Frannie closely, trying to ascertain if those tears were real or manufactured. I decided they were fake, because her nose didn't get the least bit red.

She accepted her piña colada from the cabana guy and took a long drink. Thus fortified, she continued, her voice still slightly tremulous. "I had to go to my cousin's wedding yesterday. Terrible timing, right? But I was a bridesmaid, and you know how that goes." She shot me a commiserative look. "You buy the dress, the shoes, the bag, and the poor bride's counting on you. I had to attend." She was really pouring it on.

"Of course," I murmured. It was obvious to me that she'd concocted a relatively simple lie, one we probably couldn't look into. But why lie? What was she hiding? It had to be something more than guilt over a final fight with Margo.

She rested her manicured hand on Stone's muscled forearm and seemed to slump into her own thoughts, staring out at a small yacht on the blue-gray water.

Stone, too, had turned more reflective than usual, his eyes closed against the brilliant sunlight. I extended my foot and gave his leg a little nudge with the toe of my Doc Martens, a reminder that we'd come for more than just drinks and lies.

His eyes shot open and he sat up straighter. "Frannie, it was obvious you and Margo had argued before billiards night. Do you think that's why she left early?"

Frannie wrapped her fingers more tightly around Stone's arm. "Sure, we'd fought, but so what? We fought all the time. I didn't run her off, if that's what you mean."

"I wasn't saying that," he said. "I just wondered what would make her so upset."

Frannie stayed silent.

Stone took her hand from his arm and held it. I could see her defenses melting. "Is there something you haven't told the police? You know you can trust me, Fran."

Frannie leaned in toward Stone—so close, I thought she was going to kiss him. "We fought about a man," she said.

Chapter 9

Adopting the same serious, dramatic tone as Frannie, Stone repeated, "You fought over a man?"

Frannie demurely pulled her wrap tighter around her arms to fight the chilly breeze coming from the sound. "Margo had started dating someone, but she wouldn't tell me who. All I knew was that he made her cry nearly every night. That was enough for me to hate him."

I had to give Frannie credit there. No one wants her best friend to date a total cad.

She continued. "One time, I even saw some bruising on her wrists and arms, like someone had gripped her too hard. She wouldn't tell me where they were from, but I knew it was him. Whoever he was."

Stone's jaw clenched and I could tell the abuse had hit a nerve with him. "And she didn't even hint at who he could be?"

Once again, Frannie placed her hand on Stone's arm, as if drawing strength from him. "The only thing I managed to figure out was that their relationship had to be kept a secret. I wasn't sure why."

Stone pushed again. "Was it some kind of big shot in Greenwich, do you think?"

Frannie sighed. "All her life, Margo refused to date below her station, you know? She loved her wealth and wasn't about to give it up. So I assumed her mystery man was well off. But it *is* possible that she was heartbroken because she'd fallen for someone who wasn't wealthy." She shot me a challenging look. "In my experience, those mismatched relationships bring nothing but pain."

I returned her glare with a knowing smile. "Of course. When money's your god, everything else is a poor substitute."

Frannie apparently had no idea how to respond to that, and she looked away, her mouth set in a surly line. Stone stared at the water, no longer focused on the conversation. I figured he was running down a mental list of men whose identity Margo would have wanted to protect.

Frannie sucked down another piña colada, and before she could ask for a third, I set my own glass down. It seemed we'd reached the extent of Frannie's insight—or at least what she was willing to share with us.

I took another deep breath of the fresh, salty air, then stood. "Thanks for having us over, Frannie. I'm glad we've met."

All in all, it had been a worthwhile visit. Envious, petty, and flirtatious as Frannie was, she had obviously been deeply loyal to her friend. She'd made up a story about why she'd missed the funeral, but I suspected she really hadn't attended because she wasn't ready to say goodbye.

I grabbed Stone's arm. "Let's go, honey love."

Those words got his attention fast. He roused from his near-stupor and jumped to his feet. "I'll let you know when we do another billiards party, Frannie." He held up a slim palm when she started to protest. "We'll all get together, in honor of Margo. It wouldn't be the same without you."

Frannie teared up. "I'll be there."

She didn't stand as we walked away. When I turned back, fully expecting she'd be shooting daggers at my back with her eyes, I was surprised to see her looking thoughtfully at the sound.

A shadow seemed to pass over me. What if Frannie had some crucial clue as to who the killer was, but she hadn't pieced things together yet?

That would make Frannie the next target.

* * * *

Back in the car, I told Stone my concerns about Frannie's safety.

He listened thoughtfully, but disagreed. "If she knew something, I'm sure she would've told me."

I shook my head. "But what if she doesn't *know* what she knows yet?"

"Then she'll probably tell me first when she figures it out," he said. "I'm not sure if you noticed, but Frannie has a little crush on me."

"I'm not blind," I said.

"She has for years now. But Frannie crushes on lots of guys, so I just try to ignore it."

"That's mighty big of you." I remembered the note in my purse. "There's something else. Frannie might not be the only target."

Stone fell silent as I donned my yellow gloves and unfolded the letter. I held it up for him to read.

"What do you think?" I asked.

"It definitely has a bullying tone," he said. "And whoever wrote it knows you're poking around into Margo's death. You need to give the note to the police."

He fell silent, not saying what we both knew—when I gave the note to the police, they'd probably tell me to stop looking into things.

Tapping Red on the shoulder, Stone said, "Would you mind taking us to that seafood place in Stamford? I'll treat us all."

Red happily obliged and turned at the next corner.

"We'll think better on full stomachs," Stone said.

That is exactly the kind of thing my mom would say. She'd probably approve of Stone Carrington the fifth. But what about my dad? Katrina?

Why was I thinking along these lines?

Frannie wasn't the only girl who was crushing on Stone.

* * * *

After filling up on unbelievably fresh lobster, baked potatoes, and coleslaw, I was ready to collapse into a food coma. I was wiping the last of the butter from my mouth when Stone threw another idea on the table.

"What if we walk this dinner off? I have the perfect place," he said, shooting me a remarkably non-buttery smile.

Red stood from his private table and walked over. "You ready?"

Stone looked at me and waited for an answer.

"Oh, sure. Okay. But I really should get home...and check on the snake," I threw out lamely. My introvert tendencies often caused me to try to put a kibosh on events that involved anyone other than myself. It was a habit I was trying to break, especially when that other person was as friendly and gorgeous as Stone Carrington the fifth.

Red barely hid his smile as he walked out of the restaurant. I knew I was quite the anomaly as far as Stone's regular date "type" went. If I was even *on* a date.

Outside, the air smelled of earthy fall leaves and the evening sky was bathed in shades of periwinkle and magenta. It was heady stuff, and I felt a bit off my game—whatever that was. I looked down at my *Star Wars* shirt and evaluated myself. Geeky gamer girl was my game. Exotic pet sitter who jumped from airplanes or zip lined in her free time, maybe planted a few tulip bulbs on the side.

Red waited in the car as Stone opened my door. I slid in, more than a little self-conscious.

We didn't talk much as Red drove to a location Stone had whispered to him. As Red pulled into a familiar parking lot, I recognized a beach I'd visited the first time I'd looked at apartments in Greenwich.

Red locked the car after Stone let me out, then strode over and sat on a nearby park bench. The way Red positioned himself, pitched forward like he was ready to run to our assistance, made me wonder if he was carrying a gun under that jacket. Red wasn't Security as well as a chauffeur, was he?

I made a mental note to ask Stone about that once we were out of earshot. Besides, it took all my concentration to avoid stepping into various piles of goose droppings on the grassy path to the beach.

Stone's face had taken on a half-blurry look in the falling dusk, like a glitchy game. When he spoke, it was in a subdued tone I hadn't heard him use before. It was really quite captivating.

"Belinda. I have to be honest with you."

"Please do."

He slowed his long stride, so I could keep up more easily. "Margo was a little more than a friend. At least for a while. We dated not long after she broke up with Dietrich. It was just a rebound relationship for her."

We'd reached the sandy shoreline. I considered taking my shoes off, but figured I might accidentally dig my toes into more goose droppings.

"And what was it for you?" I asked quietly.

"It could have been more," he said, and truth charged his answer. "But something happened. She seemed to lose interest. I think she was looking for something other than what I could offer."

Which was pretty near everything, as far as I could tell. What else had Margo wanted?

I turned to the velvet-blue sky, focusing on a burning-bright planet just above the water's horizon. Venus? Jupiter?

"Belinda?" Stone's voice tugged at my drifting thoughts and pulled me back.

"Yes?"

"I'm sorry I wasn't totally clear about my interest in Margo from the start, but I figured you'd suspect me. Then you wouldn't want to help me, and I really needed someone—an outsider—to look at my friends and see the things I couldn't."

I sighed. "I doubt I've done much for you. Right now, I'm just as clueless as I was going into this, except I've managed to garner a hate note from someone who must think I'm on the right trail."

Stone placed a hand on my shoulder, and part of me went completely soft. I hated it and I loved it.

"Don't say that." As if my wishes were controlling him, his long hand slid down and rested on the crook of my arm. "I'm glad you moved in next door."

Part of me screamed that this was too easy—an autumn romance with the son of the manor. Just like in the movies, it couldn't last. We were too different.

Besides, there were so many mixed signals coming from Stone, he could be a drunk referee.

Katrina would tell me to pull myself together, not to get swept away with a seafood dinner, a romantic evening walk on the beach, and the true confessions of a tennis-playing rich boy.

Katrina was a very level-headed brunette.

I was not.

Old-style metal lampposts flickered to life, bathing us in banana colored light. Tilting up on my boots, I wrapped my arms around Stone's neck and kissed his amusedly quirked lips.

His arms came around me, and he most definitely returned the kiss.

I finally pulled away. "Thanks, neighbor," I said.

And I turned and walked back to Red, who had unobtrusively trailed us to the beach. "Time to get back to my snake. Take us home, Red."

Chapter 10

Stone took my hand on the way back, and I relished the feel of our new connection. I hoped I hadn't forced it with my brazen kiss, but some irresistible urgency had driven me to take that chance and throw my feelings out there.

I was glad I had.

Red dropped me off, leaving his car lights trained on my front porch. Aware of my hesitation after receiving the warning note, Stone got out and accompanied me to the door. After I unlocked it, he followed me inside. As I flipped on the lights, Stone canvassed the small house, making sure no one was lurking inside.

"Everything looks clear," he said, returning to my living room. "If someone wanted to break in, it would be tricky. All your windows are locked and the front door has a deadbolt, too. There's just a tiny crack under the weather-stripping, which they must've used to slide the note in."

I nodded. Logically, I knew no one could get in without my knowing about it. But emotionally, I still felt violated that someone had been motivated enough to write me a "back off" note.

"I'm giving the note to the cops tomorrow," I said.

Stone nodded. "Sure. Maybe they can lift some prints." He glanced at Rasputin's cage. "He seems tired."

The ball python had stretched out behind his flower pot and his eyes looked like blue marbles.

I leaned in more closely. "He's starting to shed!" Grabbing the water bottle, I opened the cage and misted it to keep the humidity up.

Stone whistled. "You *are* a dedicated pet-sitter. That looks pretty nasty to me."

I laughed as I closed the cage. "I'm getting used to having him around. I might actually miss him when he has to leave for good."

When I turned back to Stone, his eyes trailed to my lips and lingered there. He cleared his throat. "Thank you for going with me today. I had a wonderful time."

I smiled. "I did, too. I guess we know a little more than we did yesterday."

"That we do." He leaned in and gave me a brief kiss on the cheek. "I'd better go. I'll call you tomorrow." He was restrained and gentlemanly, which I appreciated.

I walked him to the door, gave a brief wave to Red, and turned the locks.

Letting out a bottled-up sigh, I dropped into my comfy couch and touched a finger to my cheek. I needed time to mull over the events of the day, time to come to grips with the shifted dynamics of the relationship Stone and I shared.

Was it even a relationship now? Or just some kind of mutual attraction?

Of course, my mom chose that exact moment to call.

"Hey, Mom," I said.

I could've sworn I used exactly the same tone as I always did, but Mom's unfailing ability to transcend wireless signals, thus beaming herself right into my psyche, kicked in again.

"What's happened? Is everything okay? You sound different," she said.

I obligingly detailed our day for Mom, except the most burning detail of our kiss on the beach.

"Hmm. You like this boy?" she asked.

"Yes. He seems honest."

"Yes, but anyone can *seem* honest, honey. Remember the girl you found in your flowerbed and promise me you'll keep your head screwed on straight. Don't go falling for anyone until that gets sorted out."

I could have taken the time to explain that Stone wasn't a likely suspect, but Mom was certain I was in some kind of danger, and nothing was going to convince her otherwise until Margo's killer was in jail. So I did what I'd always done growing up—I said I'd do it her way. But that was no guarantee I actually would.

"Gotcha."

"Okay, sweetie. Now here's your dad." She passed the phone to Dad, and the conversation moved on to safer topics, like snake shedding.

When I hung up, I felt some of my equilibrium had been restored after that brief taste of home. Because no matter where I traveled, how many "boys" I fell for, or how many careers I pursued, Larches Corner would always be my home.

* * * *

My phone rang around seven, waking me from a nightmare in which Frannie was digging her nails into her neck, trying to untangle a twisted silver necklace that was choking her. When she turned to me in a voiceless scream, she had Margo's face.

I tried to shake off my unease before picking up the phone. Having the ability to remember my dreams wasn't fun when the dreams were nightmares, or when those dreams turned out to be portents of things to come. I'd experienced this inexplicable form of rare epiphany since I was a teen. I would never forget a vivid dream where I'd watched my grandpa get run over with a truck, because the next week, he'd been hospitalized with pneumonia and died. Another memorable example was a dream where I'd struck up a conversation with a friend I hadn't seen since grade school, and the next day, I found out he'd been in a motorcycle accident. Coincidence? I thought not.

"Hello?" I wished I'd had a cup of coffee before engaging in human interaction this morning.

"It's me—Stone. I just found out my mom is having a brunch today for Margo's mom, Ava. Would you want to join us?"

"How soon?" I struggled into a sitting position, phone cupped to my ear.

"Not until eleven. You'd have lots of time to feed the snake or whatever you have to do this morning."

"Sounds good. That'll give me time to write an article I need to finish."

"You've mentioned that you write before—what kinds of articles?" he asked.

"I review video games." I waited for the rote "how nice" reply I generally received.

"What kind? I have some older systems I enjoy playing," he said.

Surprised we had this in common, I chatted about retro games for a while and shared a little more about my freelance work. Then I glanced at the clock and let Stone know I had to get going.

He said, "Sure thing. How about you come to the front door around ten forty-five and I'll show you to the conservatory?"

I didn't even know people still used that word, much less had actual rooms labeled this way. "I'll see you at ten forty-five, in the conservatory, with a lead pipe," I quipped.

"Lead pipe? What do you mean?"

I laughed. "Haven't you ever played *Clue*? It's a board game set in a mansion—you're trying to find a murderer."

"I didn't play anything outside of tennis, golf, and video games when I was growing up," he said. "I didn't have siblings. See, after I was born, Dad had his namesake and heir—Stone the fifth—so there was no need for any other kids."

"That's sad. Those second children can really be fun. Ask me how I know."

He chuckled. "It's tragic, right? I used to beg my parents to adopt. I think Mom was partially swayed, but Dad wasn't the fathering type."

I wanted to delve further into what he meant by that, but someone started talking in the background. "Gotta run. I have to help Mom set things up. I'll see you soon."

I hung up and trudged to the kitchen. Luckily, my favorite *Zork* mug was clean, so I positioned it under the coffee pod maker and whipped up a fresh cup of hazelnut brew. *Zork* was one of the earliest computer games—way back when you typed the instructions and had no pictures to accompany the game play. Of course, I hadn't been old enough to play the text-only versions, but I had played a later video version on a retro gaming site. It had some of the best world-building I'd ever seen.

Talking about video games had been quite the satisfactory start to my morning, but now I needed to actually *play* my adventure game so I could get that article ready. I didn't have to beat the entire game to review it—my reviews weren't for walkthrough sites—but I liked to put in enough hours that I felt I could offer a comprehensive take on the game as a whole.

Rasputin didn't budge as I walked over to flip on the game system. I checked the humidity level in his cage and it was fine. Reginald had said that if the snake started shedding, he wouldn't need food for several days, so I rejoiced that I might be off the hook for handling another thawed rat.

I grabbed my coffee and sipped at it as I played. I was having way too much fun wielding my new mace when I checked the clock—it was already ten-thirty. I screeched and ran to my closet, pulling out one of the only dresses I'd had time to unpack. It was black and a bit dark for a brunch occasion, but at least this time I had the right shoes.

They didn't feel so perfect by the time I rang the front bell at the manor house. My black heels were low—maybe two inches, tops—but walking across that expanse of yard was more tiring than I'd thought.

Mrs. Lewis, the house secretary, opened the door just as I rang the doorbell again. Her look insinuated that I'd thrown all protocol to the wind when I'd decided to press the button a second time.

"Hello, Mrs. Lewis." I straightened the skirt of my dress.

"Miss Blake," she responded. "Mr. Stone had hoped to greet you personally, but something came up. He wanted me to tell you he'd be down shortly. Please follow me to the conservatory."

We turned down several hallways until reaching one that gave onto a wide area that looked like an indoor jungle. As I stepped into the sprawling room, the air morphed into something green and heavy and alive. Sunlight poured in through the glass-paned, arched ceiling. Two women sat at a white wicker table in the center. Just behind them was a small fish pond that was complete with blooming water lilies.

It was a paradise.

One of the women stood and walked toward me. She was very tan and had dark eyes and hair. She was also considerably shorter than I was, and I was five foot four. She wore a white sweater and an emerald-encrusted collar necklace.

She extended her hand. "Belinda? I'm Melissa Carrington. Melly for short—yes, just like in *Gone with the Wind*," she said, forestalling my inevitable observation. "I'm sorry I couldn't meet you before you moved in, but Mrs. Lewis assured me your credit history was good and you seemed like a respectable young woman."

Mrs. Lewis nodded and stalked back out to the hall.

Melly leaned in and grinned. "She's an old stickler, but she's solid gold when it comes to sorting the wheat from the chaff in terms of renters. I trust her completely."

She looked up as Stone strode in, his pace a bit faster than usual. Her son planted a brief kiss on her head then walked right past us, plunging down a stone-lined path of ferns and palms.

"Stone?" Melly called.

"Looking for something." He hadn't slowed down.

She shook her head. "Men." She led me to the table and introduced me to the other woman, who had remained quiet during our conversation. "Belinda, this is Ava Fenton."

The two women couldn't be more different. While Melly was tiny and dark, Ava was tall, wide, and fair. Ava's dark roots had been replaced by vanilla highlights and her nails were a perfectly-painted shade of purple that matched her sheath dress. She looked like some kind of regal snow queen.

"Nice to meet you, Mrs. Fenton," I said.

"Please, call me Ava," she replied.

We took our seats when a woman in an apron came in, carrying delicacies on a silver tray. She began to pour tea for us, but her hand shook as Stone came charging up the opposite path.

Melly cupped her hand and shouted toward her son. "In case you didn't notice, we're starting our brunch."

Stone halted near our table and gestured to our server. "I'll have an English Breakfast with no sugar, Lani. And one of those cranberry scones and some bacon." He gave us an apologetic look. "I just have to take care of something and I'll come right back."

He speed-walked into the hallway.

Finally, Ava spoke. "That's really unlike him."

Melly gave a half-nod, but she focused spearing a piece of cantaloupe on her plate. I had the feeling she'd seen Stone behave this way before, but goodness only knew why.

We fell into an easy conversation that allowed me to gather details on both women. Melly had grown up in a blue-collar family. Her father had been the plumber for the Carringtons, and that's how she'd bumped into Stone the fourth. Apparently, he'd loved how different she looked from the regular Greenwich debutantes, so he'd proposed to her and they'd married young.

Ava didn't share much about herself, but she couldn't stop talking about Margo. Margo was the youngest of three children, and the older two had long since moved away. Margo had meant everything to her mother, it seemed.

"I haven't even been able to go into her room yet, but I know exactly what it will look like in there," Ava said. "Margo was organized about most things, but not her room. I'm sure there are clothes tossed on the bed, the chairs..." Her voice trailed off and her eyes misted up.

Melly clamped a steadying hand over Ava's, like someone determined to keep the dam from breaking with one finger. "Let's not talk about that now, dear. I'm sure your household help could go through things for you, sort them out?"

Ava stiffened. "I can't let just anyone handle her things. Those policemen already forced their way into her room. I'm sure they wrecked it even further. It really needs to be cleaned, in case she left food lying around, but I simply can't do it, Melly."

The policemen had just been doing their job, but it probably felt like an invasion to Ava. I had a sudden brainstorm.

"What if I cleaned it for you? I didn't know Margo, but maybe that would make it easier for you, Ava. I could look for food and straighten up, but not do anything drastic?"

Both women stared at me as if no one had ever offered such a thing before. Finally, Ava gave a slow nod. "I think—yes, I think that would be the best route. Adam would have a fit if leftover food in Margo's room brought in mice. It needs to be done, but I really don't want the help poking around in Margo's business."

I figured most of the help had probably known Margo's comings and goings even better than her parents had, but I didn't mention that. Ava gave me her home number and I plugged it into my cell phone just as a lean older man with disheveled dark hair ambled into the conservatory. He wore gold aviator sunglasses.

Melly gave him a scalding look that could fry eggs, but she didn't say a thing. I was trying to figure out who he was when Ava said, "Hello, Stone."

I did a double-take. This man, who sported jeans, a beat-up polo shirt, and scuffed loafers, was Stone Carrington the fourth? He looked more like the hired help himself.

"Ava," he said, his rugged voice somehow evoking nights by the fire on the frosty moors of Scotland. He nodded at me, then at Melly. "Morning, ladies."

Melly pointed to a chair. "Have a seat. Lani's serving coffee—I figure you could use a cup or five."

That well-aimed zing explained Stone the fourth's indoor sunglasses and rough appearance. He was a drinker, if not a full-blown alcoholic.

Stone the fifth walked in, glaring at his father, who was easing into a seat. "Found what I was looking for," he said. "Curled up around the downstairs toilet. Which means he missed a board meeting this morning."

Ava Fenton looked as uncomfortable as I was. Melly looked bored. It was clear to see that this wasn't her first rodeo.

As Lani returned with fresh coffee, Ava turned to young Stone. "Your friend Belinda offered to clean Margo's room for me. She is a very thoughtful girl."

"Pretty, too," Stone the elder interjected.

Young Stone's eyes darkened and his hands clenched. He forced a smile. "Yes, Belinda's been the best kind of neighbor."

"I'll bet," his father said.

"That's it. Excuse us, ladies," young Stone said. He yanked the back of his father's chair and practically pulled him out of it. As he pushed him toward the hall, he said, "You can eat in your room, Pops."

Melly took a bite of quiche that had probably grown cold. Ava and I followed her lead, grazing on the remainder of our brunch in silence.

Finally, conversation became so stilted, I decided to take my leave so the two friends could discuss Stone the fourth's drunken behavior.

I leaned in. "Thank you so much, Melly and Ava. I had a wonderful brunch. The conservatory is just breath-stopping, and I'd love to visit again sometime. Ava, I'll call to set up a time to clean Margo's room."

Both women murmured polite goodbyes as I stood. As I meandered out of the conservatory, I noted that Mrs. Lewis was nowhere in sight. I could only imagine her disapproval of what had just transpired, but then again, Stone the fourth was her employer, so I was guessing she wouldn't have scolded him or forced him to leave.

As I backtracked through the maze of hallways, I caught sight of Jacques as he descended a curved staircase. The preoccupied Frenchman didn't immediately notice me and I had the distinct impression he had just completed some distasteful job. I was betting it had to do with Stone the elder.

"Hello, Jacques," I called.

The older man turned my way, a smile immediately wreathing his face. "Mademoiselle!" he cried, hurrying down the final steps and taking both my hands in his. "You look like an angel this morning. *Tres belle.* You remind me of my wife in her younger years."

"Thank you." I wondered if I should ask about Stone the fifth, but I decided to let it rest.

"What brings you here today?" He released my hands and took a polite step back.

"I just had brunch with Melly Carrington," I said.

"In the conservatory, *non*? It is her favorite place where she gets away from it all." He made a sweeping gesture, as if the rest of the house were toxic. Maybe it was.

My cheeks reddened as I decided to throw myself on Jacques's good graces, yet again. "I think I've gotten myself lost. Would you mind showing me to the door?"

Jacques offered his arm. "It would be my pleasure to do so."

As we finally stepped out into the fresh fall air, I breathed deeply and said goodbye to Jacques. My heels punched a trail of tiny holes in the lawn as I headed for my carriage house. I was already picturing curling up with fuzzy socks, an Agatha Christie mystery, and a cup of hot chocolate. Given the stressful morning I'd just experienced, I knew I wouldn't venture out of my own yard the rest of the day.

Chapter 11

That afternoon, Stone called me numerous times, but each time I let it go to voicemail. I was drained, and I simply couldn't talk about the disastrous brunch. I disliked conflict—more than once, Katrina had accused me of running from it, and she was right.

In the early evening, after I'd read quite a bit of *Ordeal by Innocence*, I ate half a can of tomato soup and a grilled cheese sandwich. Feeling awash in coziness, I finally picked up the phone and called Stone.

"I'm so sorry," he said. "Sometimes Dad gets out of hand. I swear to you, it's only a once-in-awhile occurrence. Most of the time he is actually quite a respectable gentleman."

A respectable gentleman wouldn't make an appearance when he was completely inebriated, much less voice the rude things Stone's dad had. But Stone the fifth was looking for consolation, so I lied. "Sure. I understand."

"I'm sure you don't, but you're sweet for pretending. Listen, I wanted to tell you that I caught up with Ava Fenton and she mentioned something that struck me as unusual. Turns out, over the past several months, Margo went into town a lot to talk with the Episcopal priest, Father Woods. I wonder if she had something to confess—do Episcopalians even do confessions?"

"Maybe," I said. "But confessions or no confessions, it's worth looking into. Frannie said Margo was seeing someone older, someone she was trying to keep secret. An Episcopal priest would likely fit that bill. Are their priests allowed to get married?"

"Obviously, there are quite a few things we don't know about Episcopalians," Stone said. "I can look them up tonight and get a little background. How should we approach this? Tomorrow's Sunday, you know. Should we just visit the service and then casually ask him some questions? Invite him out for a meal?"

I took a moment to think. "We should probably go right after the service, when we can catch him. Do we need a cover, do you think? Like we're looking for marriage counseling?"

"Probably wouldn't make sense, since we're not Episcopal. I'm kind of favoring a straightforward approach on this one—maybe knock him off guard? We can ask him if he knew Margo and if he lies, we'll know he's hiding something. If he says yes, maybe he'll explain why she was seeing him."

I stirred hot chocolate powder into a mug of hot water. It was a Christmas mug, but by jolly, I was ready for the holidays. "Sounds good."

We both hesitated. I wondered if he was thinking about the same thing I was—our kiss on the beach. I wouldn't apologize for taking the initiative—quite the contrary. I wanted another kiss. But it had been too soon, and in the cold light of day, I had begun to see that. I wasn't really ready for a relationship with someone I barely knew.

"About last night—" I started.

"It was fantastic." His voice was warm.

"I agree." I couldn't deny the heat on that kiss. But Stone's dad's behavior had thrown me for a loop. I didn't really know much about his family.

Silence fell again. Finally, Stone said, "Okay, so I'll find out when the service is tomorrow and text you what time we'll pick you up. Will that work?"

"Sure."

When I hung up, I sprinkled cinnamon on my hot chocolate, then walked over to Rasputin's cage. He'd been pretty quiet today. When he did move, he tended to bump into things due to his filmy eyes. It was going to be pretty epic if I could watch him shed his entire skin. I checked the thermometer, then gave his cage another light misting.

After checking in with Reginald, who sounded like he was having a horrible time with his family in Chicago, I called Katrina. She'd want an update on whether the police had caught Margo's killer. So far, I had no idea how close they were to nailing a murderer, but I guessed they were probably talking to some of the same people we were.

It was only after I hit "call" for Katrina's cell that I realized the police station had likely closed and I'd forgotten to drop off my anonymous note. And tomorrow was Sunday and it probably wouldn't be open then, either, since it was such a small precinct. I'd have to drop in Monday.

Sometimes one forgot things when one was flying by the seat of one's pants.

* * * *

The next morning, I was glad I could chill at home a little before we had to visit the Episcopal church. After taking a long shower, I read over my emails. My magazine editor was pleased with my article. He tried once again to persuade me to start my own Twitch stream, where I could share my gaming online. It was something I'd toyed with, but it would take lots of dedicated time to build up a following, and right now I was focusing on growing my pet-sitting business.

Mom had left a voicemail asking me to bring coffee and bagels for Thanksgiving, so I made a mental note to work that into my schedule. Mom never asked me to bake, and with good reason. I was a notorious bread-burner. Meanwhile, I had no doubt Katrina would bring a stash of her delectable yeast rolls.

I glanced out the back window. Frost coated the flowerbed, giving it an ethereal air that seemed to wash away any lingering taint from Margo's dead body. I pulled on a warm sweater and straight-leg pants and boots. I'd have to dig out more warm clothes before my trip to my parents', since it would be considerably colder up there.

A light knock sounded on the door and I grabbed my purse and said goodbye to Rasputin. Stone looked a little distracted, but he greeted me with a smile.

Red stayed put as Stone opened my car door. When I slid into the seat, which was starting to feel like my home away from home, Stone started talking.

"Episcopal priests can marry," he said. "We need to figure out if this Father Woods is already married—that would explain why Margo felt she couldn't even tell Frannie about the relationship, if they had one."

I nodded. "Leave that to me."

It didn't take us long to reach the quaint church right near the center of town. Red dropped us off, and we crunched up the leafy sidewalk to the quaint stone church with red doors. The morning church crowd seemed to have dispersed, so we walked into the empty entryway. Stone opened a couple of doors in his search for Father Woods's office, but they only led to a restroom and broom closet.

We walked into the main sanctuary and a man I guessed to be in his forties approached us, apparently on his way out. He tilted his blond head and raised an eyebrow. "Could I help you?"

"We're looking for Father Woods," Stone said.

"You're looking at him, but please call me Father Jesse." The enthusiastic man beamed. "What can I help you with this fine Sunday?"

I couldn't hide my shock that Father Jesse looked like he'd stepped out of a Tommy Hilfiger ad. He wasn't wearing a priestly garb, just chinos and a button-down shirt. He seemed preppy, perky, and perpetually undaunted. He was one of those men who'd aged well and probably looked better in his forties than he did in his twenties.

Stone, who wasn't above improvising a plausible story, jumped in. "Ava Fenton is a family friend, and she told me her daughter Margo had been visiting your church the past few months. As you probably heard, Margo died recently, and Ava's grief has been crippling. I wondered if you would ever stop by at the Fentons', maybe offer some comforting words?"

Father Jesse seemed to struggle to find the right answer. For a moment, I was sure he was going to lie and say he'd never seen Margo before. Truthfulness seemed to win out.

"Of course, I would be happy to visit them. Yes, Margo had stopped by a few times for counseling." He didn't elaborate.

I felt a strange urge to prod this handsome man of the cloth. "Do you make a practice of counseling single women one-on-one, Father Jesse? If so, I'm assuming you're married?"

His shiny persona faltered for a split second and he gave me a haughty look that would make even Frannie wither. A priest with attitude. Who knew?

"I'm not married, but I assure you my secretary is always around when I counsel at the church."

"And when you're not at church?" I couldn't stop myself. My imagination had taken a fast slide to the dark side and all I could picture was this priest, alone with Margo. It was dubious that he wouldn't have been tempted by her youth and beauty, not to mention her family money.

Stone gave an audible gasp, but I stood my ground. Father Jesse hadn't convinced me he wasn't involved.

The priest extended a hand and ushered us out. "Much as I'd like to answer your questions, I'm afraid I can't do that. Margo confided in me because she trusted me. I can't betray her trust, even in death."

"We understand." Stone went ahead of me down the steps.

I lingered just inside the church, because I didn't like being herded around like a sheep. I wasn't a sheep, and something told me Father Jesse wasn't the trustworthy shepherd he pretended to be.

The priest stopped short, one hand on the red door. He didn't smile anymore.

I couldn't think of an adequate parting blow, so I casually grabbed the door from the good father's hand and shut it firmly behind me.

I made my way to Stone, who stood at the bottom of the steps, his eyebrows raised.

"You're kind of savage, aren't you, Belinda Blake?"

"Just a little." I kicked at a swirl of yellow leaves that had temporarily settled on the sidewalk. "I don't like him."

"You have something against religion in general?"

"No way. But I can smell fakes, and Father Jesse reeks."

Red stood by the car. He gave me a solid half-grin and opened the door. Stone had lingered directly behind me, so I slid all the way across the leather seat to make room for him.

Stone dropped into his seat and continued. "Smelling fakes is helpful. But don't you think Frannie reeked, too?"

I shook my head. "Nope. She's a total drama queen, of course. And she lied about some things, but I don't think she was pretending to be someone she wasn't."

He shrugged. "This thing is just too complex. I doubt we're going to uncover any dastardly secrets that the police can't figure out on their own." His gaze shifted out the window as we passed a car dealership with a deep crimson Lamborghini on display. It hit me—did Stone even have a car? Why did we travel everywhere with Red?

I looked at Stone's striking profile. He might as well have been sculpted by Michelangelo with that perfect Greek nose and angled jaw line. His dark hair had been freshly trimmed, the ends curling just above his collar, showing off a smooth, tan neck. But who was this man, really? What did he like, besides tennis and billiards?

I needed to get to know him better, outside our homicide investigation mission. I leaned toward him, tapping his arm. He broke out of his Lamborghini reverie and turned those striking eyes my way.

"Stone...would you like to come over for a meal sometime?"

He smiled. "Sure. What are your plans this week? Traveling for Thanksgiving?"

"I'm heading home to Upstate New York on Tuesday. My dad's picking me up."

"So that's where you're from. I guessed you weren't a city girl."

I wasn't quite sure how to take that comment, so I brushed past it. "What about tomorrow night? I have a pecan-crusted salmon recipe that even my picky brother-in-law eats."

He seemed to waver. "It's the first Monday since Margo's death, but I wasn't planning on having a billiards party anyway. It would be great to take my mind off things." His voice grew more decisive. "You know what, sure, I'd love to have dinner with you."

I hadn't thought of it being the one-week anniversary of Margo's death. I shuddered. We'd be dining very close to the flowerbed where her body had been found, so it might not be the most conducive situation to take our minds off the tragic event.

But Stone's captivating smile convinced me. We would have a good meal tomorrow night, and we wouldn't talk about Margo, if I could help it.

Chapter 12

I woke with the sun on Monday morning, anxious to get going on housecleaning and meal prep for our dinner. As I padded out to make coffee, I stopped short next to Rasputin's cage.

A long snakeskin was draped over his flowerpot, where he must have scraped it off. I didn't really care to touch it, but Reginald had said it had to be disposed of, so I lifted the lid and grabbed it with the pincers. I gave Rasputin fresh water and he slithered toward it, moving much faster today.

I felt the absurd, momentary urge to pet the beautiful gold and blue-black pattern on his back, but I tamped it down. I'd seen online that snakes aren't really pets; they're hobbies.

But Reginald surely treated his snake like a pet.

I shook my head, walking over to write a list of foods I'd need for this evening. Excitement filled me as I anticipated an evening with Stone, then tomorrow's car trip home with my dad. Getting a chance to have Dad's undivided attention for a few hours would be a delight. Though Dad was far more logical than I was, he seemed to understand my need to be on my own and he was always a font of information concerning any new venture I attempted.

My cell phone rang as I took my first invigorating sip of coffee, and I stared, disbelieving, at the caller ID.

Frances Rutherford.

How on earth did she get this number? And why would she have any reason to call me?

Hesitantly, I picked up. "Hello?"

"Matilda. This is Frannie. I met you the other day."

"It's *Belinda*. And yes, I remember you."

"Good. Listen, Stone gave me your number. He said you're going to be cleaning Margo's room sometime."

I'd actually forgotten about that. It was something I should really do today, before my three-day trip to Larches Corner.

"Yes, I am."

Her snooty tone intensified. "I can't imagine why Ava didn't ask *me* to do that. Margo and I were best friends, after all. But regardless, I thought of something."

"Yes?" It was hard to get a word in edgewise with Frannie.

"I remember when we were younger, Margo had this place where she'd hide things from her parents. Cigarettes, fake IDs—don't ask. Anyway, she had a secret drawer in her grandpa's old desk. It's dark wood and so heavy it can hardly be moved. It's been sitting in her room for years."

I was amazed. Frannie was actually being of some help in our unauthorized investigation.

"Okay. So where's the drawer?"

She elaborated on its location and the tricky method of opening it. She bellyached some more about how she hadn't been chosen to clean the room, but I assured her it was only because she had been so close to Margo. She seemed mollified.

"Thanks. I'll keep thinking about things. I feel like there's something I'm missing, something Margo told me."

"Just let us know if you remember," I said. "And Frannie, be careful."

* * * *

I didn't want to spend half my day walking to Whole Foods, then lugging groceries back, so I called a car service. In typical form, I hadn't thought out the logistics before I moved from Manhattan to Greenwich. So far, I'd relied on walking, hiring cars, or on Red, but I couldn't keep imposing on the Carringtons' hospitality. And taking taxis or private cars would get expensive fast.

I needed to buy a car.

I made a mental note to check around used car dealerships once I got to my parents'. Vehicles would be cheaper up there, and I probably had enough savings to pick up something that wasn't too junky.

As I waited for the hired car to arrive, I called Ava Fenton's home. I was surprised when Ava herself picked up the phone. I was expecting a house secretary like Mrs. Lewis.

"Belinda. So good to hear from you. I hope you're calling about coming over?"

"I am. I'm going to visit today around noon, if that's okay? I only have about an hour to spare, and I'm heading out of town tomorrow, but if I can't get the job done, I'll drop in after Thanksgiving, too."

"That sounds perfect. Granted, it's a large room, and she could be terribly slovenly, but I know a capable girl like yourself could make headway in no time."

I savored that "capable" remark. In fact, I wished I could have Ava write it down, like a badge of approval from the Greenwich elite, so I could show it to Katrina. Yes, I did have my act together. Somewhat.

The car arrived and I said goodbye to Ava. I opened my purse to drop my keys in, then noticed I still had the anonymous note inside. I decided to make a stop at the police station first.

The car driver seemed a bit wary once I told him where I was heading, but he shrugged and dropped me off just outside the police station, assuring me he'd park and wait for my return. When I stepped out, I was surprised at the impressive size of the modern, curving police building that shared space with the fire department. I had assumed Greenwich would have a small-town police force, similar to Mayberry or the one I grew up with. Apparently Greenwich was more populous than it seemed, although I couldn't imagine it was a hotbed of crime, since all those mansions were likely protected by top-of-the-line security systems.

The woman at the desk didn't seem fazed by my awkward explanation of why I was there, and she asked me to have a seat while she called in the lead detective on Margo's case. I grabbed a magazine to cover my surprise that Margo's case even *had* a lead detective on it and not just local beat cops. Greenwich might have felt like a small town, but its police setup reminded me that it wasn't.

It didn't take long for the lead detective to stride out. He was probably in his late fifties, had close-cropped hair, and was built like a cage fighter. He extended a hand and gave mine a firm and slightly painful shake.

"Miss...Blake, was it? I'm Detective Hugh Watson. Jean said you had something for me. Why don't you step back to my office?"

I refrained from cracking a joke about his last name, feeling slightly intimidated by the entire experience. But since I was an avid fan of the *Sherlock* TV series, saying "Detective Watson" was going to be amusing.

He motioned me into a chair and dropped into one behind his desk. "What do you have for us, Miss Blake?"

"Please, call me Belinda," I said. "I'm the tenant at the carriage house on the Carrington property, and I was the one to find Margo Fenton's body in the flowerbed."

He nodded. "I read your statement in the files. Seemed pretty cut and dried how you stumbled onto her. That must've been a shock."

"Yes, sir, it was." I opened my purse and motioned to the note inside. "Just a couple of days ago, someone slid this note under my door. It says, 'If you're smart, you'll let Margo Fenton rest in peace' in a block print."

His light brown eyebrows raised. "And what do you think that means?"

I took a straightforward approach. "I've been poking around a little into Margo's death—I mean she must've died right outside my carriage house, and I feel so sorry about that, even though I just recently moved in and I was in Manhattan that night." I was rambling, so I paused and gathered my thoughts. "Basically, I think someone figured out I was looking into things and they were trying to scare me off."

"So to clarify, you've been asking questions of suspects in an open homicide case?"

I blushed, feeling like a naughty child. "Yes."

He leaned forward, his arm muscles straining against the fabric of his sleeves. All traces of amusement had vanished from his face. "I would urge you not to do that. Especially alone."

The detective had assumed I was investigating alone, and to protect Stone, I didn't correct him. Chances were, Stone the fifth was already on their suspect list, and I didn't want to draw attention to him by admitting we'd been tag-teaming this covert quest for a killer.

"Okay." I tried to inject the word with conviction.

He gave a brief nod and punched a button, asking someone from Forensics to come and take the note.

"We'll get to the bottom of this. If there are any stray prints on your note, we'll find them. But right now, I'm more interested in knowing what you make of the Carrington bunch."

Three people in a family didn't really make a bunch, but I assumed he was lumping all the house staff in, too.

Should I tell him Stone the fourth might be an alcoholic? Again, I was driven by a need to protect my landlords, who had, with the exclusion of Stone the fourth, been quite good to me. "They seem like a normal family," I hedged.

As the Forensics specialist extracted the note from my purse, Detective Watson grinned. "Belinda, I grew up in the mountains of West Virginia. We had this man in town, Bubba Craig. He was the type who'd call a black sheep white—lie right to your face. Every time someone in town fibbed, we'd say he was 'pulling a Bubba.'" His dark eyes softened and his accent intensified. "You pullin' a Bubba on me?"

There was no way I was going to lie to the detective outright. I cleared my throat. "The only thing I noticed was that Mr. Carrington—Stone the fourth—seemed to have a problem with alcohol."

"You don't say." He tapped a finger on his desk. "Nothing's popped up in the system for him. Now the son...that's a different story."

My eyes widened, and Detective Watson noticed. "Charmed you, did he? I figured as much. The boy gets picked up for OUI and it doesn't slow him down a bit."

"OUI?" I asked.

"Operating Under the Influence. Yes, we say it differently here." He peered into my face. "You been riding around with him?"

"No. I mean, he hasn't been driving any."

He chuckled. "And I can guess why. See, he recently had his license restored, but he has to use an Ignition Interlock Device—an IID. It's like a portable Breathalyzer in your car, and if you've been drinking, the car won't start. I'm guessing that breathing into an IID in front of a date isn't the most seductive technique for our man-about-town, Stone the fifth."

I stared at my purse, unable to look the detective in the eye. Was Stone really the player Detective Watson was describing?

And why hadn't he told me about his OUI?

Guess I'd have some interesting conversation starters for our meal tonight.

Chapter 13

Once I got back to the carriage house, I rushed inside and unloaded my groceries, my mind still reeling from the revelation about Stone. Hoping my visit to Ava's would clear my head, I grabbed my cleaning supply basket, then returned to the waiting car. This jaunt around town was going to cost me, but Reginald had paid me up front, so I had a little income to work with.

I called Ava and got her address, which I repeated to the driver. He seemed duly impressed by the street name.

"You are a house cleaner?" he asked, obviously referring to my cleaning supplies.

"Not professionally, no. I'm actually a pet-sitter. For exotic pets," I added.

"What does this mean, exotic pets?"

"Animals that aren't your usual pets. Things like snakes."

"Crocodiles?" A smile toyed at his lips.

"I don't know if I'd go that far," I said. But I wondered...would I? I hoped no one in Greenwich or Manhattan had crocodiles. Surely that was more of a Southern hobby?

The driver became distracted, peering at house numbers. He pulled to an abrupt stop by a gate with the number seven on it, and someone buzzed us in. We pulled up the circular drive, coming to a stop in front of a Georgian-style brick mansion.

I walked up and rang the bell, and Ava answered it, which made me wonder if the Fentons even had a house secretary. Melly had mentioned Ava's "help," so I knew she must have someone working under her. But maybe Ava was the one who handled all the daily household business. And why shouldn't she? I would think it gave her something to do.

The interior was all whites and creams and pale marble. Frankly, I found it a bit boring. The word "McMansion" sprang to mind. Greenwich seemed to be full of lovely houses with historically accurate details, but because of their gargantuan size, it was painfully obvious they were modern. Interiors were chock-full of the finest trappings, but were so tasteful they were bland. I preferred a smaller, older house loaded with character.

Ava seemed chatty this morning, perhaps excited that Margo's room would soon be food-free, so she wouldn't have to worry about a rodent invasion. As we walked upstairs, I felt comfortable enough to broach the question that had been weighing on my mind.

"I have to confess, I was shocked at Mr. Carrington's behavior at our brunch," I said. "Do you think he's an alcoholic?"

Ava remained silent, but her wide shoulders gave a nearly imperceptible drop. When she finally spoke, I was surprised at the smoldering anger in her tone.

"Melly deserves better," she said. "Sure, the Carringtons have been wealthy for years, but Stone the fourth hasn't been careful about building on his father's success. The smart thing to do would be for him to step aside and let Melly replace him as manager of his company. That woman has a head full of common sense."

She fell silent, almost reverent as we approached an eggplant purple door that had to be Margo's. It seemed to be the only spot of color on this floor. Stretching out a hand, Ava placed her palm on the door, as if sensing the presence of the daughter who once occupied it.

"I assume you have everything you need to clean?" she asked. A rogue tear spilled from her eye and bounced onto her blouse, but she didn't seem to notice. I could tell from her brusque manner that she was eager to have me get to work.

"Yes, I do. I will find every stray crumb," I promised.

She nodded and headed back toward the stairs. It was obvious she still hadn't allowed herself to look in Margo's room.

Taking a deep breath, I turned the ivory knob and opened the door.

What greeted me was so unexpected, it took me a while to take it all in.

Margo's room was a cacophony of rich colors, from purple to greens to rusts. Personality oozed from every decor choice, from her sheepskin rug to an Indian dresser that boasted multicolored drawers. Her wooden bed was canopied with sheer, tasseled drapes that had strings of lights wrapped around them. I plugged the lights in to see the full effect, and it was inviting.

As a matter of fact, I had the feeling Margo and I weren't too different in our tastes, which could aptly be described as "Pier One bohemian."

The old desk wasn't hard to locate, since it was covered in candles and an impressive collection of large rocks in various colors. I suspected they were uncut gemstones, and I thought I could pick out aquamarine, opal, and tourmaline.

Restraining my urge to handle the dazzling stones, I felt around for the secret drawer. Sure enough, it was tucked into the side, just where Frannie had said it would be. I located the twisting piece she'd described and tried turning it three times to the left, but it didn't work. Maybe it was jammed.

Glancing behind me, even though there wasn't a chance Ava was coming in to check on my progress, I did the three-turn move once again, only this time more gently. On the third turn, the drawer clicked open and I slid it out.

The flat drawer only had room for something small. And what I found myself staring at was indeed a small thing, but it had huge implications.

It was a pregnancy test stick, and a pink plus sign stared up at me.

* * * *

In a daze, I launched into my cleaning efforts, trying not to think about the pregnancy stick I'd left sitting in the open drawer. I went through a huge pile of clothes Margo had tossed onto the floor of her walk-in closet. Then I gathered up the pizza box she'd left in her bathroom (her *bathroom*?), along with several half-drunk glasses that littered her dressers.

I knew I was going to have to tell Detective Watson about the pregnancy test. I should probably pack it up in a bag for him. But I wondered if I should tell Ava. It did seem only fair—my mom would have wanted to know if it had been me.

The pregnancy added a whole new angle to everything. Because Margo hadn't seemed to be showing at all, it was entirely possible that the coroner hadn't caught hints of a very early pregnancy. Even with a thorough autopsy, things could slip through the cracks, and the focus had probably been on her neck and hands in the hunt for incriminating evidence. I suspected her autopsy was also expedited out of respect for the Fentons, so they could have a funeral before Thanksgiving week.

But even though Margo had been buried quickly, Thanksgiving would probably be charged with nothing but grief for the Fentons for years to come. I hated to add to it by revealing that their daughter was pregnant when she died. The Fentons had lost not only a daughter, but a grandchild that night.

My phone rang in the midst of my ponderings, and I wasn't surprised to see it was Stone.

"How's it going?" he asked.

"It's going well. I'm actually cleaning Margo's room right now."

"You are? Did you turn up anything interesting?"

I didn't even hesitate to answer. Something told me to protect Margo's secret, even from Stone. "Not yet."

"Let me know if you do. Her room was always such a dive," he laughed.

For some reason, that bothered me, his disrespect for a dead woman's room. Sure, he'd known her—even dated her—but did he really have to be so cavalier?

"I like her room." My voice had an edge to it I didn't even recognize.

He got serious. "Oh, sure. Well, she had unique tastes in just about everything. Show her a Ferrari and she'd say she preferred a Prius."

Now that our talk had turned to cars, it would be a great time to ask him if he had one. Instead, an equally invasive question escaped my lips. "So, are you at work today? Where do you work again?"

He answered quickly. "I work from home for my dad's hedge fund business. I've been training with Dad's partner, who's basically in charge of the day-to-day aspects of the company."

"Wow. I had no idea you were so busy." And so smart. I felt like a heel for sticking it to him with my cross-questioning today, but the omission of his OUI past needled me.

"Speaking of which, I should get back to work. See you at seven." His voice was a little curt.

"Great." I couldn't even fake exuberance, feeling more nervous than excited about tonight.

I hung up and picked up my dust cloth, fresh determination filling me. Margo's room was going to sparkle by the time I finished with it. It was the very least I could do for this woman who might not have been so very different from me.

* * * *

It was almost three-thirty by the time I finished cleaning. I felt grimy and exhausted, and I still had to go home and clean and cook. Granted, housecleaning wouldn't take long, since I was fastidious about wiping down my bathroom regularly.

Margo's room, on the other hand, had been a more massive project than I'd anticipated. The bottom line was that she'd had far too many clothes, shoes, and accessories. Many of them still had tags on them. I made a pact with myself that if I ever became rich, I'd keep a Spartan wardrobe by donating my extras to shelters.

I plopped into an overstuffed chair and called a car service, fingering a church bulletin I'd discovered that was jammed into a Bible under Margo's bed. The police had probably glanced over it. But I'd noticed it was a bulletin for Father Jesse's Episcopal church, and when I opened it, I'd found a handwritten note scrawled inside.

I hung up the phone and reread the personal message in the bulletin. It had obviously been charged with both longing and familiarity.

How I'd love to wrap my hands around your beautiful waist. Come see me tonight.

I couldn't stop switching the word "waist" for "neck" in my mind.

The bulletin was yet another thing I'd need to drop off with the police. I could run the pregnancy test and the bulletin in on my way home and get them off my hands before I left town.

If Stone asked if I'd found anything, I could share about the note, which seemed to point to Father Jesse as Margo's secret lover. And what I didn't necessarily have to share with Stone was that if Father Jesse had discovered he was the father of Margo's baby, he would've had a really strong motivation to kill her. He couldn't afford that kind of scandal in a small community like Greenwich.

The pieces seemed to fit together, but I still felt like some critical fact hadn't surfaced yet. Maybe it was something Frannie had overheard, something that would give us some definite, direct proof of motive.

I sighed and stood, shoving the bulletin in my purse. I knew it would have my prints on it, but I hadn't thought to wear gloves before rummaging through Margo's Bible.

Taking one last glance around Margo's cozy room, I felt satisfied that everything was in order. Ava could walk into this bedroom at any time and feel closer to her daughter, but she didn't have to worry about sorting through trash and messes to do so.

"I'm sorry, Margo," I whispered, pulling the door closed behind me. I nearly jumped when something moved in my peripheral vision. It was Ava. She'd been sitting in a chair in the hallway, for who knew how long.

She stood and moved toward me. I reached to shake her outstretched hand, but she flipped it over. Several hundred dollar bills uncurled in her palm.

"Thank you, my dear. Please take this."

I shook my head and withdrew my hand as if I'd been scalded. "No. I can't take your money. I wanted to do this to help you out."

She gave me a curious look. "I've never met anyone who rejected my money."

I couldn't explain how wrong it felt to take money from a grieving mother. Plus, I was about to drop a bombshell on her.

"I appreciate it, but I really can't accept your kind offer." I held her gaze. "I wondered, did Margo ever talk about a boyfriend, maybe to you or to her siblings?"

Ava thought a moment. "She wasn't close to her siblings, since there was quite an age gap between them. Of course, her father and I knew some of her boyfriends—Dietrich Myers was especially sweet on her when they were growing up—but she hadn't mentioned any recently."

"I need to tell you something, but you might want to sit down first." I had a feeling that news of Margo's pregnancy would come as a serious shock to Ava.

Her face blanched and she sank into the chair. "Did you find something in her room?"

"I did. It was something she had taken pains to hide. A pregnancy test."

Ava's fingers locked over the armrests like talons and she leaned forward. Her horrified look told me she'd guessed what I was going to say next.

"It was positive," I confirmed.

Chapter 14

Detective Watson wasn't in when I visited the police station again, so I dropped off the pregnancy test and the church bulletin and scrawled a hasty note, telling the detective I suspected Father Jesse Woods had left the message in Margo's bulletin. I left him my cell phone number so he could call for more details.

When I got back to my carriage house, I kicked off my shoes and said a hasty hello to Rasputin, who seemed a little slithery and restless. I grabbed a handful of peanuts to quell my growling stomach, then donned my cleaning gloves and got to work.

Once I wrapped up the cleaning, I took a little break for a quick cup of coffee. After that, I cut up root vegetables for roasting, then washed and tore lettuce for a Caesar salad. I'd made sure to pick up some almond croissants for dessert, so that was one thing I didn't have to worry about.

As I applied the pecan crust to the salmon, my mouth started watering. Even if Stone was feeling miffed tonight because of the questions I'd asked about his job, I determined that I was going to enjoy this meal, if for no other reason than the salmon and pecans hadn't been cheap.

By the time I'd changed to a flowing skirt and sweater, I was swimming in nervousness. Unlike a dog, Rasputin didn't seem to sense my mood and he continued slithering back and forth in his cage, almost like he was pacing. Maybe he was already hungry again? I'd have to call Reginald tonight and ask.

Stone's now-familiar knock sounded and I opened the door. He wasn't smiling, which made his dark good looks all the more spectacular. He could play the Count of Monte Cristo or the Scarlet Pimpernel in movies.

"Thank you for coming," I said, waving him inside.

He trailed behind me, gently kicking his shoes off inside the door. Thankfully, his presence wasn't intimidating in the least; in fact, I seemed to relax the closer I got to his proximity. I tried to imagine him getting pulled over for driving drunk, but I was literally unable to do it.

"Have a seat," I continued, motioning him toward the small pine table Katrina had given me. It was a quaint antique, scuffed and dinged by many who had gone before me. He settled into the chair and finally spoke.

"How'd it go at the Fentons'?"

I was ready for his question. I began to arrange the rosemary root vegetables on a platter as I answered. "I found a note written on a church bulletin. It was from the Episcopal church we visited." I shared what it said.

He steepled his long fingers, thoughtful. "Definitely sounds like something a secret love interest would say. You think it's Father Jesse?"

"I do. I mean, who else fits the bill?" I froze, realizing I'd referred to Margo's hidden pregnancy without thinking. Trying to cover my slip, I turned to the fridge for the Caesar salad.

But my comment hadn't gone unnoticed. "What do you mean, 'fits the bill'? Do you have some other hint as to who Margo's lover was?"

It still felt wrong to share about Margo's pregnancy. I supposed I had some misplaced notion about protecting her honor, even in death.

"I just meant that he struck me as someone she would have confided in, and it *was* a church bulletin, after all."

"Hmm." He sounded doubtful of my reasoning, but he didn't push it. His gaze slid to the snake's cage. "When does the snake go home for good?"

"Next Sunday. His owner swears he'll never leave him for that long again. He's having snake withdrawal." I laughed. "I've had to text him photos of his little buddy so he knows he's doing okay. I can't say he's the most photogenic ball python on the block, either. Sometimes, I have to send a photo of a tail sticking out of a flowerpot."

"I wouldn't call that thing *little*," Stone said. "After all, I've seen how it stretched around your body that first day we met."

"So awkward." I opened two bottles of sparkling water and sat down to serve our food, but Stone began to do that for me.

"You've had a long day," he said, placing a huge hunk of salmon on my plate. "The least I can do is dish up the food for you. It looks delicious, by the way."

A man who served me food was hard to resist. "Sure. Thank you."

Our conversation drifted to random topics like TV shows and books. Stone turned out to be an avid mystery reader, which really shocked me. His knowledge of Agatha Christie books fell somewhat short of my own, but the very fact he knew who Parker Pyne was blew my mind. Many Agatha readers had never heard of him, yet *Parker Pyne Investigates* was one of my favorite books.

I was discovering that Stone and I had more than a few things in common, which probably explained why I felt so comfortable around him. Had Margo ever felt the same way? What had made her throw Stone over? From what Stone had said, it sounded like she'd set her sights on someone else.

I stood to fix decaf coffee to go with our almond croissants, and Stone took that as his cue to clear the table. I was surprised that a rich boy who had hired help in the kitchen knew how to pitch in with cleanup duties.

"Have you ever lived on your own?" The question sprang from my tongue with no regard for how it sounded.

Stone didn't seem offended. He scrubbed at a plate as he answered. "I did live in Manhattan for a while. Spreading my wings and all that. I actually worked as an investment banker for a while, but I hated the hours. About that time, Dad's hedge fund business was taking off, so I ditched banking and started working from home. Saves money, and as you might've noticed, my parents' house is huge. It's like I have my own apartment anyway."

He was right, of course, but I wondered if Margo had been looking for someone more independent, someone with a house of his own. Someone not so beholden to his parents in nearly every way.

I leaned against the counter, listening to the comforting sound of coffee brewing. "So, did you have a car in the city?" I rushed on, giving him a chance to formulate an answer. "I didn't, and now I regret it. I really need a car here."

"Parking in the city isn't worth it. I just took the subway or buses like everyone else when I lived there. But you're right, in Greenwich you need a car." He accepted the cup of coffee and added caramel creamer to it.

He hadn't answered the real question I'd been asking, so I tried a different angle. "I saw you lusting after that red Lamborghini. Couldn't you buy yourself one? Then you wouldn't have to hitch rides with Red. Though don't get me wrong—he's a great driver and a nice guy."

I must've hit the magic button, because Stone's face did something extraordinary. It literally crumpled.

He took a bite of almond croissant, chewing on it so long I feared he'd soon chomp into his tongue instead of the disintegrated pastry.

After taking several swallows of coffee, he finally spoke. "Belinda, I need to be up-front with you. I should've told you earlier, but I couldn't bring myself to do it. It's honestly the most humiliating thing in the world. I *have* a Lamborghini—it's yellow, actually. But I haven't been driving it because it has a Breathalyzer installed in it. Basically, if I've had any alcohol, it won't start."

I feigned shock, hoping I wasn't overdoing it. "But why?"

"I was driving drunk. It was stupid. I really hadn't had much to drink, but I hadn't eaten yet, so it must've filtered right into my system. I ran a red light and there was a cop parked nearby."

"I'm so sorry."

I was glad for his sudden honesty, but what if I hadn't known to ask those questions? Stone hadn't been forthcoming about a lot of things.

Unable to sit down, I walked over to my back window, the one overlooking the flowerbeds. Stone seemed to sense why I was drawn there, and he came and joined me.

"Hard to believe she's gone," he said.

"Hard to believe how she died," I added. I glanced back out and stiffened. "What's that?"

I pointed to a small light that was bobbing in the darkness. It was definitely moving around, and rather rapidly, as if someone was afraid of being caught.

Stone wheeled around and strode to the door. "Someone's out there. I'll check on it. Do you have a light on that patio?"

I nodded.

"Okay. I'm going to sneak out the front door. As I round the corner, I want you to throw that light on so I can catch the person. I doubt they'll try to jump the stone wall, so the only way they could get out is through me."

It seemed like a plan fraught with hazards. What if the intruder had a gun, for instance? But Stone was already heading outside. I peeped out my front door, and as he rounded the darkened corner of my house, I hit the back patio's light switch.

There was a brief shout, followed by loud talking. The intruder sounded like a man. I edged back into the house, unsure what to do next. If Stone thought he was in mortal danger, surely he'd yell for me to call the cops?

Just as I was pushing the door shut, a light knock sounded on it. Stone's voice rumbled through the crack in the door. "Belinda, it was Val. It's okay. Open up, because he has some explaining to do."

I opened the door, trusting that Stone had Val in hand. What was he doing, creeping around in the flowerbed?

Val looked apologetic as he walked in, wearing jeans and a leather jacket in place of his security uniform.

"Were you doing some kind of undercover security tonight?" I asked.

He dipped his head. "No. I'm sorry to scare you like that, miss. I was looking for something I'd lost."

I frowned. "At night? In the dark?"

Stone motioned Val to a kitchen chair, then took a seat next to him. I leaned against the kitchen counter, uneasy about getting any closer.

"Walk me through what you were doing back there again," Stone said, in a tone that implied he wouldn't accept any shenanigans.

Val gave us a beseeching look. "Like I said, I'd lost one of my security badges."

"In the flowerbed," Stone said.

"Yes," Val confirmed.

I butted in. "And how did it come to be there?"

Val looked from me to Stone, then back to me. "I'm going to tell you the truth, because Stone here is a great boss and his family has done right by me all these years. What happened was that Miss Margo spoke to me that night she came to the billiards party. I let her in the gate, you see. She was all jumpy and such and I asked her what was up. She said, 'I can't talk about it now, but I'll meet you around eleven here at the booth so we can talk.' So I was waiting at the Security booth at eleven—past my shift, but I told Rick to come in later that night."

His voice cracked and he took a deep breath. I decided to have mercy on him, because he did seem to be telling us the truth.

"Would you like a glass of water?" I asked.

He nodded appreciatively. "Yes, please."

Once he'd drunk a few sips and gotten a second wind, Val launched back into his tale.

"To tell the truth, I was hoping she wanted to meet me since the Monday before, I'd finally worked up the courage to ask her on a date. She had never responded. But when she said she wanted to meet at eleven to talk, I hoped she was going to agree to go out with me."

Stone's face expressed shock and disbelief, and Val noticed.

"I know I'm not in her class," Val said. "She was like an angel, you know? Always friendly, not stuck up like some of them." He looked at me. "Kinda like you."

I ignored that remark, which seemed honest but a little creepy, especially if Val had killed Margo. "So did she show at eleven?"

His eyes darkened. "No, and when I think that all the time I was sitting there waiting in the booth, she could've been screaming for help out here...I can't stand it."

I'd thought of that, too—that if I'd been here that night, instead of babysitting Rasputin in Manhattan, I might've heard Margo's cries. Then again, something told me she didn't even have time to cry out. The person who'd killed her had been close to her, I was sure. It hadn't looked like she'd put up much of a fight and the police must not have found any DNA under her nails, or they'd have arrested someone by now.

Val looked so genuinely distraught, I was finding it hard to believe he would've killed Margo. Then again, maybe he was the type that became so infatuated, they couldn't deal with it when their feelings weren't reciprocated.

"But what does this have to do with the security badge?" Stone asked.

"Oh, that," Val said. "I'd taken a permanent marker and written my cell number on my badge. I gave it to Margo that night and told her to give me a call when she was heading my way. She never called."

"Did you find the badge out there?" I asked.

"No. I figure the cops never found it, either. I didn't see them pick it up that day they were crawling all over the place, and if they had, they would've contacted me by now. I couldn't stop thinking about it—what would happen if they came back and found that badge—so I thought I'd try to find it."

Stone frowned.

Val rushed on. "I swear, I wasn't trying to cover anything up. I didn't kill Margo. But I knew the cops would go down the wrong rabbit trail if they found the badge, wasting time looking at me when there's a real killer running around." He squeezed his fingers into a fist.

Val's story seemed to hold water, and on top of that, the man definitely seemed protective of Margo. I took a moment to try to picture the wealthy rich girl dating a security guard who was twice her age, and I was shocked to find that I could. Cleaning Margo's room had offered me a narrow glimpse into her head, and what I'd seen seemed to indicate she was anything but the stereotypical socialite.

Val had gulped down his entire glass of water, so I refilled it. As he accepted it, his eyes slid over to the snake's cage for the first time. The glass tottered in his hand and he brought up his other hand to steady it.

"Is that what I think it is?" he asked.

I finally sat down at the table. "Yes, it's a snake. A ball python, to be exact."

Val inhaled. "You gotta be kidding—"

Stone interrupted. "That'll be all, Val."

I could hear the dismissal in his tone, and I knew Val could, too. I felt the urge to smooth things over for the earnest security guard, because Stone hadn't even tried to mask his rejection.

And being rejected by Stone was a terrible thing, I suddenly realized.

Chapter 15

Our date night fizzled as soon as Val walked out the door. Stone seemed lost in thought, probably shocked his loyal security guard had kept things from him.

As for me, I was disappointed our relationship seemed to be going nowhere. And how could it, when Stone had deliberately hidden things from me, like his interest in Margo and his drunk driving episode?

I walked him to my door and he launched into an awkward goodbye.

"I'll text you if something comes up," he said.

Text. Not call, which would indicate he actually wanted to talk with me—would miss me, even.

I swallowed my dejection. "Sure. And I'll text if I think of anything. Hope you and yours have a great Thanksgiving." *And I hope Lani doesn't serve alcohol.*

He waved and walked out into the small circle of light cast by my porch light. Then he blended into the darkness of his lawn.

Had Margo walked through that same darkness on the night she died? Had she made her way to my little carriage house to meet someone?

I did some quick thinking and realized it would've been the dark of the moon that night, so there would've been no moonlight and the yard would've been even darker than it was tonight. Although the manor house had plenty of stylish lampposts surrounding the house itself, the huge lawn was like a sea of darkness.

I shivered as I took my analogy a step further. Like a small rowboat bobbing in the ocean, my little place was stranded too far from the giant ship of the manor house for anyone to hear if someone tried to break in.

Or kill me.

I strode past Rasputin's cage, strangely thankful for the snake's company, which was precious little company at all. He peered up at me, but seemed a bit more lackadaisical than he did earlier. I decided to call Reginald, just to check in and have someone to talk to.

Reginald picked up on the first ring. I could hear children cavorting in the background, which I figured annoyed him to no end. I wouldn't peg Reginald for a doting uncle type.

He sounded harried. "Belinda? Everything okay?"

"It is. Rasputin's doing fine. I was just wondering—do you think he'd be hungry so soon after he shed?"

"It's possible, sure. Is he at your place or mine?"

"I have him in Greenwich with me—we're heading up to my parents' tomorrow."

Reginald sighed. "I wish I could be back by then. Believe me, I do. Hang on." He put the phone down and I could hear him shouting at kids in the background. The noise died down a bit, but not for long. He picked up again. "I don't know why I put myself through this. My brother has this huge place in Chicago, but his kids are wild. Absolutely wild. If my mom didn't come in for this, I swear I wouldn't show up."

"I'm sorry," I said.

"I'm just thankful I don't have to worry about Rasputin," he said. "You're a godsend, Belinda. At least he doesn't have to be in the middle of this mess again. I can't even begin to tell you how these kids have treated him in the past."

I could imagine. "Okay, well, that was all I needed to ask. I'll give him another rat soon, then."

Reginald's voice softened—a bit too much. "I hope you know you're one of a kind, Belinda. Most girls wouldn't even touch a ball python." He sounded like an awestruck teenager.

"Oh, I'm sure there are lots of snake-loving girls out there, Reginald. I hope you have a great Thanksgiving and I'll see you Sunday at your place."

I hung up before he had a chance to respond. Katrina had warned me that some of my employers might get a little enamored with me. I had ignored her warnings, figuring I wouldn't be spending as much time with my employers as I did with their pets. But I was starting to see what Katrina was getting at. It wasn't just that I was a single woman, it was that I was willing to handle creatures most people wouldn't. It upped the danger factor, like being a Harley driver. Gave me a little edge that might be attractive to some men.

I went to the freezer and took out a rat, then dunked its plastic package in a bowl of warm water. Although I'd only planned to feed Rasputin in his own home, I was glad I'd had the foresight to bring an extra rat here, just in case. If I fed the snake in the morning, he'd probably spend our entire car trip digesting his meal. Luckily the process wasn't really loud, like the human digestion system.

After thoroughly washing my hands, I broke off half an almond croissant and sat down to play my new video game. I needed some time to reset my focus. I was leaving Connecticut and heading home tomorrow, for goodness' sakes. I would be surrounded by my loving family and I'd be far away from the unease I'd felt over Margo's death.

I hoped.

* * * *

I woke to a blinding carpet of snow outside. Dad had all-weather tires on his car, but I gave my parents a call anyway. When Mom answered, I told her the snow was falling heavily in Greenwich.

"Oh, honey, your father will be just fine. You know he's driven through blizzards up here, tending to sick animals. But I'll let him know it's snowing there, too."

After feeding Rasputin his rat, I finally located my winter clothes box and pulled out several turtleneck sweaters for New York. I also found my adorable orange tiger hat and its matching gloves. I had picked those up in Hong Kong, and I'd never regretted that totally random purchase. They reflected the whimsical side of me, plus I could wear them during hunting season so I wouldn't get shot if I had to walk out on my parents' property.

Dad arrived promptly at eleven. As he stepped out of the car, I felt a swell of pride. Tall, trim, and dapper, with prematurely white hair, my dad actually looked like he belonged in a place like Greenwich. I burst through the door, plowing through the snow to hug him.

"Belinda!" He returned my hug, patting my curls. "Didn't know you missed me so much," he laughed.

I hadn't known either, until that very moment. My words formed clouds in the frosty air. "Come on inside where it's warm! Want a cup of coffee?"

"I wouldn't turn one down," he said. "You all packed?"

"Yes. And the snake is, too."

Once inside, Dad kicked off his shoes and began to check over the plumbing, lighting, and weatherproofing of the carriage house. Finally satisfied, he settled down with his cup of java. "You did a good job picking this one. They must be attentive landlords, since everything's up to date."

I grinned. "Would you expect anything less than the best for me?"

He sipped at his coffee. "Well, I seem to remember this one particularly atrocious lean-to you lived in right out of college...that house was so small and had such thin walls, the big bad wolf could've blown it down."

"Very funny. I guess I've moved up in the world now."

He nodded. "Fancy area. Couldn't believe some of the car dealerships I passed in town." He jerked his chin in the direction of the manor house. "They're quite wealthy, I take it?"

"Definitely."

"Mom said they had a son about your age?"

I nodded.

Dad thankfully didn't pursue that train of thought. He knew me well. Instead, he walked over to Rasputin's cage and peered in. "Just feed him?" he asked.

Of course, being a longtime veterinarian, Dad had immediately noticed the huge lump partway down the ball python. It was always fun to see Dad's skills in action.

"Sure did," I said.

"What say we take this boy on an extended field trip to Larches Corner? We'd better get going. It was snowing there when I left, but they weren't calling for more than four inches."

I grabbed my suitcase. "Nothing could please me more," I said.

Chapter 16

We were nearly home when my cell phone rang. I figured it was Detective Watson since "Greenwich Police Department" popped up on the caller ID.

"Thank you for dropping off the pregnancy test and the church program," the detective said. "I'm surprised my people didn't find those when they went over Margo's room. Then again, Mrs. Fenton was distraught, so they were searching as quickly as possible."

"They were kind of hidden," I said. I didn't see any reason to mention Frannie's tip about the secret drawer.

"Could you explain why you felt Father Jesse Woods might be involved?"

"He's the priest at the church the bulletin came from, and on top of that, Mrs. Fenton mentioned that Margo had been seeing him for counseling or something."

I kept it vague, since she hadn't specifically shared that information with *me*. Dad shot me a questioning look as he turned the car into our driveway, skidding a bit on the layer of snow that hadn't been plowed yet. Dad maneuvered the car's tires into the grooves he'd cut earlier, then slowly drove toward the house.

Detective Watson gave a light whistle. "You don't say. Mrs. Fenton didn't mention that to us."

"Like you said, she's been really distraught. I doubt she was hiding that from you. But Father Woods seemed like someone you should look into, given the personal nature of the note on the bulletin."

"I'll look into it. And as for the pregnancy test, they're telling me they can't pull a father's DNA from it."

"So what's that mean?" I asked, placing a finger on my lips to shush my mom, who'd run up to my window, excitement shining in her eyes.

"Probably means we'll ask for an exhumation. But not until after Thanksgiving weekend. Too many people out of the office, not to mention it would be an awful thing to do to the Fentons during the holiday."

I pictured what an exhumation would do to Ava. "I agree," I said.

"Thanks for your help, Belinda. Have a nice Thanksgiving."

"Thanks, and same to you."

I hung up, glancing around. Dad had already jumped out and started unpacking my things. I turned to open my door for Mom, who was still standing out in the cold, rubbing her hand-knit gloves together.

I got out quickly, and Mom took a long look at me—the compulsory mom inspection to make sure her daughter was healthy and happy—then pulled me into a crumpling hug. Her familiar fruity scent surrounded me and her blonde curls danced around my face.

"You're okay," she said. "Did they ever find out who killed that girl?"

I hated to be the bearer of bad tidings, especially since I knew Mom would worry. "They haven't yet. But there's a really nice detective on the case."

I realized too late that it had been the wrong thing to say. Sure enough, Mom gave a little gasp.

"You've been talking with a detective? Are you a suspect?"

"No. I mean, I don't think so. They haven't pulled me in for more questions or anything, just my witness report when I found her."

Mom kicked her heavy barn boot into a snow bank. "I don't know about you staying in that house, Belinda..."

"It's fine. I'm not worried," I lied.

Dad bustled back out. "Come on in, ladies. It's too cold to talk out here. Belinda, could I carry that snake cage inside for you?"

"Sure, Dad, just be sure to use both hands on that handle." I grabbed Mom's arm and rubbed it as I surveyed our white farmhouse with its Christmassy wreaths and dark green door. The coziness of home beckoned me like a siren. "Let's get some coffee and I'll show you the snake."

Most other moms would've cringed or declined my offer. My mom was not most moms.

"I can't wait," she said.

* * * *

Despite her initial enthusiasm, Mom tired quickly of our snake talk, since Rasputin was lethargic and boring today. After serving me a cup of organic coffee and a sugar-free scone that crumbled apart like sand in my mouth, Mom took me outside for a tour of her latest homesteading endeavors.

She'd built a chicken tractor in the summer, so her chickens could have a more portable home. It was rather impressive and I told her so.

"It's nothing compared to my turkey roost. I built that thing in a day! Imagine."

"Turkeys? I didn't know you were raising those."

"I sure am. And I've picked the one we'll be having for dinner on Thursday. She's plump as plump can be."

"Mom, do you know how to kill turkeys? I mean, they're bigger than chickens."

"I've read up on it. Your father will help if I need him."

How many times had I heard those words? I could just picture my dad's joy at having to kill his own Thanksgiving meal.

"Maybe I could help." I threw myself under the bus to save Dad.

She looked delighted, as if this would be mother-daughter time of the highest caliber. "Sounds like a plan."

A dark Lexus pulled up and it took me a moment to realize it was Katrina's new car. I rushed over to meet her, Mom close on my heels.

Katrina opened the door and stepped out from the driver's seat, because my sister was always the driver. She said it helped her unwind.

As usual, she looked like a modern-day Scarlett O'Hara. Katrina was the kind of girl who made men look twice, then steal a few more looks. There was substance to her beauty, something elegant and high-class. Her dark curls were twisted into a high bun and she wore pearl stud earrings.

I looked closer. Was it just me, or did she look unusually radiant? Her cheeks seemed a bit rosier and fuller. And her dark jeans...they definitely fit a little tighter than usual.

"Are you pregnant?" I blurted.

Mom gasped and Tyler stepped around and gave me a high five. Katrina shot Tyler a glare. "See? What'd I tell you? So much for our grand Thanksgiving announcement."

Mom gave a whoop and we rushed to hug Katrina.

"It's true?" I whispered.

Katrina grinned. "I'm not that far along, but I *knew* you'd notice."

Mom launched into a spiel on natural birthing techniques, as if Tyler wasn't an obstetrician who could probably recite these methods in his sleep. He pretended not to hear, pulling suitcases from the trunk.

I already felt like a proud aunt. Whether the child got Katrina's dark hair or Tyler's red-blond hair, it would certainly be the most perfect baby ever.

As I looked at my happy, glowing sister, I felt a pang of loss. I didn't know if Margo would have kept her baby or not, but the very fact that she'd kept the pregnancy test seemed to indicate she viewed her pregnancy as a special thing. She died without having the chance to share her excitement with her family. To kill a woman and her unborn child took an especially heinous type of murderer.

We made our way inside, so Katrina could share the good news with Dad. As the gushing continued in the kitchen, Tyler joined me by the bay window. We didn't look at each other, just out at the sweeping white yard that contrasted with the leafless, umber trees lining the driveway. Tyler and I were often on the same wavelength, and today was no different.

"You're upset about something, aren't you?" His voice always held a deep, musical note.

"Yes." Snowflakes drifted from the dove gray sky. Everything suddenly felt dark and overcast in my own soul. For a moment, I was tempted to tell Tyler everything. All my doubts about Greenwich, all my suspicions about Father Jesse...but Tyler wouldn't know how to make me feel better. Katrina would. And she would have a plan of action, which was what I desperately needed.

We fell back into silence until the voices died in the kitchen. Katrina made her way to my side and gave me a squeeze.

"It's girl time," she said. "Let's go to our room. Dad's got a house call and Mom's heading to town for some last-minute stuff."

Tyler took this as the unspoken dismissal it was and meandered into the TV room. I patted my sister's hand and we walked upstairs to the room we'd shared when we were small. Since that time, Dad and Mom had built an addition on the house, so our bedroom now functioned as a guest room and home office.

Katrina talked a while about the woes of pregnancy, but I could tell she was ecstatic and simply trying to play it down for me. She'd always been convinced I was jealous of her, and in some ways I supposed I was. Katrina had always gotten the highest grades, been the most popular, and attracted the most attention from men. And she'd landed a loving, supportive husband. But I was truly happy for her, and I knew I wasn't ready to settle into marriage yet, much less start birthing babies.

Finally, we wound our way back to the subject of Margo's death. I brought her up to date on my latest discoveries. I was interested to get her thoughts on the suspects we'd talked to, since she was usually spot-on about reading personality quirks, even from afar.

"Hmm," she said, placing a hand protectively over her still-tiny stomach. "That Frannie sounds like a real corker. Fiery, unpredictable...and maybe jealous? But she did tip you off with that secret drawer information. Have you followed up and told her what you found?"

"No, I need to do that. Maybe I'll call her tonight. What about Dietrich? Does he sound likely?"

Katrina looked out the window as she thought. Mom and Dad had never replaced the original windows in this room, so ice trickles had formed inside the glass panes.

Finally, she answered. "Dietrich is a bit of a strange one, isn't he? Obsessive, sure. But obsessed to the point of killing the object of his desire? I wonder. Maybe he just channels all his angst into those freaky paintings."

I sighed. "Kat, I've already thought of this stuff. I need some new insight, you know? I feel like I'm swimming in circles. What about my anonymous note? Should we start there?"

"Sure, we could. Who do you think sent it? My initial hunch is Val, since he's always nearby."

Her hunch lined up with my thoughts. "I wondered about Val, too," I said. "But wouldn't he have admitted sending the note when Stone caught him in my back yard? Also, what reason would he have to kill Margo? He thought he was on the brink of a date with her!"

"So he *says*," Katrina said. "But he could be lying. Maybe she turned him down cold and he grabbed her on her way out."

I shifted on the bed and tucked my cold feet under a weathered quilt. "How about this. Let's talk about *Margo* and what she was like. For starters, she seems to have had a bit of a gypsy-wanderer soul, because she decorated with eclectic things from other countries. She was approachable and had a sense of humor, Stone said. Frannie said she was high-class and liked wealth, and I can tell she lived large from her overstuffed closet. But whoever she was seeing was somehow unacceptable, so she had to keep her relationship secret."

The front door slammed shut and Mom shouted, "Girls! I need some help down here."

"Flashback to my childhood," Katrina said.

"Unloading the groceries will always be our job," I said, extending a hand to help Katrina up. "Let's do our daughterly duty, then we'll continue this conversation later on."

"Sounds good." Katrina stopped short behind me and I turned. Her face was paler than usual and she gripped my hand. "BB, you've been asking a lot of questions, and the person who killed Margo probably knows you're looking into things. I'm thankful you're here for a few days, but when you go back, promise me you'll be extra careful?"

I gave her a hug. "I promise."

But I was pretty sure I'd already poked the sleeping tiger, and if I didn't watch out, it would be coming for me next.

Chapter 17

Wednesday was official turkey-killing day. We all knew it and we all dreaded it—even my mom, given her nonverbal cues. But she was determined to be a homesteader through and through, so by Jove, she was going to finish what she'd started when she'd picked up those baby turkeys (or "poults," as she called them), earlier this year.

Somehow, everyone else was too busy to help—Katrina was working on her yeast rolls for tomorrow, Dad took off for the clinic to check on a sickly cat, and Tyler...I wasn't sure what Tyler was doing that precluded his involvement in the turkey killing, but I suspected it had something to do with watching a ballgame on cable.

The process was not a pretty one, but not nearly as inhumane as what I'd pictured. Although Mom and I both nearly froze our fingers off messing with the bird in the twenty-six degree weather, we managed to wrangle the huge carcass into the laundry room sink for plucking and gutting.

By the time we'd finished the monumental task of prepping the turkey, Katrina had baked three pans of rolls, a pan of cinnamon rolls, and a batch of gingerbread cookies.

Lured by the smell of nutmeg that had infiltrated every inch of the house, I stole a gingerbread man from the cooling rack. Katrina playfully smacked at my hand. Smearing flour on her cheek as she brushed a stray hair away, she glanced out the window.

"Who's that?" she asked.

Mom glanced out the window at the white delivery truck parked in the driveway. "Oh, that's Randy Jones. He's coming to load up the rest of my turkeys. He's an organic grocer—he's been doing big business, especially with all the New Yorkers who've moved up here."

We said "New Yorkers" to refer to people from New York City, even though technically, we were all New Yorkers. But New York City was like a state unto itself. And many Manhattan residents had bought land up our way, dreaming of wide open spaces and leaving a smaller footprint. Sometimes the only footprints they left were their own, as they pulled up stakes and ran away from our heavy snows. But some had settled in pretty well, so the demand for organic foods had continued to skyrocket.

Mom rushed out to help Mr. Jones with the turkeys. Katrina's stare shifted from Mom to me, and she slowly took in my feather-encrusted work overalls and dirt-smeared face. She gave a demure cough.

"I'll take a shower," I said.

"That'd be nice," she said. Katrina was a stickler for cleanliness, whereas I was the kid who'd once gone two weeks without a bath. Until Katrina had told on me.

I skulked upstairs, reaching my room just in time to make out a muffled ring from my phone. I dug around in the covers until I located where I'd haphazardly tossed it.

"Hello?" I asked brusquely.

"Belinda? This is Dietrich."

"Dietrich?" I couldn't hide my shock. "What're you doing calling me?"

"And a warm hello to you, too, little lady." He laughed. "Sorry for being so random, but Stone said you'd been over at Margo's to clean her room, and I wondered if you'd found anything."

I smelled a rat, and if anyone knew what rats smelled like, I did. "Why didn't you just ask Stone?" I countered.

"You know Stone, *dahling*," he said. "Cagey as ever. You can't ever get a straight answer out of him, but you struck me as the more forthcoming type." His playful tone turned serious and he said, "Actually, I wondered if you found any of my artwork."

"Why, did you want it back? You'd have to ask the Fentons about that."

"There was a little sketch I did for her—something she didn't want anyone else to see. I thought she might've tucked it away in that plunder palace she called a room."

My phone lit up and I jabbed at it, accidentally hitting the view button. Dietrich's face popped onto the screen, and I could tell from the uneven pink splotches dotting his cheeks that he'd been crying.

In similar fashion, he was gaping at my filthy, feathered face. The horror in his expression sent me into a gale of laughter.

I finally pulled myself together, realizing how unhinged I must seem. "Sorry. I'm at my parents' and we've been doing...farm chores." Something told me Dietrich might not understand that turkeys were not born in the freezer section, so I didn't elaborate on my adventures of the day. "Anyway, I didn't run across a sketch of any kind."

Come to think of it, I hadn't seen any of Dietrich's artwork on her walls. Why did she allow him to paint her if she didn't even care for his work?

We continued to stare at each other. Behind Dietrich's slim shoulders, I caught a glimpse of canvases that had been toppled to the floor. Had he had some kind of an artist's tantrum?

"You doing okay?" I asked in all sincerity.

He gave a sniff. "Not really. I mean, it's nearly Thanksgiving and Margo is gone. I thought I was okay with it, but it's hitting me now."

I nodded. "Perfectly normal. You're grieving." In reality, he could be emotional for any number of reasons, including guilt over murdering her in a fit of rage.

Something moved behind me on the inset phone screen. Katrina adjusted her hair and smiled. "You talking to someone?" she asked innocently. She was angling to see Stone.

Dietrich peered at the screen. "What a lovely friend you have, Belinda."

"Sister," I corrected. "And she's married and pregnant. But thanks for noticing."

His face gave an odd twist when I said *pregnant*. Like a wake-up slap, I realized Dietrich had known about Margo's pregnancy. It was so blatantly obvious. So why had she confided in him instead of Frannie? There was no logical reason...unless he was the father.

I struggled to hide the disgust that simmered inside me. I couldn't think of one decent thing to say to Dietrich. Luckily, Katrina sensed I was a bit thunderstruck, and she spoke up.

"And are you Stone?"

I blushed furiously as Dietrich shot me a look. "No. I'm Dietrich Myers." He paused for dramatic effect, and I nearly dropped through the floor when Katrina provided his hoped-for response.

"Oh, the artist? You're in New York City, right? I went to your show in Albany last year."

Dying. I was literally dying. What on earth would possess Katrina to go to one of Dietrich's art shows?

While Katrina and Dietrich chatted about his painting process, I geared up for a polite goodbye. Before I had a chance to offer it, Mom's irritated shout sounded from the kitchen.

"Belinda!"

I jumped from the bed, leaving my phone in my sister's hand. "Oops, sorry. I'd better go, Dietrich. Thanks for calling. Hope I helped a little."

I raced downstairs, trying to guess how I'd dropped the ball in the Thanksgiving preparations. As I burst into the kitchen, Mom's back was to me. She was digging in a cabinet, pulling things out and setting them willy-nilly on her counter.

"I was sure I had honey," she said. "I've looked through everything and I'm totally out. We need it for those yeast rolls—you know how your father loves honey on rolls."

I nodded, unsure what she wanted me to do about it, but she didn't hesitate to supply the solution.

"Thank goodness Jonas had lots of honey this year. Could you run over and pick up a couple of jars? You can take the snowmobile."

Mom knew my weakness. There was nothing like the feeling of gliding across our fields at less-than-cautious speeds, frosty cold snapping the breath from my lungs. And Jonas was our closest neighbor, even though he was almost a mile away. Not only had Jonas maintained his deceased father's organic dairy farm, he also sold honey, blueberries, apples, and pumpkins. I never could figure out how he kept up with all that work, but he did have some hired help.

"You got it," I said.

Mom heaved a huge sigh. "Thanks." She glanced around. "Where's Katrina?"

I knew another shout was soon to follow. Mom didn't like being left alone in the kitchen, especially when a big family meal loomed. I skittered out to the garage, donning my outside attire before steering the snowmobile out into the yard.

I welcomed the bracing air. Maybe it would clear some of my conflicting thoughts about Dietrich.

Chapter 18

The snowmobile bounced over a small hill and I gave a sigh of exhilaration. I wanted to revel in the fields and forests that always welcomed me, that never demanded anything more than my rapt attention. I throttled up and hunkered down, flying like a bullet toward Jonas's Greek revival farmhouse.

Still, I couldn't stop mulling over the conversation with Dietrich. Could he have killed Margo? Sure, but he really was small-built. He would've had to reach up to pull a necklace tight around her neck, and she could have easily broken free.

Besides, why would Margo have kept it secret if Dietrich had fathered her baby? Dietrich was from an established family, and he would've had income to take care of Margo in the style she'd grown accustomed to. Their families knew each other; they were probably friends. I couldn't see any way a relationship between Dietrich and Margo would've been taboo.

I geared down, narrowly missing one of Jonas's snow-covered beehives. By the time I pulled alongside his long front porch, I had dropped to a perfectly respectable crawl.

Jonas's front door opened. He stood in the doorframe and waited for me, since he wasn't wearing a coat or shoes. This allowed me the chance to take a good, long look at him, one of my secret pastimes, because there wasn't a man alive who was put together exactly like Jonas Hawthorne.

Jonas's head was shaved, which gave the initial impression that he was a Marine. He wasn't. He had a strong brow that was emphasized by oft-quirked dark eyebrows. He wore a trim beard. His mouth was nearly always drawn in a serious, tight line, which explained my perverse temptation to crack jokes every time I was around him. Because when Jonas laughed, it filled up the room and went on a few seconds too long. It was like the one thing he couldn't seem to control.

He was in his mid-thirties and already had the air of a man who'd pulled himself up by his own bootstraps, which I supposed he had. He'd taken risks his father never would have taken, and from the look of the updated paint on his house and the new truck in his driveway, it was clear his entrepreneurial spirit was treating him well.

He waved me inside. "Your mom called and said you were on your way. Come on in. My mom's asleep right now, but I know she'd love to see you."

I crunched across the snow to him. "Don't you dare wake her. She needs her sleep." Mrs. Hawthorne had been battling an aggressive form of breast cancer for two months, and there was no way I'd interrupt her rest.

"Your call," he said, taking a long look at my hat. "Nice tiger. You going hunting later?"

I grinned, then stepped in the door and shed my snow-encrusted boots and coat, along with my vibrant hat and gloves.

Jonas motioned toward his study and I followed. "We won't wake Mom in here," he whispered as I walked past him.

It really was more of a man-cave library than a study. Stained wood planks stretched to the ceilings, and bookshelves lined two walls. I cautiously perched on the edge of a worn leather couch, suddenly aware of my still-dirty state after the turkey killing. Jonas closed the door, then settled into an oversized peach chair I was pretty sure he'd commandeered from his mom's living room set. I stretched my hands toward the gas fireplace, enjoying the warmth.

Something was different about Jonas, but I couldn't put my finger on it. "What's new?" I asked.

He crossed an ankle over his knee. "Not much. I had a good honey year, so I'm glad your mom's taking some off my hands. Tell her it's no charge. Merry early Christmas."

"Thanks," I said. I absently fluffed my curls, which had likely been flattened by my hat.

Jonas's mildly disinterested gaze sharpened and followed my hand movement. Rushing to cover the thrill of surprise that shot through me, I asked, "And how are your animals?"

"The cull rate was down this spring, so I have a lot of healthy heifers coming up," he said.

"Cull rate" was a fancy way of saying "death rate," so I was glad to hear more calves had made it this year. Jonas had some of the prettiest Jerseys I'd seen.

His silvery blue eyes twinkled. "I should ask how *your* animal's doing. Your dad said you've been snake-sitting?"

"Yes—a ball python. He's fairly small."

"Be careful. You know that's a constrictor."

I didn't need a lecture. "Yes, I know." I curled my socks under my legs in an attempt to warm my cold toes. "I noticed balloons on the way in. Was your mom in the hospital or something?"

"No, actually that was for a book club that meets in town. We call ourselves the *Kaffeeklatsch.* We're reading through the classics. Yesterday was Delia's birthday, so we celebrated."

I'd forgotten how active Jonas was in the affairs of our small town. He always seemed to be plugged in. If I recalled correctly, Mom had mentioned that Jonas was now on the town board.

But Jonas mentioning a girl was something new. I tried to place her name. "Delia...?"

"Delia Jensen. She was in my graduating class. Moved to Buffalo for a while, then came back. She runs the bakery."

"Oh, okay." I wanted to find out more about Delia, but couldn't think of a roundabout way to ask more questions. My silence dragged into awkwardness.

He jumped to his feet. "I'll go get the honey. You have some way to carry it back?"

"I'll put the jars in my coat pockets. What're you reading? For the book club, I mean." I couldn't stop myself from returning to the topic burning in my head.

"*Tess of the d'Urbervilles.*" He shook his head. "Talk about bleak. Even though I already know the ending, I can't bring myself to read it."

"I need to read that book," I said.

"You won't like it."

"I'll be the judge of that," I said, trailing him into the kitchen. It was a small space, but cozy as could be. A row of open-shelved cabinets ran along the wall and showcased honey and multicolored jam jars.

He took out a couple of honey jars. They were topped with black and white gingham cloth that was cinched with white rickrack, a touch I knew his mom had come up with. "While we're discussing the untimely deaths of young women like Tess, your mom said something about a murder in your neck of the woods in Connecticut? Some woman who was strangled?"

He handed me the honey and our eyes locked for one second. What I saw in Jonas's eyes flummoxed me. It went beyond simple neighborly concern and belied the casual tone of his voice. It flew in the face of my theory that Jonas was dating Delia.

What that look said was, "I want to protect you."

I took a step back. I was seeing things.

A truck roared into Jonas's driveway and we both rushed toward the front door, concerned.

Jonas took one look and said, "It's Gerald Klein, come to pick up his hay. But he's driving too fast." He threw the front door open and Gerald rolled his window down.

"Cows out!" Gerald shouted.

The words every farmer dreaded.

Jonas moved fast, pulling on his boots, coat, and gloves before I managed to struggle into my damp coat.

"What're you doing?" he asked.

"Going with you," I said.

I figured he'd tell me to stay there, but he didn't. When the cows were out, it was usually all hands on deck. Everyone around knew the story of the time Jonas's dad's cows had broken through the fence, making their way across pastures until they hit the main road, where they'd formed a herd and walked straight into town.

We jumped into Gerald's truck and he skidded up the narrow back road until we reached the animals, who were milling around not too far from the fence line.

Jonas's tone was grim as he looked over the situation. "Someone's run into the fence, taken out a wire. Of course, I don't have electric running to the wires right now, since the cows aren't out long in this snow. But the animals must've pushed against it and realized it was down."

Gerald turned to me, explaining. "Since Jonas is organic, he has to keep the cows out a certain number of days a year, no matter the weather."

Jonas was already out of the truck, though in a very gentlemanly move, he turned back and offered a hand to help me out.

Jonas spoke mostly to Gerald. "I'm going to round up the bull, if you two can handle the others?"

Gerald nodded with more confidence than I could muster. I'd only rounded up cows once, when I was on a house call with my dad. He hadn't wanted me to join him, but it was obvious they'd needed more bodies to direct the animals.

But there hadn't been a bull loose that day. I stared at the big beast who was rubbing against the fencepost. He looked beefy and belligerent to me, even with those pretty chocolate-brown eyes.

Fear gripped me as I saw Jonas walking directly up to the bull. I had to look away, but I heard him say, "Get in there," with the tone of one who would not be disobeyed.

Gerald nudged my elbow. "You ready?" Without waiting for my answer, he strode over to the cows. Throwing his arms wide, he yelled, "Go on! Get back in there!"

Adrenaline coursed through me and I followed suit, forming a human fence for the wayward animals. "Go on!" I shouted, trying to seem more intimidating than I was.

The cows mooed and balked, but we kept at it. Finally, I took a moment to glance back at Jonas, and he was standing near the fence, pulling on a broken fence wire.

His eyes met mine. "C'mon out," he said. "They're all in."

I glanced around, realizing he was right. Amazingly, the bull was safely in the fence and moving away from us, toward some fresh hay. Gerald and I backed out and Jonas pulled the wires tight, wrapping them around the pole.

"I'll have to get my tools and come back and fix that," Jonas said. "Thanks for letting me know, Gerald."

We climbed into the truck and Gerald cranked the heat. As the men fell into a conversation about milk prices and hay quality, I leaned back into the cracked upholstery of the seat. I felt strangely content and more than a little proud of myself. Maybe I should add cow wrangling to my list of exotic pet-sitting capabilities.

But I'd done nothing today compared to what Jonas did. What kind of man walked straight up to a bull and bossed it around? A man with some kind of serious confidence, that was what. I hadn't ever seen that side of Jonas Hawthorne, and it was impressive.

When we got out at the farmhouse, I realized how much time had passed. "I'll get the honey and head home. Mom will wonder what's taking so long."

Jonas's arm shot out and his hand gripped my sleeve. "Don't go yet—I want to talk to you a second. Let me load Gerald's hay and I'll come right in. You can wait in the study where it's warm."

Drying my wet clothes by the fireplace sounded good. "Okay," I said.

I tiptoed inside, carrying my coat into the study to warm it up before I had to leave again.

I perused the book titles on Jonas's shelves—mostly classics, thrillers, and farm manuals—then I segued over behind his desk. He had quite a few pictures of his parents, as well as old pictures of the farmhouse. He had a picture of him and his older brother, Levi, running a lemonade stand when they were children. Levi had moved to Alaska a few years ago, where he worked on oil rigs and pretty much eschewed human interaction, from what I could tell.

The front door shut and I scuttled over to the couch just as Jonas strode into the room. He walked straight over and dropped to the couch next to me. He placed his calloused hand over both of mine, which were demurely clasped in my lap. "You didn't have to help us. I could tell you were scared."

"Was not," I said childishly.

"You were," he said, brooking no argument. "You don't mind living dangerously, do you, Belinda?"

I shook my head.

He leaned back and met my eyes. "According to your mom, you've been looking into that girl's murder. Why don't you tell me what you've found out so far?"

I hesitated, then gave in. If anyone could assimilate the facts into something that made sense, it would be Jonas. He was used to fixing unfixable problems on the farm, so maybe he could take the information I'd gathered and arrange it into something cohesive.

Yet when I finally finished speaking, he made the one suggestion I didn't want to hear.

Chapter 19

"You need to look at Stone," Jonas repeated.

He'd listened patiently as I'd rehashed our interviews with Dietrich, Frannie, Father Jesse, and Val. I'd filled him in on all I knew about Margo and her family, as well.

But for some reason, he'd decided to come back around to *Stone*?

"What do you mean?" I asked, knowing full well what he meant.

"Stone the fifth. He's the most obvious suspect. She was at his house—probably in his yard—the night she was killed. Stone said he'd wanted to date Margo, but she wasn't interested."

"That was a while ago. And why would he lead me all over creation to look for the killer?"

Jonas leaned forward. "Yes, why *would* he?"

He was probing for an answer, making me dig deeper.

Like a bolt, it hit me. "You mean he's trying to make himself look innocent—"

"While getting closer to you," Jonas finished. He rubbed a hand over his shaved head. "You might be next, Belinda. What if this has nothing to do with Margo's hidden pregnancy and everything to do with Stone being a serial killer?"

I stood and turned my back to Jonas, grabbing my coat from in front of the fire. "I need to go."

In a heartbeat, he was standing right behind me. He didn't touch me, but his presence was so strong, he might as well have.

"Don't run off like this. You know I'm right. You have to keep your distance from Stone Carrington the fifth. He's already been busted for drunk driving, he can hide behind his wealth and family name, and he's been using you, Belinda."

I yanked my hat over my ears in an attempt to muffle not only Jonas, but the accusatory thoughts he'd set loose in my own mind. Stone, a murderer? No way.

"I have to get back," I said, shoving the honey jars into my deep inside pockets. I fumbled for the cash Mom had sent and thrust the bills toward Jonas, ignoring his suggestion that the honey was a gift. "Thanks for the honey and happy Thanksgiving to you and your mom. Tell her I said hello."

I clomped out the front door, closing it behind me. Jonas didn't open it, but as I drove away, I could see his face in the narrow window by the door.

I'd hurt his feelings, but I didn't care. He'd hurt mine, by suggesting I'd let Stone lead me around on a wild goose chase.

I wasn't that stupid. Was I?

* * * *

By the time I got back, Mom was asleep on the couch, HGTV blaring in the background. I clicked the TV off and went to look for Katrina. She was curled up next to Tyler, who was still watching the ballgame.

Katrina uncurled and gave me a hug. "Sis! Where've you been? Were you at Jonas's this whole time?"

I nodded, unable to explain. Tears had probably frozen to my cheeks on the way home, but I didn't care. Jonas Hawthorne was too nosy. Jonas Hawthorne was too cautious. Jonas Hawthorne might be right.

Tyler stood and stretched. "I'm hungry, how about you two?"

Katrina pointed to her stomach. "Always hungry. There's probably a little mini-Tyler in there."

Tyler laughed and kissed Katrina's cheek. "How about I run get some pizzas for tonight? Mom's wiped out, and Dad's showering after that house call."

I'd always thought it was sweet how Tyler spoke about our parents like they were his own mom and dad. Effectively they were, but he didn't call them "Drew and Leanne," like he could have.

"Pizza sounds amazing. I'm going to shower and get into some dry clothes," I said.

Katrina gave me a long look. "Then we can talk."

Sometimes having a psychologist sister who seemed to see into your brain was rough.

* * * *

Once the pizza was in the house, Mom and Dad materialized and we sat around the farmhouse table to eat and talk. After an hour or two, we moved into the living room and played a few rounds of *Trivial Pursuit*, which were pretty much dominated by my dad and Tyler.

When our parents started yawning and making their way to bed, Katrina suggested we go to my room to check on the snake. I knew she had no such intent—she wanted to cross-examine me about the day—but I was too tired to argue.

Katrina closed the door behind us. "All night slumber party!" she shouted.

"Are you hopped up on hormones? I'm pooped. Don't forget, I helped butcher a turkey today," I said.

"*And* you visited Jonas," she said slyly. "Don't think I couldn't tell you'd been crying. What in the world happened? Did he hurt you? I'll kill him."

I grinned. "Of course not. Well, maybe a little. I mean in a different way—"

"Just spit it out," she said.

I fell face-first into my pillow, turning my head only slightly to say, "He thinks Stone's a serial killer."

I expected Katrina to laugh at the implausibility of it all, but she said, "I'd thought of that, too."

I twisted around and glared at her. "What?"

"I hate to break it to you, but you're so gullible sometimes, BB. Remember that time you bought into a pyramid scheme?"

"That was a legitimate phone card business," I retorted.

"Or when we were kids—remember when Mom gave us the huge box from her new oven? We wrote Grandma's address on the outside, and I told you we were going to mail ourselves to her in Colorado. You totally believed it! You managed to lure Blitz in there—poor bewildered dog—then you poured us a couple of cups of Kool-Aid and got some cookies and you thought we were really shipping out. Mom played along and taped some of the box and dragged it into the living room."

"Yeah, I remember." I distinctly remember the tantrum I'd thrown when I'd finally poked my head out and discovered we weren't even at the post office, much less in transit to Colorado.

Katrina's voice softened. "So if Stone recognized that about you, he could play on it. That's all I'm saying."

"Ugh. Why do you and Jonas have to be so suspicious of everyone?"

Katrina patted my leg. "We all let our experiences shape us to a certain degree. The thing is some look at the rosy side of said experiences, while some see the more...*aubergine* side." She laughed. "Dietrich was telling me about his masterpiece portrait of Margo."

"Oh, mercy."

"Exactly. I mean, his artwork is good—very fresh and unique—but he talks like he's in love with himself," she said.

"Would a guy like that kill someone?"

Katrina raised an eyebrow. "Oh, sure. But what I keep coming back to is what we talked about yesterday. Who was Margo? That'll give us the answer."

I sat up, ticking things off on my fingers. "I already told you. Spoiled, loveable, eclectic—"

Katrina placed a hand over mine. "Not her characteristics. I'm wondering what appealed to her. What kind of man would've pulled her in? Think about the men she talked to—Father Jesse and Val. Seems like she was more open to them, for whatever reason. But what do they have in common?"

"They're not wealthy," I said.

"True...but what I'm seeing is that they're *older*. She wasn't really interested in Dietrich or in Stone, right? Think about it—they're younger. So what if our Margo had a father complex?"

"Like she wanted to fall for a father figure?" I shook my head. "Kind of a long shot."

"But not outside the realm of possibility," Katrina said. "I've counseled girls like Margo before. For whatever reason, they crave the love and approval of an older man. Or conversely, they'll allow older men to take advantage of them—maybe even abuse them—to assuage guilt or sadness. Maybe their dad wanted a son instead of a daughter, or maybe they never felt they lived up to their dad's standards, that kind of thing."

I hadn't met Adam Fenton yet, but I had to admit a father complex might explain some things about Margo.

"So you don't think it's Stone the fifth?" I asked hopefully.

She took a slow sip on her water bottle. "I didn't say that. It's still wise to watch your back."

Chapter 20

The sounds of melting snow streaming through the gutters woke me on Thanksgiving morning. I pushed back my curtains to see that the sun was out in full force. Rasputin shifted a bit in his crate, but compared to a week ago, he seemed pretty docile. His last feeding, coupled with his earlier shed cycle, seemed to have worn him out.

I pulled on my nut-brown turtleneck sweater and slim plaid pants and felt a little Audrey Hepburn-esque as I followed the mouthwatering smell of roasting turkey to the kitchen. Today would be hectic and tiring, and I didn't want to miss a minute of it.

* * * *

I'd forgotten all about used car shopping until Dad brought it up after our meal. A woman at his office had decided to sell her seventeen year-old Volvo, and he'd mentioned I might be interested. I agreed to look at it, hoping it was somewhere within my budget. Dad gave her a call and she said we could come over in an hour.

The car turned out to be more than just practical—it was so pretty, I fell for it immediately. A dark, metallic blue with tan leather seats, I wouldn't be the least bit embarrassed driving it in Greenwich. Of course, it had some issues, but the owner explained them to Dad and he thought it was a good deal for the price.

I drove my new old car home, pleased as punch to finally have my own wheels. Tyler had to take it for a spin to see if the tires were snow-worthy (they were), and Katrina dug up a few music CDs for my trip home, since it had a CD player.

I'd always named our family cars, so I dubbed this beauty "Bluebell." I had a feeling Bluebell and I were going to be fast friends.

* * * *

Several hugs and desserts later, Katrina and Tyler headed back to Albany, because they'd scheduled appointments on Friday. I was reluctant to watch my big sis go, knowing she had already slipped into a whole new era of her life.

Since I had my own car, I revised our earlier plans of having Dad drive me back to Greenwich this afternoon. Instead, I kicked back and reveled in having Mom and Dad to myself for a while. Even though Dad watched TV and Mom mostly talked about her need for solar panels, I felt thoroughly loved.

My phone rang around ten thirty, which was rather late for a social call. When I saw it was Stone, I wondered if he'd missed me.

But his first words dispelled that notion. "Something terrible has happened."

Possibilities of things that could be deemed "terrible" paraded through my head. Val had killed himself. Stone the fourth had beaten up Melly. Ava Fenton had put out a hit on Father Jesse. Stone the fifth was calling me from jail after driving drunk.

Instead, the only words I could manage were, "On Thanksgiving?"

Stone's voice was dulled, like he was pressing his phone to his face. He gave a sniffle. "She's dead."

"What? *Who's* dead?" My stomach lurched.

"Frannie. Police are saying she was strangled, too."

"Oh, no!"

He continued. "Trust me, it gets worse. She was here with us for Thanksgiving. Her parents were vacationing on the Riviera and she wanted a home-cooked meal, she said. I thought she was just trying to get close to me. But once she got here, I could tell she wasn't herself. She couldn't sit still, and finally she excused herself to use the restroom. It literally took her forever to return to the table, so Lani went ahead and cleared things for dessert."

"And?"

"And Frannie came back, all right, but she looked paler than ever."

"But what happened? When was she killed? Where was she?"

He dropped his voice. "This is where things take an odd turn. Belinda, I hate to say it, but after she left, she was found out in your flowerbed, right near where Margo was."

I sucked in a breath. "Tell me you're kidding."

"I'm not. Jacques found her—Mom had asked him to check on the carriage house while you were away."

He fell silent. I could hear people rustling around in the background. Probably police.

"Obviously, you're not a suspect." He was trying to appease me.

"Well, of course I'm not," I snapped. "I'm in Upstate New York."

"I know." His voice grew a little stronger. "If it's any comfort, they're saying she must've put up a fight. She had some hair in her hand."

Good for Frannie. I didn't even have to speculate—I knew why she was killed. She'd remembered something, something that would've pointed to the killer. Had she confronted him, I wondered? Was she actually strangled in my back yard or somewhere else?

Stone rambled on about Frannie's fighting spirit and I was only half-listening until he said, "Mom was wondering if you were coming back soon. The police are crawling everywhere today, but she really wants someone in your house, to keep an eye on things."

"I'll be back tomorrow. Does she want someone in there tonight?"

He took a moment to murmur something to Melly, who must've been sitting right behind him. I could hear the desperation in her voice as she answered, "It's just not safe sitting empty. If she's not coming back tonight, I'll have Mrs. Lewis housesit."

Stone returned to the phone. "She said—"

"I heard. That'll be fine." Although I wasn't super-comfortable with anyone staying in my house, Mrs. Lewis was better than no one.

Stone spoke with Melly again, then said, "Thanks. Mom will give her a call."

I hung up with Stone, trying to formulate my plan of action. I couldn't tell my parents about the latest murder or they'd beg me to stay home longer. And I had to get Rasputin back to the city, because Reginald would freak out if he wasn't there on his return.

I could hole up at Reginald's place until Sunday, but it could still take weeks or months to find the killer—or the police might never find him at all. I couldn't afford booking a hotel until they nailed the murderer. Anyway, Mrs. Lewis couldn't stay at my place indefinitely. I needed to be there, to hold down the fort and maybe, if I was honest, to do a little more sleuthing.

Because Jonas was right. It was time for me to face the facts and take a closer look at Stone Carrington the fifth.

Chapter 21

Mom gave me a jar of honey as I left on Friday morning. "It might help your allergies. Just eat some every day."

I thought it only worked against allergies if it was local honey, but I didn't mention it. I'd still savor that golden taste of home on my morning toast.

After Rasputin was loaded into Bluebell and goodbyes were said, I pulled out. As I drove onto the main road, I had an impulse to turn left and run by Jonas's house again so I could offer a proper goodbye. I'd been curt and snippy when I left him, but what he'd suggested had wounded me. I didn't like people interfering in my relationships, telling me I'd made a poor choice in friends.

More than that, I had to admit Jonas had shattered my illusions. I had believed that Stone the fifth felt something for me, that our attraction was mutual. But if he had been using me, as Jonas and Katrina both suspected he was, I needed to end our snoop sessions and branch out on my own.

Stone claimed he'd lied since he feared I'd suspect him if I knew he'd been interested in Margo. Now I suspected him because of the lies he'd told.

I was thankful we hadn't rushed into a relationship, although I couldn't deny I'd harbored feelings for Stone. The man had a level of natural perfection rarely seen, but more importantly, he had acted like a true gentleman at every turn. That impressed me more than his good looks or his wealth ever would. Most people liked him, from Red to Dietrich to Frannie. He had seemed genuinely thankful that I'd joined him in the hunt for Margo's killer.

Whether it was all an act or not, I wasn't sure. But I would treat it as such, stepping carefully and not giving away too much.

It was time for gullible Belinda to grow up.

* * * *

It was after lunch when I pulled up at my carriage house. Mrs. Lewis came out to greet me, looking more casual than I'd ever seen her in what could only be described as "mom jeans."

"Miss Blake. I wasn't sure when you'd arrive. Give me a moment to pick up my things and I'll be out of your hair."

Even stranger than the casual attire was the apologetic tone Mrs. Lewis was employing. I'd always fought the urge to kowtow to her, and now here she was, rushing out on my behalf.

"No hurry," I said to her retreating back. I was about to offer her hot tea or coffee when it hit me that she wasn't being apologetic. She was genuinely anxious to get out of my carriage house.

I sighed, hauling Rasputin's cage out onto the driveway. When she emerged, Mrs. Lewis hardly gave the snake a second look. Pulling a small rolling suitcase behind her, she hightailed it toward the manor house, like she feared my house was ground zero for murders.

I unloaded my things, then spritzed Rasputin's cage and gave him fresh water. I'd be interested to watch the snake's reaction when he saw Reginald again. Did snakes know their owners? Did snakes care one way or another about humans? It almost seemed Rasputin recognized me, but that could've just been coincidental. Maybe he didn't like my shadow crossing his cage or maybe my smell gave him indigestion.

Stone called soon after I went inside, but I let it go to voicemail. I hadn't yet come up with a legitimate excuse for not hanging out with him.

I played a few shooter video games, just to get my adrenaline up. I had a new plan to put into play. It could be dangerous, but I figured my innocent demeanor might come in handy if I got into a tight spot.

I was going to spy on the Carringtons.

It couldn't be that hard. I could lurk any number of places in and around their huge house and never be seen. I was fairly certain they didn't have security cameras, or Stone would've mentioned them. Plus, the police could've pulled the footage and found the killer by now. I figured they counted on their security guards to keep the place safe from outsiders.

It was the insiders they hadn't counted on.

The snow had melted and the day seemed to be warming up nicely, so I dug around for an outfit that would blend into the landscape. Finally, I found an olive green shirt and camo pants. I added my brown boots and a brown knit hat, figuring I could skulk around behind trees and bushes in this garb.

Stone called again. Once again, I let it go. I wondered if he was working from home today. Or maybe he'd gone into the city. Or possibly it was Frannie's funeral today?

I stopped my speculations and headed outside. I debated climbing behind the boxwoods and edging along the stone wall until I approached the house, but I figured that would seem more suspicious if someone happened to notice me. Instead, I would pretend to study flowerbeds while making my way to the back patio. I would avoid the kitchen entrance, but I knew there were other doors around back.

I didn't see Jacques working the grounds today. Much as I liked him, I had to entertain the possibility that he could've killed Margo and Frannie. He'd mentioned having a wife, which made him an unlikely pick for Margo's hidden love interest, but he was generally around, like Val. Although I hadn't seen him working evenings, so he likely wasn't here the night Margo died.

I returned to the serial killer angle. It could have been a killer who didn't have any personal motivations—someone looking for women around a certain age.

My age.

Goosebumps rose on my arms, but I pushed on, focusing on the close-clipped rosebushes interspersed between silvery clumps of lavender. I skirted the fountain and moved quickly toward a small door that looked to be a good distance from the kitchen. Double-checking that no one was on the patio, I jiggled the knob and was pleased to find the door gave, just a little.

But something had pinned the door shut, and it wouldn't open another inch. Clearly, the door was left unlocked because they felt no idiot would try to break in this way. I worked up a light sweat, shoving with all my might, and I finally managed to open it wide enough that I could squeeze through the crack.

Once inside, I moved the heavy boxes blocking the door, then slowly crept into the pitch-dark room. Holding my hands in front of me, I walked forward until I bumped into a shelf of some kind. I ran my fingers over the shelf, quickly ascertaining from the rolls of toilet paper and boxes of tissues that this was some kind of storage closet.

I made out a crack of light coming from under a door, so I carefully tiptoed that way. Twisting the knob, I pushed the door open slightly. I was in some kind of hallway. No one was around, though I heard bustling voices not far off. From the sound of clinking dishes and cookware, I thought it was probably the kitchen, so I decided to head the opposite way.

As I walked, I could almost hear Katrina asking me what kind of half-cooked plan this was. What if I was caught?

I answered the Katrina in my head. "Good question. I'll say I was looking for Stone and I got lost."

I continued to make my way down the hallway, exiting just as voices approached from the other end. I found myself staring at the sunlit entrance to the conservatory, so I crept along the wall toward it.

Female voices were chatting inside, and I guessed that Melly had come here to soak up some rare November sunlight. I peeked out to see who she was talking with, but small palm trees—palmettos?—blocked my view. I flattened myself behind narrow tree trunks and inched my way toward the central area.

Finally, I was able to make out Mrs. Lewis, who was settled at the table like a friend, not merely a hired secretary. She had leaned forward, oblivious to the steam rising off the cup of tea before her.

I couldn't hear what she was saying, so I took a chance and dove to the ground under an oversized, draping fern.

"Tell me," Melly said, an urgency in her voice. "I have to know."

Mrs. Lewis muttered almost to herself, then answered. "All right, I'll tell you what I heard. Of course, as a loyal employee, I knew it would be unwise to share this information with the police."

Mrs. Lewis's voice held a smug note, and I realized this wasn't a little heart-to-heart between two friends. This was starting to sound like extortion.

Melly's voice flattened. "I understand."

"On the night of Margo's death, I was heading home when I passed the study. I overheard Margo telling someone she was sure she was pregnant."

Melly gasped. "Who was it?"

"I couldn't tell," Mrs. Lewis said. "Someone closed the door and I kept walking."

"Who could it have been?" Melly asked.

Mrs. Lewis dropped her voice, so I crawled a bit closer, giving a little rattle to the fern leaves. Mrs. Lewis didn't seem to notice, so enrapt was she in sharing her sordid gossip.

"I have an idea of who it was," she said. "But you're not going to like it, Melly. In fact, it's probably best if you don't know." She was directly in my line of view as she straightened in her chair, her thin back like a ramrod. Prim and proper to the end, that Mrs. Lewis. Except for the blackmail she was about to dabble in.

Melly pressed again. "You have to tell me, Esther."

Mrs. Lewis hesitated. "Of course, I would need some time off after this. An extended break, you understand. With a little spending money?"

And there it was. Would Melly fall for it?

When Melly answered, there was no waver in her voice. "I have to know if there's a killer hanging around my house, Esther. So yes, I'll give you the time off and the...bonus."

Mrs. Lewis gave a brisk nod. "I'd parked off the side drive the night Margo was killed. I had just settled into the driver's seat when two people ran out the front door. I could see them clearly because of the overhead lights. One was Margo, and a man was following her. More like chasing her."

She hesitated, and I'm sure Melly wanted her to spit it out as much as I did.

"And?" Melly sounded dubious.

"And the man was Stone."

Melly burst into tears and I heard her swearing Mrs. Lewis to secrecy. Lani came in at that moment. I realized I might be visible to her, so I crawled backward for a short distance, then turned and inched out into the hallway. Once there, I brushed the fern leaves off my pants—walking straight into someone in the process.

Narrow hands grabbed my elbows and I drew back. I looked up, blushing to realize I'd run right into Stone the elder. Since he was wearing flannel pajamas, I assumed he was home from work again. It was clear from the smell on his breath that he'd already been drinking.

He smiled. "Miss...Brown, was it?"

"Blake." I wriggled free from his lingering grasp.

His smile faded into something less than friendly. "In the conservatory, were you? Is my wife in there? I can't seem to find her about."

"I don't know. I was just looking for your son and I got lost."

He arched an eyebrow. "Hmm. Lost under the ferns, looks like?"

"I have to go." I rushed down the hallway, then took a quick turn into another hallway that should have led back to the kitchen.

Of course, it didn't.

Instead, I had entered a hallway with a curving staircase, and sure enough, Stone the fifth was stomping down toward me. He was glowering and looked like he wanted to deck someone.

I froze in place, wondering if he'd stalk right past without glancing up. But of course, I had no such luck.

He stopped mid-stride and his gaze traveled from my boots to my face. "Belinda? What're you doing over here? I've been trying to call you."

"My phone's been weird lately. I came over to let you know I was back."

I hated lying, but I had to protect my own hide right now. Especially given what Mrs. Lewis had shared. Stone had chased Margo outside on the night of her death. If that wasn't suspicious behavior, I didn't know what was.

I didn't want to be alone with him. Yet here we were, just the two of us.

He seemed distracted, though. "I have to run down to the police station. That detective wanted me to stop by. They must be talking to everyone who was here on Thanksgiving. Mom and Lani already went down and gave statements."

"Oh, okay." I tried to sound neutral.

He stepped closer and I forced myself not to flinch. "Belinda, you're going to have to keep up the search. I was thinking maybe we didn't question Dietrich enough. He was so crazy about Margo—unhealthily so."

"But how does that explain *Frannie's* murder?" I asked.

His eyes were stormy. "I don't know. Frannie must've figured something out. Why didn't she tell me what it was?"

The answer was obvious to me—Frannie hadn't trusted him. But I didn't answer him.

Stone draped an arm over my shoulder. I stood very still, taking shallow breaths. Thankfully, I'd shoved my pepper spray in my pocket before I'd left the carriage house, and I knew I could pull it out and unleash havoc if Stone's hands wandered toward my throat.

Instead, his voice and demeanor grew gentle. "I wanted to thank you for all you've done to find this killer. I know it wasn't easy, returning from a vacation and walking into a homicide scene...again. It was my fault for dragging you into this mess." His luminous eyes beseeched me to understand, and in that moment, I did.

I believed every stinking word he said, and that was my problem.

His phone buzzed and he glanced at it. "That's Red—he's waiting outside. I'll call you soon as I'm back. Or you call me."

To my utter astonishment, he leaned down and kissed my cheek. It wasn't a careful kiss, more like a loose kiss charged with sadness. His lips slid toward mine and it took everything in me to place my hands on his chest and take a step back.

"I'll see you later," I said, hoping my offhand manner masked both my attraction and my fear.

"Sure. Okay." He strode toward the door and I couldn't take my eyes off his long-legged swagger.

Once he was out of sight, I followed his footsteps and finally made it out the front door. I didn't stop, though. I kept going straight to my carriage house, where I bombed into my room, grabbed my cell phone, and called Detective Watson.

Chapter 22

The detective's warm voice seemed to reach right through the phone, calming a little of my anxiety. "Belinda. Sorry I haven't contacted you yet. It's been crazy around here. You know what happened, of course."

"I do. And I'm calling because I overheard something that's probably relevant to the case."

His chair squeaked like he had leaned back. "Fire away."

I took a deep breath. I couldn't overthink this; I had to spill the facts. What Mrs. Lewis said, however deviously intended, made sense.

"I know more about what happened the night of Margo's death. The house secretary has been holding out on you."

"Go on," he said.

"She told Mrs. Carrington that she overheard Margo telling someone she was pregnant that night. Then later, when she was in her car, she saw Stone chasing Margo out the front door. She said *chasing* her, not following her."

I waited for Detective Watson's reaction, but when he spoke, it certainly wasn't what I'd anticipated.

"Thank you for sharing that. I can't elaborate, but I've asked Stone the fifth down to the station today—in fact, he just checked in at the desk. I have some questions I need to ask him."

"What are you saying? You mean he's a serious suspect?"

"Evidence has come to light that has me concerned, I'll tell you that much. I'd like you to stay put at your place the next day or two until I can wrap some things up. Don't meet up with Stone the fifth again during that time."

I agreed. As I hung up, I let the full impact of our conversation hit me and I sank to the carpet in my room. Detective Watson hadn't said it outright, but he must be considering Stone as the killer. That meant the man who'd taken me out to The White Peony, who'd walked along the beach with me, and who had shared a meal in my house could be a ruthless murderer.

Because it did take sheer ruthlessness to strangle a woman, to relentlessly grip her neck as she gasped for her final breath.

And if Stone had murdered those women, he had taken advantage of me by feigning grief, then talking me into a pointless quest for a killer. As Jonas and Katrina had suspected, he had ulterior motives.

I felt dirty and used. I felt unattractive and idiotic. Why else would someone as gorgeous and wealthy as Stone have looked twice at me, if not to manipulate me so I was putty in his hands?

A rap sounded on my door and I jumped, then reminded myself Stone was down at the station.

I slunk over to the door and took a brief peep out the window. It was Dietrich. How did he know where I lived?

I fingered my pepper spray to make sure it hadn't fallen out, then opened the door.

Dietrich looked artsy as ever, wearing suspenders and a gray flannel jacket over slim jeans. The jeans emphasized just how thin he was. Druggie thin, if you asked me.

He mistook my perusal as interest and smiled. "I was looking for Stone, and they said he wasn't home, so I scouted the grounds and found your delectable little house, just as Stone had described it."

I glanced again at his slight size and motioned him in. It seemed impossible someone so small could have strangled both women, so I figured I could trust him to some degree. "We need to talk," I said.

"Exactly what I was thinking, love."

His familiarity always warmed me. "You want some coffee?" I asked.

"No, thanks." He stopped by Rasputin's cage, transfixed. The snake obligingly slid out of his flower pot and draped himself at the front of the cage.

"Glorious. Look at those markings. Have you picked it up, Belinda?"

"Yes."

He pressed his hands together, like he was praying, and gave a little bow. "Hats off to you, brave goddess."

"Um, yeah. It's really not that big a deal. Now I need to tell you something."

He gave one of his little hops, raising his hand. "Oh, please, let me go first."

I sat on the couch and he sat near me. "Go ahead."

"After I spoke with you and your sister—by the way, you both have the most perfect green eyes. Yours are a bronze-dusted deep green, and your sister's are a foggy green, like moss. I'd love to paint them. Anyway, back to what I wanted to say. I thought you and Stone deserved to know the truth. On the night she died, Margo told me she was pregnant."

I remembered what Mrs. Lewis had said about overhearing Margo's revelation that night. "Was it in the study?" I asked, before stopping to think.

"Yes. Wait—how'd you know she was pregnant, much less that she told me in the study?"

Instead of explaining, I demanded my own answers. "You and Stone definitively said no one left the billiards room with Margo that night."

Dietrich touched two fingers to his lips as if smoking an invisible cigarette. "Oh, honey. Stone was three sheets to the wind that night."

"He was drunk?"

"Yes, he was hammered. He wouldn't remember, though. Stone's a sorry drunk, like his dad. They tend to black out and forget things the next day."

That shed a whole new light on things. I'd thought Stone's drinking was controlled. He'd certainly acted disgusted enough with his dad's alcoholism that day in the conservatory.

Dietrich continued. "Now don't get me wrong. I think after Margo's death, Stone had some kind of epiphany. The last few times I've talked to him, he sounded downright repentant. In fact, he said he was determined to make it up to Margo, but he didn't tell me how."

"He was looking for her killer," I said. "At least that's what he was pretending to do. But I have some news to share too."

Dietrich swirled a lanky finger in the air as if conjuring something. "Do tell."

"Stone is down at the police station now for questioning."

Dietrich's face fell. "What? Why? Do we need to get a lawyer for him?"

"Stone will probably have to get his own lawyer, if things go the way I think they are."

I stopped speaking as recognition crept across Dietrich's face. He was putting things together, and in just a moment he'd see—

"Hang on. Do you mean they're looking at Stone for Margo and Frannie's murders? Is that what you're saying to me right now?" His eyes turned wild.

I placed a steadying hand on his arm. "It's possible."

"I never should've trusted him. And if he was the father of Margo's baby, she didn't trust him, either," Dietrich spat out.

"Why do you say that?"

"That night Margo told me she was pregnant, she wouldn't say who the father was. But she told me he was dangerous, and she was afraid he'd do something crazy. I told her she had to get protection and she said she was going to talk to some kind of security guy about it."

Val. So she really had planned to talk with him, but not about dating. About protection.

Dietrich was getting worked up. He bounced his legs in a frenzied beat. "I knew I should've walked her out that night, but I couldn't get past the fact she'd had a baby with another man. It blew my mind, you know?"

I nodded. "So where'd you go after talking with her?"

"Back to the billiards room. Stone stuck around for maybe ten more minutes, then he stumbled out and said he was heading to bed. The party basically broke up then. I walked Frannie out to her car, and I think Stone's driver took Jet and Sophie back to their place. As far as I knew, Margo left directly from the study after she dropped her big news on me. "

"That still means it's possible Stone killed her," I said.

Dietrich pondered. "I guess so. I mean, I saw him putting quite a few drinks down, but he could've been faking somehow. Being drunk off his gourd would be a great alibi, right?"

"Except he didn't use it. He told the cops he was in the billiards room all night." I was getting confused. What if Dietrich was feeding me a line of baloney? Why had he come all the way to Greenwich just to volunteer information, anyway?

I stood. "You need to go. I have to think about things."

He stood and rubbed his goatee. "You and me both. I don't know whether I should go in to the police with my story, especially since Stone's down there right now."

"You could call them," I offered. "Detective Watson's the one you'd want to ask for."

"Got it. I'll do that," he said. "And Belinda, seriously, you have to be more careful. You were running all over town with Stone. He could've killed you, too."

"You don't have to tell me twice." I walked Dietrich to the door. "Thanks for coming by and filling me in. I guess we'll both have to wait and see how things play out."

I didn't offer to meet Dietrich again, because I was having second thoughts about his story and I needed to figure out how it held up. At the very least, I could hunt down Jet or Sophie, whoever they were, and verify whether Stone had been drunk or not.

I closed the door behind Dietrich and flipped both my locks. It was time to retreat in my little carriage house and try to make sense of things.

I could scrounge meals from what I had in the house while I mulled things over; maybe work up a new game article to clear my head.

I absently picked up my phone and flipped through my phone contacts, wishing I had someone local to confide in. Scrolling down, I saw Frannie's name, which triggered an unexpected torrent of tears. What had she ever done to anyone? All she'd wanted was a warm, home-cooked Thanksgiving dinner, for the love of everything.

I noticed my voice mail symbol had lit up. I glanced over my unopened messages. The most recent ones were from Stone, and I couldn't bring myself to play them. But there was an older one—from Thanksgiving Day.

Frannie had called me.

I turned the volume up and pushed the play button. Her familiar voice sounded so alive.

"Hi, Belinda. Listen, I'm over at the Carringtons' for Thanksgiving dinner today. I want to test a little theory I have. I'll let you know how it works out. I'm not telling Stone yet"—she gave a nervous giggle—"but you'll know when I do!"

That was it. She gave no clue as to what her theory was, though her manner and words seemed to indicate she could've suspected Stone for some reason. The poor woman hadn't known she was going to die the same day.

I cried even harder when it hit me that for once, she'd gotten my name right.

Chapter 23

By nighttime, Rasputin had gotten a bit more active. Although I could never tell when he was asleep, because snakes didn't have eyelids, he was definitely moving around more than he had recently. I hoped he'd be in top form for his reunion with Reginald on Sunday.

After fixing myself some pancakes and drenching them with syrup Mom had sent, I proceeded to binge-watch three hours of TV, because I didn't feel like writing. Then around midnight, my phone rang.

Stone's number popped up, so I guessed this wasn't his one call from jail.

"Belinda, sorry to bother you, but I wanted to let you know what's going on. We need to talk. Can I come over?"

He had to be kidding me. After two women showed up dead in my flowerbed, he thought I was going to open my door to *any* man in the middle of the night?

"I was just about asleep. Can you tell me on the phone? Were you at the police station all day?"

"Yes. There's something weird going on. From what I can gather, things are starting to point to me. They didn't tell me what, but I swear they asked me every question in the book."

Frustration rose until I had to say something. "Dietrich came over while you were gone."

"Really? That's strange."

"He was looking for you. But the thing is, he said you'd lied about that night. He said you were drunk."

I waited for some kind of rebuttal, but none came. Finally, Stone said, "Yeah. I think I was."

"You *think*? Seriously, you don't remember?"

"I'd really like to talk to you face-to-face. This is going to sound really bad on the phone."

Predictably, I felt an urge to give in to him. I cut that down quickly.

"No, I can't do that." I was tired of making allowances. "I don't know if I can trust you now."

"Okay," he said. "What if Red came along?"

"What, is Red at your beck and call now? You sound like a mob boss. Listen, I'm telling you I need some space, so you're going to have to back off."

The harshness of my words made me feel like I was channeling Katrina. But I felt cornered and unsafe.

Stone finally seemed to understand. "I know you're feeling betrayed. I lied about being drunk because I couldn't admit I didn't know what happened that night." His voice dropped. "I also couldn't admit what you might've already figured out—that I was turning into a drunk like my dad."

Now I regretted not letting him come over, so I could've watched his face as he confessed this to me. Was he being truthful, or just playing on my emotions?

"Dietrich said as much," I said noncommittally.

"I figured he'd tell on me sooner or later. For some reason, he went along with my story at first."

"He probably thought you were innocent then."

His voice deflated. "And now? Even my friends are turning against me?"

Did Stone even have any friends left? I changed the subject. "Why did they keep you so long at the station? Did they have something on you?"

"I don't know. I'll have to get a lawyer, I guess. Dad knows a good one."

I thought of my run-in with Stone the fourth and his flannel pajamas. "You're taking advice from your dad now?"

"Dad might be going through a rough patch, but he'll pull out of it."

I didn't relent. "Just like you will?"

Stone gave a short laugh. "Whoa, Belinda. Like I said before, you're savage. Here's the deal: when I realized I couldn't remember anything about the night Margo was killed, I decided to quit drinking. Cold turkey."

I thought of Stone's obvious inebriation the day we went to Frannie's. Did he think I hadn't noticed? "And have you stuck with it?"

"I've had a lapse or two, but the bottom line is that I'm sick of not driving. I'm sick of forgetting things. It's like I can't give all of myself to anything. I'm only half there."

Dude. This was some heavy stuff, the kind of deep reflections Katrina would try to get her clients to share. Only I had no training as to how to help Stone work through things.

"I'm sorry," I said, hoping he heard the truth in my tone.

"I just want you to know that no matter what they think they have on me, I didn't hurt Margo. I *know* I would've remembered that. I didn't have any reason to kill her. Do I seem like a psychopath?"

I had no clue what psychos seemed like, but Stone's miserably broken state didn't seem to fit the mold. And I was pretty sure if he'd fathered Margo's baby, being of such a gentlemanly nature, he would've stepped up to the plate instead of trying to strangle her.

"No, I don't think you do. Call me when they tell you anything. I'm going to be hanging around my house."

"That's wise," he said.

"Alone," I emphasized.

"Gotcha. I'll stay away, I promise. I guess you ruled Dietrich out when you talked with him?"

I sighed, unsure. "I think so."

"Who's left? Father Jesse?"

"I guess so, but what can we do about him? He's not talking to us."

Stone grunted. "Maybe I could work on him tomorrow. I went easy on him during our last visit, but it's time for the games to end. Margo was covering for someone, and if he knows who it is, he has a duty to tell the cops."

I figured if Stone brought the full force of his family name to bear, the reluctant priest might pay attention. The Carrington family had probably been around long enough to fund half the buildings in the town, including the Episcopal church.

I capitulated. "Okay, Father Jesse is all yours. He didn't like me anyway."

Stone laughed. "I can't imagine why not. Oh wait, maybe because you came at him with both barrels blazing."

I laughed in spite of myself. I really missed hanging out with Stone. He never shot down my ideas and he was more than ready to step out on a limb with me.

"Call me tomorrow," I said.

"You got it, Blondie."

I hung up and couldn't wipe the grin from my face. The clock read twelve forty-three, way too late to be up chatting, but things felt more settled in my mind. My instincts flew in the face of Mrs. Lewis's story,

Frannie's phone call, and Dietrich's misgivings about Stone. Not to mention whatever evidence Detective Watson thought he had.

It didn't matter. I finally went to sleep, resting easier now I knew Stone was still next door. Because I was almost totally convinced he wasn't the killer.

* * * *

Katrina called in the morning as I was loading my coffeemaker. As she talked, I leaned against the sink, staring out at the flowerbed I hadn't visited since before Frannie's death. It seemed I should arrange a pile of decorative rocks, or maybe plant some perennials, to memorialize where the women's bodies had been.

"Sis? Did you hear me? I asked how the car's doing for you."

"Fine, fine. I mean, I haven't driven it much."

"Why not?"

She was going to drag it out of me one way or another. I went ahead and pulled the pin on my verbal grenade and tossed it out in the open. "There's been another murder. The police detective suggested I stay home a little while."

"You're kidding! And why are you supposed to lie low? Is he making an arrest?"

"I hope so." Only I hoped it wasn't Stone.

"You'd better tell me what's going on, or I'm driving down today."

I had no doubt my sister would do just that. And if Mom knew, she'd do the same. I tried to ease Katrina's misgivings by sharing what Dietrich and Stone had said, but it only made her more apprehensive.

"Sounds like Stone's moved to the front of the pack as lead suspect," Katrina said. "Under no circumstances should you open your door to him."

"I'm not utterly dense. I don't plan to."

After several more warnings, Katrina had to get back to work. When I hung up, I caught movement outside and peered out my back window. Jacques was clearing my back patio with a leaf blower. He wore ear protection, or I would've shouted a hello to him. I wanted to thank him for checking in on my carriage house...and maybe probe for details about how he found Frannie.

A surge of stir-craziness hit me and I decided to get out into the mild weather. I was tired of being cooped up alone. I changed to jeans and a hoodie, but by the time I went out, Jacques was nowhere to be found.

I ambled around in front of my house, unable to relax at the backyard bistro table I had previously enjoyed. Driven by the certainty that I shouldn't be wasting my time when Stone had probably gone to question Father Jesse, I made a brief jaunt into my kitchen and grabbed a jar of honey. I'd take it over to the manor house, spy around, and if someone ran into me, I'd offer the honey as an early Christmas gift.

Like most of my plans, it was flawed, but I'd make it work.

Chapter 24

I thought I'd follow my stealthy bush-lurking route from last time, but when I neared the house, that idea crashed and burned. Melly stepped into her driveway and immediately caught sight of me. She leaned into the car and said something to Red, then made her way to me.

It seemed to take a while, thanks to her petite legs and high heels. I continued walking toward her and met her in the grass.

She was beautifully turned out today, wearing a ruby necklace and numerous large-gemstone rings. She had an oversized silk scarf draped around her arms. She smelled soft, like candy and jasmine. Her dark hair was pulled back in a twisted chignon.

In fact, she looked like the business end of the Carrington business, even though she wasn't even involved in it.

"Is everything okay at the house?" she asked breathily. "Mrs. Lewis said everything was in order, but it has to be so trying for you right now. The police assure me they're doing all they can to deal with this unpleasantness."

Yes, two murders would qualify as some serious "unpleasantness."

I extended the honey jar, the pale golden alfalfa honey catching the light. "I'm doing fine. As a matter of fact, I was just bringing this early Christmas gift over. It's honey from my parents' area."

She took it. "Delightful. I was actually just heading out. Would you mind running it into the kitchen for me? They'll know where to store it."

"Of course." I smiled. "Please don't worry on my account." It was her son she needed to worry about, but I didn't point that out.

She gave my hand a squeeze and we walked back to the car together. Red politely tipped his hat as I approached. I wondered where Melly was off to, but it was probably some high-class Greenwich society meeting.

Regardless, I had my excuse to go into the manor house, so I went inside and headed to the kitchen. Lani emerged from the pantry, carrying a large carton of tomatoes.

"Hello, Miss Blake," she said.

I hadn't realized she knew my name. "Hello. Lani, is it?"

We made small talk, then I tried to work around to the topic of what happened on Thanksgiving. "I was up at my parents' house on the day Frannie died," I said. "I was so sorry to hear about it. That must've been horrible."

Lani held a fluttery hand up to her chest. "Oh, Miss Blake, it was. A tragedy. And she loved my pumpkin trifle so much."

Sadly, the ardent love for a pumpkin trifle had no power to stop a cold-blooded murderer.

"So Jacques found her soon after she left?" I asked.

"Not even an hour later," she lamented, her coffee brown eyes filling with tears.

"I'm surprised Jacques worked on Thanksgiving," I said. "Wasn't he with his family that day?"

Lani considered. "I believe he has a son, but I think he's grown and out of the house. As I recall, Jacques dropped by to shut down the fountain on Thanksgiving. It was after that first snow, and Mrs. Carrington worried the concrete would freeze."

"And he checked on my carriage house," I added. "Which must've been when he found Frannie." I sighed, feeling like I was going in circles. I tried a different approach. "After Frannie left, did you see any of the Carringtons heading outside?"

Lani set a couple of heads of garlic on a chopping board and began to expertly crush the cloves. "I'll tell you exactly what I told the police—I didn't pay much attention because I was clearing the plates. But the last I saw of them, Mrs. Melly was talking to Jacques in the entryway, Mr. Stone the fourth was heading upstairs, and Mr. Stone the fifth came in to help me in the kitchen." She smiled. "That boy is a sweetheart. He always tries to help me do my job."

Somehow I wasn't surprised to hear Lani's glowing assessment of Stone the fifth's humility. A large part of what drew me to him was his lack of pretense about his station and family wealth.

Since Melly had been talking with Jacques, I didn't think she would've had the chance to attack Frannie. Besides, why would she? But Stone the elder was a different story. Sure, he'd *looked* like he was going upstairs, but there were plenty of ways he could've redirected his course and trailed Frannie outside.

I thanked Lani for her time and let her get back to her food preparation. Judging by the ingredients she had laid out on the granite countertop, it looked like a delicious Italian meal was on the agenda for tonight. My stomach growled and I wished I'd eaten more than half an English muffin.

I headed into the dining room, slowing to gape at its ornate decor. The long, polished table looked straight of *Downton Abbey*. Plush red roses adorned the cherry wood table, and paintings that were likely real, not reproductions, lined the walls. Predictably, I didn't see any of Dietrich's work. What would it be like to eat a meal in this room? I thought I would probably feel like royalty.

I wished I could poke around the house, maybe check out the study or the billiards room, but that would definitely be too risky. Casting about for something to examine next, I determined I'd have to go back outside. Maybe I could somehow retrace Frannie's steps when she left the house.

Had Frannie driven herself over that day? Unlike Stone, she didn't have to rely on a driver all the time. If she'd driven, she had probably parked in the side gravel lot. The police would've checked her car and returned it to her family by now, but maybe they'd missed something.

I crunched around to the side of the house. Only a handful of cars were parked there, and they were all older models, so I guessed this was where the hired help and visitors parked. I walked between the cars, eyes fixed to the ground in case Frannie had dropped something or left a clue.

Suddenly, a small cavalcade of police cars hurtled up the driveway. The lead car stopped in front of the manor house door and someone jumped out. I immediately recognized him as Detective Watson.

Something must've turned up. Maybe the detective's evidence, whatever it was, had finally pointed to someone definitively.

But who?

I stood frozen, realization sinking in that they might be here to pick up Stone the fifth. And this time, I doubted they'd allow him to walk out of the station.

A dull thud sounded in one of the cars nearby. What on earth?

I glanced around. I was probably hearing things because I was so on edge. My attention returned to the police cars out front.

But there was another light pounding noise, and this time, I was sure it was coming from a car. I turned and began speed walking between them, but there was no one in sight.

Then I heard a metallic clunk, like someone had kicked something.

The trunk. Someone was in a trunk.

Chapter 25

I hurried from car to car, banging on every trunk. "Who's there? Are you in here?"

When I pounded on the trunk of a small silver car, a weak thump sounded in return. I raced to the front door to try to get to the trunk release lever, but the door was locked.

"Hang on!" I shouted, taking off for the cops.

I hurriedly explained the situation to the nearest officer, and he grabbed a slim metal tool and followed me. After jimmying the car door, he pulled the trunk release. I stood by the trunk as it opened, and it took me a moment to recognize the person inside.

It was Mrs. Lewis, but her face had been badly beaten. Duct tape covered her mouth, so I tried to pull it off as gently as possible. Her eyes were hazy, and I suspected she was about to lapse into unconsciousness. The police officer barked some kind of code into his radio, then rushed to check her pulse.

"Help is on the way," I murmured, hoping she understood.

"I can't...too strong," she slurred.

"You're going to be okay," I said, hoping against hope this would be the case. But Mrs. Lewis was no spring chicken, and it looked like someone had beaten her with the intent to kill. I also noticed red welts around her neck, like I'd seen on Margo. Someone had tried to strangle her.

She tried to say something else as the officer spoke into his radio again. Her words were garbled and hoarse, so I leaned in closer. "Wasn't...working," she croaked.

Well, that much was obvious—whatever she'd done to fend off her attacker hadn't worked.

I held her hands in mine until the ambulance appeared. When the paramedics gingerly lifted Mrs. Lewis's body from the trunk, she looked like a mere wisp of a woman. Nothing like the commanding house secretary I'd met the first day I came to the Carrington estate.

Had I just stumbled across a near-murder scene? Did the killer run away as I approached the parking lot, before he had time to finish the job?

I followed the ambulance as it wheeled out into the driveway. As I rounded the corner of the house, I tried to catch a glimpse of what was happening with the police cars.

The front door of the manor house opened, and Detective Watson walked Stone the fifth out. It looked like the detective had thrown a friendly arm around Stone. I wondered what they were talking about. Maybe Stone had stumbled onto some new evidence.

But when Stone turned in front of the police cruiser door, I saw that the detective had been guiding Stone by the elbow.

Stone's hands were cuffed behind him.

He was under arrest.

* * * *

I didn't even stop to think. I ran to the police car, then banged on the closed rear window. Stone was mouthing something, but with all the officers talking around me, I couldn't make it out. Detective Watson threw his door open and walked over to me, like I was Public Enemy Number One.

"What's got you in such a dither?" he asked, his Southern twang strong. "I told you to stay away from Stone the fifth, so this can't come as a surprise to you."

"I know, but are you sure this is the right thing to do? We just found the house secretary in the side parking lot, nearly beaten to death! Her attacker could have been there when I walked over, and that was right about the time you came—"

The detective's voice grew stern. "Belinda, I want you to give a full statement to Officer Lindstrom." He gestured to a tall blond man who was observing our conversation. "But right now, I'm taking Stone in. We have evidence he was there around the time of Frannie's death."

"Evidence that makes you one hundred percent certain he was with her when she died?"

Detective Watson leaned closer. "I can't tell if you're hoping to exonerate this man, or if you're just anxious to make certain we're taking the right man in. Rest assured, we are. Now, obviously, I can't share what our evidence is. All I can say is that you'll be safe now—I'm sure of it."

I glanced into the back window, horrified. Stone stared straight ahead, as if in a trance.

Like a wet wool blanket, doubts threatened to suffocate me. I'd suspected Stone, then I'd talked myself out of the notion. He'd seemed so convincing the last time he called, when he'd said he would talk with Father Jesse today.

I waited until Detective Watson turned to speak to one of his officers, then I gave a covert tap on the police car window. Stone blinked, turning my way. "Father Jesse?" I asked.

Stone gave a short nod. He said two words, so I dipped down, pressing my ear against the closed window. Stone repeated the words again—first once, then twice. Although the sound was muffled, I was fairly sure he'd said, "Your phone."

Detective Watson began to turn, so I straightened and gave him a bored look. The detective abruptly dusted his hands together, like he was washing them of this entire business. "I'll call you later, Belinda. Officer Lindstrom?"

The tall man moved my way and I threw a final glance at Stone. His despondency seemed palpable, even through the closed window.

Gathering my thoughts, I was somehow coherent as I walked Officer Lindstrom through the events in the parking lot. By the time he had my statement, I was feeling chilled and ready for a hot cup of anything. The moment the officer gave me leave, I ran back to my carriage house, not caring how anxious I looked.

Once safely inside, I locked the door, then threw myself directly onto the couch. Sobs overtook me, and I gave in to them. Memories swirled to the surface, reminding me of failed love interests through the years. There'd been Lee, my high school crush who'd hardly known I was alive, at least until my "friend" Tammy had blabbed that I was the secret admirer who'd sent him a hand-crafted Valentine's card. After that, he'd actively started to avoid me. In college, there was my boyfriend Colin, with his delightful British accent and his utter disdain for how American I was. Needless to say, that didn't last. I'd all but sworn off love until I fell hard for Micah, who'd longingly shared how perfect I was for him...right before he decided to leave the Peace Corps and start medical school.

Love seemed to have it in for me, or maybe I just really knew how to pick 'em. Either way, this was exactly where I always ended up. In tears. Alone. Again.

"Oh, Rasputin," I wailed. "Every time I think I've found a good man, it turns into a miserable disaster. What is *wrong* with me?"

The snake didn't have an answer, and neither did I.

* * * *

After I'd fixed a mug of hot chocolate and eaten a few crackers to settle my stomach, I pulled out my phone to see what Stone had been talking about. It must have been on vibrate all morning, because I found a message he'd left around eleven.

"I went to see Father Jesse," his message began. He sounded relaxed and confident. "Somehow I managed to talk him into a chat. He said Margo had never mentioned a name, but she'd voluntarily asked for counseling about a relationship she was in. He got the feeling she felt threatened somehow, but she never elaborated on it. He said he'd recently talked to the police and told them the same thing." He paused. "Okay. That's about it. Call me and we'll talk."

I replayed the message, trying to discern any hidden meanings behind what Father Jesse had said. There seemed to be none, except for the fact that he'd actually confided in Stone, which seemed to indicate that he didn't think Stone was Margo's dangerous love interest.

I didn't either.

Despite the overwhelming evidence that Stone the fifth was likely the murderer, it just didn't add up. Stone may have liked Margo in the past, but from everything he and everyone else said, it seemed they were nothing more than casual friends now. Not exactly the type of relationship Margo would've feared extricating herself from.

I needed some outside perspective on Stone's habits. Val might know something, but judging from how surprised Stone was that Val was interested in Margo, I figured they didn't tell each other everything.

Dietrich was out too, because he'd already shared all he knew about Stone. Maybe he could give me Sophie and Jet's number, though. I didn't hold much hope that those two had any information, given how everyone said they were so wrapped up in each other, they were oblivious to anything else.

I absently glanced out the window, experiencing a small thrill when my gaze fell on my blue Volvo. I finally owned a car. It seemed surreal, after all these years without one. I'd gotten through college borrowing my parents' old beater cars. Then I'd traveled with the Peace Corps and gotten used to bumming rides. I hadn't really minded.

Unlike Stone, who was used to driving his own Lamborghini around.

That was it. I knew who I needed to talk to, the one person who could give me the perspective I needed. Not a friend, but someone who knew just about every move Stone made.

Red.

Chapter 26

I took a deep breath and called Red. I wasn't sure what information I was looking for, but I had a feeling I'd know it when Red shared it.

He picked up the first ring. "Miss Blake?"

I could hear men talking in the background and I wondered where he was. He'd driven Melly somewhere. Was he killing time with the other chauffeurs? Taking a quick drink at some kind of watering hole?

I decided to tackle the most pressing issues first. "Red, the police were just here. They arrested Stone and took him to the station. And Mrs. Lewis was attacked. She's at the hospital now. She was in very rough shape."

Red didn't skip a beat. "I'll bring Mrs. Carrington home now. Thank you for letting me know."

I plunged on. "Also, could we talk when you get back? I could meet you at Dunkin' Donuts."

I was proud of myself for thinking of meeting in a public place. Even Katrina would be impressed that I hadn't thrown caution completely to the wind. While I was nearly one hundred percent certain Red couldn't be the murderer—he was out driving around when Mrs. Lewis was attacked, and he probably wasn't even around on the days Frannie and Margo were killed—I was playing it safe.

"Of course, Miss Blake. I'll call you when I arrive."

I liked the way Red took me seriously. He didn't ask why I wanted to meet at Dunkin' Donuts and he didn't question the nature of our meeting. He just assumed I had a good reason.

Feeling hopeful as I hung up, I checked the temperature in Rasputin's cage and gave him new water. It was hard to believe we'd be trekking back to Manhattan in the morning. I wanted to head in early so I could tidy up at Reginald's a bit before he returned. It would also give Rasputin a chance to acclimate to his larger cage again.

I fixed an easy lunch. The sunlight pouring into the windows seemed to flood me with fresh strength. Although I was tempted to sit at the bistro table, I settled for scooting my kitchen chair into a pool of light as I ate.

Looking out at the flowerbeds, I guessed at their dimensions. Then I scrolled through flower bulb websites, adding pink daffodils, red and white tulips, and a couple of peonies to my virtual shopping cart. It was too late this year to plant bulbs, but I could prepare for next fall. I'd make every attempt to take away the stigma of the deathly flowerbed.

The sunlight had made me drowsy, so I snuggled under a blanket on the couch. I picked up a book to kill time until Red called back. I couldn't stop thinking about how Stone had sat in this very room and opened up to me about his life. I had reveled in our similarities, hoping we could become closer.

I wasn't ready to give up on Stone yet.

* * * *

Red called me around two. It had taken longer to return home since Melly had asked him to stop at the police station first. I didn't probe, but he did say that when she came out of the station, she'd been more furious than he'd ever seen her.

Dunkin' Donuts was surprisingly busy. I ordered a medium coffee with cream and sugar, then caved and bought a cream-filled chocolate donut. Red got a black coffee and a bear claw that was the size of four donuts put together.

As usual, Red was easy to talk to. We chatted about the weather, then I told him I was following up on some things for Stone, which was partly true.

"Did Stone visit Margo's house frequently over the past few months?" I asked.

He blew on the hot coffee. "You talking about Stone the fifth?"

"Of course. He's the one who was just arrested."

Red shifted in his seat, and a couple of people darted glances our way. I had a feeling he could be quite intimidating, should he so desire. "Stone the fifth never went to Margo's house."

He fell silent, and I scrambled to fill in the blanks. "Wait. So did Stone the *fourth* go to her house?"

"No."

He took a huge bite of bear claw and munched.

I put two and two together. "But Stone the fourth met Margo somewhere else."

Red grinned and gave a slight incline of his head.

I took a wild stab. "Stone the fourth and Margo were having an affair."

Red gulped his coffee. "I'm sure I couldn't say."

I leaned forward. "And you never mentioned this to the police?"

He didn't answer, but he didn't have to. The one who controlled the purse strings was the one who controlled Red. He probably made a good income working for the Carringtons, and if he'd squealed on Stone the fourth, his job would've been forfeit.

My mind raced. Stone the fourth made sense. He was volatile and maybe even dangerous due to his alcoholism, Margo would feel the need to hide their relationship, and he did seem to have an eye for younger ladies, given his bawdiness that day in the conservatory.

And when Mrs. Lewis said she'd seen Stone chasing Margo out the door, what if she'd meant Stone the fourth? It was entirely possible I'd misread that conversation.

I nibbled a piece of my donut, the white cream oozing onto my tongue. Washing it down with the strong coffee, I finally formulated another question.

"I wonder if Melly knows?"

Red shrugged as if unwilling to say more.

I took time wording my next thought. "Stone the fifth was all too aware of his father's alcoholism. I'm betting if he knew anything about this affair, he would've done all he could to stop it."

"Sounds like you know Mr. Stone quite well," Red said, polishing off the last cinnamon-iced bite of the bear claw.

It seemed Red agreed that Stone the younger hadn't known of his father's dalliance with Margo.

So apparently, Red and I were on the same page. We both didn't really believe the younger Stone could've strangled two girls and attacked Mrs. Lewis.

Red drained the last of his coffee as I wiped my mouth with a napkin. Apologetically, I began to overexplain. "I'm sorry you had to come over here. I just couldn't meet you at my house. I mean—"

He interrupted. "That was smart. You're a young girl, living alone. There've been two strangulations right next to your place. It's wise to exercise caution—with everyone in the Carrington household." He stretched his legs to their full length, and as his pants rode up, I could've sworn I saw a holster strapped around his ankle. Gun? Knife?

The sight of the holster might have made some people nervous, but I felt just the opposite. It was comforting to know that Red was prepared for anything, and I made a mental note of it. Even though I knew next to nothing about Red, besides the fact he'd been in the Army, I was sure he wasn't pulling any punches with me. In fact, he seemed almost protective of me, in his reserved way.

But as Katrina would point out, I was sometimes too trusting, so I kept my guard up when Red walked me to my car. After he pulled out ahead of me, I let out a huge breath. It was exhausting, being suspicious of everyone. I didn't know how Katrina managed to be so wary all the time. My sister expected people to earn her trust, because she certainly wouldn't bestow it on them otherwise. I preferred to give everyone the benefit of the doubt, until they let me down in some major way.

I imagined what a relief it would be if Katrina could come live in my carriage house. She could be observant and distrustful and cautious *for* me. I could live the carefree life of exotic pet-sitting and video gaming I'd signed up for. Stone the fifth and I could have dazzling picnics on the beach and eat at the best Manhattan restaurants.

But of course, reality had already given my leisure-life dreams a swift and hard kick to the pants. I had to gear up with my own armor and charge forward, weighing each story and each person's intentions, just like Katrina would.

Besides, I wasn't entirely incompetent. I'd been on my own for years, starting with college and the Peace Corps. Sure, I tended to live like a hermit, but I'd learned that I needed significant blocks of down-time— *alone*-time—and if I didn't have those, I never recharged and I became a grouchy brute.

Life in the carriage house hadn't left me much time alone. I seemed to constantly be interacting with people here, from the Carringtons and their staff to Stone's billiards friends.

I broke from my thoughts as I pulled back into the gate at the manor house. Val sat in the Security booth, so I slowed and rolled down my window. "Any news?" I asked.

He shook his head. "Far as I know, they're still holding Stone. Oh, and you have a visitor."

Puzzled, I drove around to my carriage house. A shiny white BMW sat in my driveway. I edged up behind it and stepped out.

Ava Fenton rolled down her window, sliding her oversized sunglasses down her nose. "Belinda. I heard about Stone and it's *dreadful*. And Melly told me about Mrs. Lewis—the poor woman is hanging on by a thin thread. Now, listen—I've determined to give you a proper thank you for cleaning Margo's room and for...being honest about what you found in there. Besides, I thought you would probably like to get away from all the uproar around here. So I'm extending an invitation for a meal at our house tonight. Please don't say no—cooking helps me take my mind off things."

I started to refuse, but Ava's hopeful look spoke volumes. The poor woman only wanted to cook for me. "You know, that sounds wonderful. I'd love to visit."

"Excellent. Let's say six o'clock? I just bought the ingredients. We'll have prosciutto-stuffed chicken with mushroom sauce, green beans with brown butter, and plenty of other deliciousness."

I could practically taste it. "I can't wait. Thank you."

Ava pulled away, and instead of driving toward the house, she circled back to the gate. She must've already visited with Melly. I wondered how Melly was doing, given what Red had said about her angry exit from the police station. Maybe Ava had stopped by to help her calm down. I imagined Stone the fourth had offered little support, given his near-constant state of inebriation.

Why would Margo have fallen for someone like that? How long had Stone the fourth been a drinker? Stone the fifth had said his dad was going through a rough patch, so maybe the drinking had picked up after Margo's death.

Maybe it was because he was grieving—or guilty.

Just as I got in the door, my cell phone rang. Dietrich was calling to see if there had been any new developments today.

Had there ever.

I told him about Stone's arrest, and he gave a small screech. "Should I drop by, maybe stop in at the station?"

"I doubt it. Stone is probably lawyering up and I figure things are crazy at the station right now. But you could help by giving me Sophie and Jet's phone number, so I can ask them a few questions."

Dietrich rattled papers in the background. "You're still digging into that night? I hate to say this, but it sounds pretty conclusive that our chum Stone jumped the rails somewhere and started killing people."

"I can't quite believe it," I said.

"I do, and I've known him for years," Dietrich said calmly. "He was drinking that night, and like I said, he's a bad drunk."

"Whatever. Can you just give me the number?"

Dietrich clicked his tongue as if unable to believe my naiveté, but he retrieved Sophie and Jet's phone number for me. I scrawled it down and we said our goodbyes.

Even as I punched their number in, I had the sinking feeling that whatever the lovebird couple saw, *if* they'd seen anything that Monday night, would only corroborate the theory that Stone was drunk and had followed Margo outside.

But I would go down every trail to find out what really happened. And hopefully, I'd stumble onto a trail or two that didn't point to Stone the fifth.

Chapter 27

Sophie picked up the phone after the fourth ring. She sounded stoned. When I explained that I was Stone's friend, she seemed fairly disinterested.

Until I told her Stone was in jail, at which point she perked up considerably and shouted to someone in the other room. Presumably it was Jet.

"Guess what? Stone-boy got himself thrown in the slammer," she yelled.

A man with a deep voice responded to Sophie, then he took the phone. "Who's this?" he growled.

After explaining who I was and why I was calling, the man seemed to calm down. "This is Jet," he said. "Yeah, we were there that night. Played some pool—I mean billiards—and hung out."

"And did you notice when Margo left?"

"You know, the cops asked us that, too. Honestly, Sophie and I were kind of otherwise engaged."

Sophie gave a nervous giggle, and I realized Jet had put me on speakerphone. I directed my next question to both of them.

"Was there anything unusual about that night? Did Margo or Stone act strangely?"

"I don't think so," Sophie said.

Jet spoke up. "Yeah, I mean the weirdest thing that night would've been Dietrich. Usually he's hanging around Margo like a leech, but they went out to talk and when Dietrich came back, he'd turned into the Ice King. Margo wasn't with him."

"The Abomadorable Snowman," Sophie said, in a sleepy voice.

Jet continued, ignoring Sophie's made-up word. "Dietrich didn't want to play anymore, so he went and spoke with Frannie, who was also sulking around, but that's nothing new. Not long after that, Stone said he had to go to bed—he was smashed as usual—so we had him call his driver to take us home."

"We were smashed, too," Sophie added helpfully.

Their side of the conversation abruptly digressed into kissing noises. I made a desperate attempt to pull things back on-track.

"Did Dietrich do anything out of the ordinary, though? Or he was just sulky?"

After one particularly smacking-loud smooch, Jet answered. "Let's see. He walked Frannie out to her car while we waited on Red. Frannie drove off, I know that much—that girl drove like a maniac—but Dietrich never left, even after we pulled out."

Sophie said, "Yeah, Dietrich the *artiste* is usually the first to roll. He always has to get back to his precious parking place in the city. Too good for the subway. We're not like that, are we, angel-eyes?"

More kissing ensued, and it was obvious I wasn't getting either of them back. I murmured a brief thanks and hung up.

So Dietrich hadn't been as honest as he'd seemed. He had stuck around after Frannie left...to meet up with Margo?

And had Stone the *fourth* or Stone the *fifth* followed Margo outside that night? If only Mrs. Lewis would have elaborated on that. I was inclined to think it was Stone the fourth, and Melly swore Mrs. Lewis to secrecy so her husband wouldn't be incriminated. But would her husband have inspired such an outburst of tears?

Maybe I could go over and talk to Melly. She'd seemed so concerned about me this morning. I could play up my distress, maybe fill her in on what happened with Mrs. Lewis, and try to probe around for information. If Stone the fourth was wrapped up in this, he surely wouldn't harm me in front of his wife.

I slid my pepper spray in my pocket and walked briskly toward the manor house. I was crunched for time due to Ava's meal, but I wanted to do as much sleuthing as I could before I headed to Manhattan tomorrow. Who knew how long they'd hold Stone in jail?

I rang the doorbell, hesitated, then tried the knob. The door wasn't locked, so I quietly stepped into the hallway. I really needed a map to this place. Without Mrs. Lewis around, how would I ever locate Melly?

As if in answer to my thoughts, Stone the fourth waltzed into the room. "Thought I heard someone ring the bell," he said. "We need to get a butler or something, don't you think?"

What I thought was that it was extremely rude for a father to be cracking jokes the same day his son had been thrown in the slammer.

I forced a slight smile. "It would be helpful, especially now that Mrs. Lewis is in the *hospital*." He seemed oblivious to the seriousness of the situation.

"Of course," he said, running a hand through his thick, dark hair. That was one thing he had going for him, I guessed. I scanned his face, wondering afresh what he had that could have possibly attracted Margo. His eyes were blue, only bloodshot. His face looked haggard and his pants rode down on his thin waist.

I glanced at his hands. He had long fingers, like his son's, but they were bony. It seemed the only realistic thing Stone the fourth could've tempted a younger woman with was his wealth.

And if what Frannie had told us was right, wealth could very well have been Margo's biggest temptation. Had Stone the fourth pledged his love to her? Declared he would divorce Melly? That's what I understood older men did in these kinds of affairs. Then the mistress was left high and dry and the men stayed unhappily married to their society wives.

I stood up straighter, determined to complete my mission. "I'm looking for Mrs. Carrington."

"Ah, my beloved wife," he said, and I wanted to smack his facetious mouth. "She's up in her room, but I'll warn you, she's been crying and shouting for hours. I'm staying away from her, and you might want to follow suit."

I narrowed my gaze. "I believe Ava Fenton visited earlier," I said. "I'm sure I'll be fine."

"Really? I didn't see Ava. But sure. I'll take you upstairs." He gestured to the stairs so I could go first, but I had a sneaking suspicion he just wanted to check me out as I walked.

I stayed rooted in place. "Please, lead the way."

As I followed him up the curving staircase, it was even more evident how slight his frame was. Was there any way he could've overpowered young, tall women like Margo or Frannie? Or cruelly beaten the daylights out of Mrs. Lewis?

He glanced back at me. "Have you visited the conservatory lately?" His tone was charged with amusement. Clearly, he was letting me know he hadn't overlooked my little spying expedition.

I remained unflappable. "No."

"Poor Mrs. Lewis," he said, abruptly switching tracks. "She might not make it."

He made me sick. Even though Mrs. Lewis was a blackmailing piece of work, she'd suffered a brutal attack—in Stone Carrington the fourth's parking lot.

"I hope you have insurance," I spat out.

He turned, giving me a surprisingly astute look. "I assure you, I do, Miss Blake. Our company is one of the wealthiest around." His lips curled into a scornful smile.

So he did have *some* pride, despite his pajama-clad, housebound days of wine and roses. Even if it was only pride in the business his son was basically running for him.

Skimming around a glossy-finish Queen Anne table in the center of the hallway, he led me to a door and banged on it several times. Placing a hand to the side of his mouth, he whispered, "Good luck."

When glass cracked and shattered into other side of the door, Stone the fourth tore off as if he'd personally been hit. I gave a gentle knock and shouted, "Melly? It's Belinda."

After a moment, I heard someone crunching over glass to open the door. When Melly opened it, I couldn't help but gape at her.

What stood before me was a woman I hardly recognized.

Chapter 28

If I hadn't met Melly Carrington before, I would've mistaken her for a teenager. No longer did she look like a well-heeled matron of Greenwich society.

Melly's hair tumbled around her in a dark, unruly cloud. Every speck of her makeup had been cried off and her face was reddened and puffy. She wore flat slippers, making it noticeable that she didn't stand much over five feet tall.

She snuffled. "Belinda, I'm so sorry you have to see me like this." Her gaze traveled down to the pile of broken glass on the floor. "This is something Mrs. Lewis would've taken care of," she said, launching into a fresh fit of sobbing.

Thankful I hadn't taken my shoes off, I crunched into the room. "Do you have a broom? I'd be happy to sweep."

Melly sniffed again, but her practical side was beginning to take over. "Come to think of it, I believe there's one hanging in my bathroom. Hang on." She walked into a side door and finally emerged with a broom and dustpan. "You'd think I would've thought of that," she said hoarsely.

"It's okay," I said. "It must've been a shock, what happened to Mrs. Lewis. And then with the police and Stone...you're not yourself."

"That's so true," she said. "My poor Stone. But trust me, he has the best lawyer money can buy. And anyway, I don't think the police have anything on him."

I hoped she was right. I gave long, gentle strokes with the broom, distracted by the lustrous colors of the glass shards. "You seemed so upset with Mr. Carrington," I observed, trying to sound nonchalant.

She dropped into a chair. "Yes. Stone has been under my feet from the moment I got home, suggesting this and that, driving me up the wall. I simply couldn't stand it anymore and I told him to get out."

To me, Melly seemed to be the one who'd taken a long dive off a short plank. But I didn't mention that.

I changed the subject. "Have you heard anything about Mrs. Lewis?"

She fiddled with a pillbox on her table. Maybe she'd already taken a couple of Xanax too many. That would explain her unusually moody behavior. Then again, being married to Mister Cheater Pants could also explain her behavior.

"Mrs. Lewis's daughter called and she said her mother's prognosis is grim. She seems to have slipped into a coma."

I picked up the full dustpan and glanced around for a trash can. "I feel horrible. I must've been the last one to see her when she was lucid."

Melly gave me a sharp, curious look. "I'd forgotten they'd said you found her." She clasped her hands together. "Did she say anything to you?"

She probably wondered if Mrs. Lewis had spilled the story of Stone's chasing Margo out the door the night she was killed.

"Nothing important," I said.

Melly looked unconvinced. "But surely it took an effort to say anything at all?"

I attempted to smooth her ruffled feathers. "Like I said, it was literally nothing that made sense. Are we allowed to visit Stone, do you know?"

She shook her head. "Just his lawyer. He's the only one Stone's asked for."

It didn't take a psychology degree to pick up on the pettiness in Melly's tone. It seemed I was just one more nuisance in her life today.

"I understand," I said easily. "I'll head back over to my place. Thanks for filling me in."

Melly scrunched deeper into her chair, picking up her cell phone as I pulled the door shut.

I wondered who she was calling, given her exasperation with Stone the fourth.

* * * *

Outside, the weather had shifted. The sky had faded from blue to dove gray and it smelled like a snow front was moving in. I pulled up my hood and jogged toward the carriage house. Just as I shoved thick curls out of my eyes so I could actually see where I was going, I ran full-force into Jacques.

Thankfully, the solid man didn't teeter. Instead, his hands shot out to grab my elbows and he steadied me. "Miss Blake! Where are you rushing off to, *mademoiselle*?"

"I'm so sorry, Jacques! I'm just getting cold and I need to get ready to go to Mrs. Fenton's house tonight and I'm kind of in a hurry."

I wasn't sure if I'd made sense, but Jacques gave me a knowing nod. "Of course. You are a busy woman, Miss Blake. I, too, must get back to my work."

I gave a vigorous nod. "I saw you leaf blowing this morning, even with so few leaves left on the ground. You certainly are a meticulous gardener." I hoped it was clear how impressed I was.

He gave me a strange look and stalked off. Had I offended the Frenchman somehow? I'd thought we were getting along royally.

I'd spent my Peace Corps years in China, which undoubtedly had different social norms from France. Still, I'd always been openly friendly with Jacques, the man who'd extracted me from Rasputin's vise grip. Maybe my friendliness was lost in translation.

I shook off my confusion and jogged into my house. Time was ticking, and I needed to make an effort to fit into Ava and Adam Fenton's world tonight. Though if my strained conversations with Melly and Stone the fourth offered any indication, I doubted I could even pretend to fit in with the upper crust.

Rasputin slithered around a bit hectically. I wondered if he had some sixth sense that he was going to see Reginald tomorrow.

I was anthropomorphizing a reptile. Just like I anthropomorphized my car. Katrina would probably tell me I had issues, befriending inanimate objects and critters more easily than I befriended human beings.

But I felt no shame about it. Unreliable as cars were and unresponsive as Rasputin was, at least they didn't lie to me.

Unlike almost all the Greenwich crowd I'd talked to thus far.

Chapter 29

Finally settling on a gold sweater that seemed glam in an understated kind of way, I dressed quickly. I took a little more time with my makeup and hair, then added a pair of knee high boots and my wool coat to stave off the cold outside.

Glancing at the humidity level in Rasputin's cage, I stopped to give it one last spritz of water. I grabbed my keys from the side table and locked the door, leaving my porch light blazing. Maybe it would offer a slight deterrent to anyone lurking around with evil intent. As an added precaution, I pulled my rubber doormat up just a little, propping it against the bottom of the door. If someone wanted to sneak in that way, they'd have to move the mat.

But it didn't really matter, because if the police were right, the murderer was already behind bars. Stone the fifth would be out of commission for a good long while.

Yet I wasn't comforted by that thought.

* * * *

Ava Fenton herself let me in, looking dazzling in a rose silk blouse and gold link necklace. Her cheeks had a slight flush and she seemed a bit nervous.

"Adam will be down soon. I know he'll be glad to meet you," she said. "I told him about...well, about what you found in Margo's room. He won't come out and say it, but he is very thankful you told us about it." She gave a hesitant smile. "Now in the meantime, would you like to try some crudités?"

Ava led me into a cozy sitting area where a real-log fireplace crackled. I settled into a wide plush chair and helped myself to roasted cauliflower and dip.

Ava layered some kind of leafy things on her plate. Noticing my bewildered look, she explained, "This fennel is really delicious with the blue cheese dip, I've found."

Ava Fenton had a natural way of putting me at ease that I truly appreciated.

We munched our crudités in pleasant silence. I imagined Margo sitting in this very room, unwinding with her parents, and I felt a pang of guilt. I wished I could give my parents a hug, right then and there.

Distracting me from my morbid thoughts, Adam Fenton strolled in. The weather-worn crinkles at his eyes gave the impression he liked to sail—likely a yacht club type. Radiating confidence, he extended a hand and walked straight over to me. I placed my hand in his and he squeezed it heartily.

"Belinda Blake. Ava has told me so much about you. Welcome to our home."

As Adam settled into a chair next to me, Ava busied herself preparing a plate for him. It was sweet how she knew exactly what he'd want to eat, once again reminding me of my own parents.

Adam grew serious. "How are they treating you over there, Belinda? I hear you're tucked into the Carringtons' carriage house?"

I nodded. "I do love it. Very snug. The back yard seems like a fairy wonderland or something."

Ava blanched at the same time Adam turned to look at her. Realizing what I'd said, I stumbled to retract it. "Not to make light of what's happened there. Oh, my, I don't—"

Adam's eyes softened. "You don't have to apologize, Belinda. Besides, *you're* the one who has to live right next to such a cursed spot. Are you doing okay with that?"

Ava's voice caught as she spoke up. "Be honest with us."

I hesitated. "I can't really say. You know they arrested Stone the fifth yesterday, so I guess I should assume he's the killer."

Ava's eyes rounded. "You don't think he is?"

I positioned my plate on the coffee table. "I'd love to know your thoughts on it. Did Stone hang out with Margo often? Did you get the feeling he was capable of violence, especially something...so terrible?"

I couldn't bring myself to say the word *strangulation* to Margo's parents.

Adam tipped his head up, as if working through memories. Finally, he answered. "I wouldn't have thought it."

Ava's light brown eyebrows furrowed. "Nor would I."

I shivered. "Then that can only mean one thing." I didn't want to elaborate.

Adam filled in the blanks for me. "They haven't found the killer yet," he said.

* * * *

Ready for a break from such heavy thoughts, I joined Ava as she went to the kitchen to dish up food. She had a lovely food-warming setup, complete with gas-heated metal platters. Chatting as we worked, we transferred the food to dishes, then arranged it in the center of the dining room table.

Going about the rote food service tasks that had brought families joy for centuries, I suddenly realized I wasn't feeling anxious or fearful. I just felt like *me*.

"I can't tell you how much I appreciate your hospitality," I said. "I needed this break so much."

Ava smiled. "And we needed to have a young woman in this house for a while. It's like being in a severe withdrawal, one you know you'll never recover from."

Adam swooped into the kitchen, planting a kiss on Ava's head as he caught the tail end of our conversation. His voice cracked. "We will learn to live again, somehow."

Tears welled in my eyes as I filled the glasses with bottled water. It was obvious these two really supported each other. "It's good you have each other," I said.

Ava motioned us to sit at the table. As we arranged napkins on our laps, she said, "Adam grew up right down the road from my family. We know each other so well, we can—"

"Finish each other's sentences," he said, winking.

Ava's smile fell. "That's what made it difficult to watch Margo's dating relationships. She seemed to seek the exact opposite of the stability we'd given her."

I took a bite of my prosciutto-stuffed chicken, pausing a moment to savor it. "Sometimes people rebel and they don't know why," I offered. "Maybe Margo just wanted to know what she'd be missing if she settled into the same life her parents had."

Ava looked thoughtful. "You're probably right."

Adam stabbed up a forkful of green beans. "I only wish I knew the identity of the blaggard Margo had entangled herself with at the end. Do you know that Frannie called us the day before Thanksgiving, saying she might have figured it out? And then someone took her life, as well."

I straightened in my chair. "Did Frannie say who she suspected?"

Adam shook his head. "No. She only hinted that he wasn't Margo's usual type."

"Men like Dietrich Myers were her usual type," Ava said. "Affluent boys who never grew up. They might have houses and cars and everything they could possibly want, but they have no clue how to work for a living."

That brought me back to my theory that Margo wasn't dating a boy, but an older man. And Red had clued me in that Stone the fourth was seeing Margo before her death. Had they been romantically involved? Or had he been meeting her for some other reason?

"Tell me more about the Carringtons' relationship," I said. "Unlike you two, it sounds like they were from entirely different worlds?"

Adam nodded. "Stone grew up in this area and his parents were cornerstones of this community. Stone's parents were huge philanthropists— they made so much money, they could throw plenty away."

Ava took up the tale. "But Melly came from a whole different playing field. Her family's income fluctuated wildly, depending on how much plumbing work their father had. They lived in a really rural part of Connecticut, until her mother pushed her dad to move to Greenwich, in hopes he could make more money."

"And he did," Adam continued. "That's how Stone and Melly met, but I'm sure Ava's already told you that."

"She did," I said, turning back to Ava. "So it must've been a huge adjustment for Melly to take over at that huge house and fit into socialite circles?"

Ava mused on that for a moment. "You know, I don't think it was. Melly once told me she'd determined to have a posh lifestyle when she was small." She chuckled. "She said she'd never let herself date until Stone the fourth asked her out."

"Knew what she wanted," Adam affirmed.

And yet, if my suspicions were correct, Melly had sacrificed love on the altar of wealth. She had married an alcoholic who was possibly also a philanderer.

I wondered if the tradeoff had been worth it.

Chapter 30

I hated to take my leave of Ava and Adam Fenton, but the hours had slipped past and it was already nine at night. Adam offered to follow me home and see me into my carriage house, which I thought was a very thoughtful thing to offer, but I refused. I needed to take care of myself and maintain my independence, otherwise, I might as well pack up shop and move back with my parents.

I figured Margo had been fighting for her own independence, too, no matter how ill-advised her choices were. If only she'd opened up to someone, shared her struggles, she might have received some valuable counsel and gotten out of her dangerous relationship before it destroyed her.

Val was still in the Security booth as I drove in, and he waved me through. Pulling into my well-lit drive, I scanned my front porch. The doormat remained in place, blocking the very bottom of my door.

I patted the Volvo's cold dashboard. "Bluebell, you stay close, in case I have to make a fast getaway." I gave a little chuckle, but I left the car doors unlocked, on the off-chance I had to do that very thing.

The first of my front door locks opened easily, but the second seemed stiff with the cold. I wished I'd worn gloves, as the temperature had really dropped. I repeated the unlocking process and the door finally opened.

I'd left the kitchen light on, so I walked straight in and locked the door behind me. After making a quick check of the rooms, I finally let out a breath. Time for a bath and a good book.

As I poured the water, my phone rang. It was Dietrich.

I remembered how Sophie and Jet said Dietrich had lingered after the billiards party the night of Margo's death. How easy would it have been for Dietrich to meet Margo, strangle her, then take off? But then again, wouldn't Val have seen him pulling out, if he was still in the Security booth, hoping Margo was coming to accept his offer of a date?

Or had Val left soon after Margo didn't show? I needed to ask him that.

The ringing stopped abruptly, and I realized I'd missed my chance to pick up. When I saw Dietrich had left a voicemail, I played it.

"Hi Belinda, it's me, Dietrich." He gave a nervous laugh. "I found the sketch I was looking for. Turns out Margo must've forgotten to take it home."

Maybe she hadn't wanted it around, and had only pretended to leave it behind at Dietrich's loft. Especially if it was one of his nudes that looked nothing like a nude.

Dietrich continued. "I still can't figure out why she was so secretive about letting anyone see the sketch. She was fully clothed in it, after all." He gave a braying laugh. "Sure, I think I caught a certain vulnerability in her eyes, but there was strength there, too. Resolve, maybe? I'd sketched that the week before her death, so maybe she worried it would show her pregnancy? But her stomach is totally flat in this sketch. And she wore this elegant little ruby necklace that nestled right into her clavicle, like a kiss from the—"

His voice cut off as the message ended.

I poured in more of my coconut-scented bubbles, then sank into the tub. Dietrich was obsessed, for sure—it seemed he would never stop rehashing his time with Margo—but he didn't seem the killer type. More like the "please take care of me and be nice to me" type. And I suspected Margo didn't have time for that kind of neediness.

The phone rang from where I'd left it in the kitchen, but I didn't bother jumping out to get it. The bath felt so warm, I wanted to let my troubled thoughts float away. What a gourmet-level meal Ava had cooked. It was interesting that I felt so comfortable with the Fentons. Despite the unthinkable circumstances that forced our paths to cross, it was like I'd finally found real friends in this town.

I reluctantly toweled off and pulled on my warmest black pajamas, which were patterned with frolicking red reindeer. When I stepped into my jingle bell slippers, I felt a surge of Christmas spirit. I would enjoy returning to my parents' house for the holiday season. I wondered if Katrina would be showing any by then.

I padded out to the kitchen, poured water in my teapot, and dumped an envelope of instant chai latte in a mug. Noting another voicemail on my phone, I hit *play.*

"Belinda." It was Stone the fifth.

I hit *pause*. Was he out of jail already? I was sure his parents could post a high bond, but seriously, was it that easy for the wealthy to get out, even if they were murderers?

I turned the volume up and hit *play* again.

"I'm still in jail—a friend of mine works here, so he let me give you a call. The police have a warrant, and they're planning to search the house tomorrow. They've found some evidence—I don't know how, but for some reason, my hair was in Frannie's hand. I...I can't bring myself to tell Dad and Mom. Mom's a wreck—I guess you've probably seen her?"

He lowered his voice. "Listen, I'm not worried, because I have a great lawyer, but also because I know I didn't kill anyone. I am worried about *you*, though. Two murders right outside your carriage house can't be a coincidence, and I know the killer's still on the loose. You shouldn't be alone so much. Maybe you could stop in at Mom's tomorrow morning, make up some excuse about going Christmas shopping? Red will take you anywhere, and that would get you both out of the house when the cops come. Is there anywhere else you can stay for a while?" He turned away from the phone and spoke to someone in the background. "I have to go, but I'll call when I can."

The fact that Stone wasn't even worried about the hair in Frannie's hand screamed *innocence.*

Had Stone somehow been framed? But who would ever want to frame Stone Carrington the fifth, and why?

It seemed so many questions could be answered if the police would just exhume Margo's body and test the baby's DNA. I didn't want to bother Detective Watson at this time of night, but I wasn't above texting him. I typed out my message.

"Hi, Detective Watson. I wondered if you were still planning to exhume Margo's body to find the father's DNA? I am worried that Stone isn't guilty and I hope you are planning to follow up on that angle?"

I was hoping that wasn't too pushy, but at the same time, it bugged me they hadn't done that yet.

I swirled the hot water into my chai, then took a sip. A text binged on my phone and I checked it.

Detective Watson replied that they were exhuming the body tomorrow. I could almost hear his West Virginia accent through his text:

"I told you you'll be safe if you stay put. I'm for dang sure we got the right man. It's those slick ones who do it every time. Born with a silver spoon. I'll check in with you in the morning."

Despite the detective's certainty Stone the fifth was guilty, I remained unconvinced. But he was right on one count—I should be safe enough if I stayed home. And tomorrow I had to return to Manhattan to take Rasputin back, anyway. Maybe I could honor Stone's request and ask Melly if she'd like to come with me and do some shopping.

Right. With a ball python in the car.

Pretty dubious, but for Stone's sake, I'd try.

Chapter 31

I woke in the night, chilled. The wind seemed to whistle through the cracks and crevices in the old carriage house. I walked into the dark hallway, using my phone light to locate the thermostat. After I bumped the heat up, a light movement sounded from Rasputin's cage. He would be feeling this chill even more than I did. I stumbled into the living room and cranked up the temperature on the snake's heat pad.

I headed back down to my room, jumping into bed and yanking the covers up. I hated waking up in the middle of the night. It nearly always resulted in nightmares, for some reason.

Sure enough, I startled awake again and grabbed my phone. 3:22 and a nightmare had jolted me up. What was it again? Someone...yes, it was Margo. She was at Dietrich's, posing nude with a red necklace tight against her throat.

A dainty red necklace...

A ruby necklace...

Just like the one Melly was wearing when she left yesterday.

A crash sounded in the living room and I shot to my feet. But as I cleared the end of my bed, I stopped short.

There was a shadow blocking my doorway.

I dropped to the floor, trying to think. I reached for my phone and the screen lit up.

"You do not want to touch that, Miss Blake."

I knew that voice, but it was so out of place in my tiny house, I refused to believe who it was.

Besides, it was dark. Maybe I was wrong.

The shadow moved and I hesitated. Should I reach for the phone and risk getting shot if the intruder had a gun? Or should I focus on beating him out of my room? I couldn't get to the door, but maybe if I could open a window...

I inched back, toward the windowsill. I mentally rehearsed the steps it would take to escape. I'd have to unlock it, open the glass, open the screen or push it out, then climb out onto the back patio.

Too many steps.

The figure advanced. I rose to my feet. Dangerous as trying to get out the window was, waiting around to be attacked promised to be more dangerous.

Wait—where was my pepper spray? I cast about to remember when I'd last had it. It was probably in the jeans I'd worn today, which were now crammed into my overflowing laundry basket in the bathroom.

So much for that option.

Suddenly, the man gave an "*Oof!*" and thudded to the floor. It sounded like he had tripped over something, which was odd, because there was no furniture between the door and the bed. It was a conveniently straight shot.

I didn't hesitate, but turned and opened the window. I shoved the screen up and scooted out, just as I heard someone scrambling toward me again.

Now what?

I took off running up my driveway, in the general direction of the Security booth. I prayed Val was still there, but as the booth came into view, I could tell it was dark.

On top of that, the gates were closed—most likely locked.

I had no other option but to head for the main house. As I plunged into the dark lawn, I slowed, trying to recall where trees were located so I could avoid them.

As I approached the manor house, the outdoor lamps began to illuminate dark tree trunks, so I picked up speed. By the time I reached the front door, I was winded. I jammed at the doorbell repeatedly, trying to catch my breath. Had Mrs. Lewis been around, she would've been completely appalled.

A half-asleep Melly finally cracked the door. "Yes? Who's that?" She wiped at her eyes, letting her incredulous gaze rove over me.

I glanced down, realizing I was wearing my reindeer PJs and my hair was doubtless a tousled mess. "It's me, Belinda! Someone's in my house! We have to call the cops!"

Melly peered into the darkness behind me as if trying to ascertain the truth of my story.

"He might be following me!" I shook her shoulders, trying to wake her up. "Let me in!"

Melly slowly stepped aside and let me in, locking the door behind me. She tried to focus, but I suspected she'd taken some kind of sleeping aid. "Tell me again what's going on?" she asked.

"Melly, we need to call the police. Right now."

The petite woman headed straight for the kitchen. That was good. I guessed Lani had already gone home, but at least the kitchen was safe and bright. And it probably had a phone.

Melly gave a prolonged yawn as she flipped on the kitchen lights, flooding the room with an unnaturally bright glow. She glanced around, bewildered. "Now, where does Lani keep that phone again?"

A quick scan revealed it wasn't sitting on a counter, so I raced around throwing drawers and closet doors open. As I did so, I recalled the voice I'd heard in my carriage house bedroom. Was he who I *thought* he was? But why on earth would he break into my house?

It didn't matter why. Anyone who broke into someone's house at three in the morning had nefarious intent, unless they happened to be a relative or a close friend.

And he was neither.

Melly trailed around like a slug, a dramatic change from her well-organized, level-headed persona. She must have taken some strong meds tonight.

"Where's your husband?" I asked, wondering if she had any clue.

"I...don't know. He went to bed early, I think."

I slammed a drawer shut. "But you don't *know*?"

She shook her head just as a click sounded at the kitchen's Dutch door. I whirled around, and the heavy red door swung open.

Jacques strode inside, key ring in hand. "Everything okay in here? I saw lights and heard voices."

I shook my head, incapable of believing this kindly French voice matched the one I'd heard in my carriage house.

But it did.

"Run!" I shouted to Melly. "He's the one who broke into my house! Go get your cell phone!"

Melly gave me a blank stare of disbelief. She didn't even budge.

Jacques continued to move my way. The knives were too far away from me, but I grabbed the first thing I could.

A metal colander. Brilliant.

I edged closer to Melly, who was positioned closest to the hallway door. "Get out," I hissed at her.

Jacques came to an abrupt halt about three feet in front of me. What was he waiting for? I knew he was going to turn me into a victim, like the other women he'd attacked. I raised the colander, trying to shoot daggers at him with my eyes.

To my absolute horror, Melly began to laugh. It was literally an evil laugh, like an animated villain. Her gaze narrowed and her lips twisted up. When she spoke, it became obvious she was both one hundred percent lucid and one hundred percent deadly.

"You *really* didn't know, Belinda? You're kidding me. We were quite sure old Esther Lewis had squealed on Jacques when she croaked her parting words to you."

Chapter 32

An electric charge seemed to shoot through my body. Surely these two weren't working together. Surely this was a huge misunderstanding. Digging deep to find my voice, I finally managed, "Mrs. Lewis told me something wasn't working. I think she meant she wasn't able to fight off her attacker."

Jacques gave Melly a thoughtful look.

Melly snapped her fingers. "Of course. She meant you, Jacques. *You* were the one who wasn't working. She knew you weren't scheduled to work the day Margo was attacked. But she must have noticed you or your car that night, when you came over after I called you."

Jacques looked irritated. "I thought I'd parked where no one could see me, but there is one angle from that side parking lot that gives a view of the back of the carriage house. Esther Lewis must've parked in a spot that gave her a glimpse of my car that night."

Melly sighed as if terribly inconvenienced. "It was only a matter of time until she realized what she saw and tried to blackmail me again. She'd already seen my son chasing Margo outside—probably in some drunken, lovesick gesture—and she wouldn't have hesitated to tell the police about it if I hadn't agreed to pay her. It was good we got her out of the way, Jacques." Melly's gaze swung back to me. "And you've certainly been a busy little bee, haven't you, Belinda? Buzzing around, trying to put all the pieces together? You didn't back off like you should have when we gave you that warning note. Then you interrupted Jacques's attack on Mrs. Lewis, and we knew she'd said something to you—something you might figure out."

"Poor Esther," Jacques said, but his tone was jubilant.

"The hospital called me just before you came, Belinda," Melly said, pulling a faux sad face. "Sadly, Esther Lewis just slipped from our world."

I gripped the metal handles on the colander until they dug into my hands, trying to force myself to acknowledge what was playing out in front of me. Melly had given Jacques orders to kill people. And Jacques had carried those orders out.

"But...what about your son?" I asked, unable to understand how any mother could be so heartless. "Why would you plant his hair on Frannie, knowing it could send him to prison?"

Melly's smile wavered and she shot an accusatory glance at Jacques. "That was a mistake," she said. "Stone had borrowed his father's new hairbrush. Jacques went into my husband's bathroom and took the wrong hair sample."

Comprehension swept over me. Melly had tried to frame her *husband,* only it had backfired.

Noting my stunned look, she ranted on. "As you might have guessed, my husband isn't the brightest. He thought he could have an affair with that...*floozy*...and I wouldn't find out. I had guessed about my husband's relationship, then I found a text he'd sent her, insinuating he was going to be a father again. My husband even gave her a ruby necklace from Chopard and he thought I wouldn't *notice*. Can you imagine—as if I'm not fully informed on our bank accounts at all times? I suppose it doesn't matter, because I got it back in the end."

It was the ruby necklace she'd worn yesterday—the necklace in my dream. Stone the fourth must not have seen it on her.

Jacques huffed impatiently. "Her husband's an idiot."

I wished he'd back up or sit down. Instead, he seemed to have inched closer.

"But he's a *rich* idiot, dear." Melly smiled at Jacques. "See, Jacques understands. He's always understood me, from the time we were young. It only made sense for me to hire him as groundskeeper. I needed someone close who could protect me."

Jacques's eyes darkened. Hatred simmered in his voice, the hatred of a man who had long ago been spurned by the woman he loved. "Stone's a drunk, too."

Was Jacques completely oblivious to the fact that Melly had used him all this time? She'd married for money, leaving her old French friend in the dust until she'd wanted him to do her dirty work. Couldn't he see he was going to be the patsy for her, since he was the one who had killed three women?

I tried to wake him up. "That doesn't justify murder. Margo and Frannie were so young. They had their whole lives in front of them. And now Mrs. Lewis is dead, too. You have to tell the police about Melly's involvement, Jacques."

Jacques took two quick steps forward. I started to run, but he slipped behind me, wrapping a strong arm around my neck. I jabbed the colander backward, hoping to jam the prongs into his stomach, but the metal bowl was too large and unwieldy.

His arm tightened. I flailed at him and squirmed, but couldn't extricate myself. I tried biting his forearm, but I couldn't force my chin down against the strength of his grasp.

"Enough talking," Jacques said. "You escaped from me once tonight, thanks to your enormous snake, but not this time."

What was he talking about? What did Rasputin have to do with anything?

Jacques spoke calmly as he pulled his arm back. I kicked at him, but he had already clamped a hand around each side of my neck. "Melly, you probably won't want to see this. I'll dispose of her and we'll talk in the morning."

Melly nodded and walked into the side hallway. In a practiced move, Jacques locked his fingers together and began to choke me.

I tried to scream, but nothing came out. In a last-ditch effort, I gathered all my strength and hurled the colander to the hard tiles on the floor. It gave a satisfyingly loud bang, then bounced to a stop.

"You should not have done that," Jacques said. He spoke rapidly, his French accent growing stronger with every word. "I owe Melly everything. When my parents came to this country, she was the only one who would talk to me." He squeezed tighter. "Once her idiot husband is out of the picture..."

His words faded out and things were growing dim. I gave one final kick toward his knee, but my strength was so depleted, it didn't make contact.

Suddenly, there was a muffled cracking sound, and Jacques's hands fell from my neck. He thudded onto the floor behind me.

I took several shuddering breaths, then locked eyes with my rescuer.

Stone the fourth gripped the handle of a wide, cast iron pan. His thin hands were shaking, but his eyes weren't the least bit bloodshot. Instead, they seemed lit by a righteous fire.

He kicked at the prone body of Jacques. "Who's the idiot now?" he asked.

* * * *

Stone the fourth didn't waste any time. He raced into the hallway to make calls—on a phone we'd probably walked right past before Melly had trapped me in the kitchen.

When Stone returned, he dug twine out of a drawer and tied Jacques's hands and feet. He dragged Jacques, who seemed unconscious, to the pantry, shoving him in like a sack of potatoes. After pulling the pantry door shut, Stone turned back to me, full of newfound determination. "I'm going to get Melly. I've called Val and he'll be here any minute for you, and the police and ambulance are on their way."

"But what if she has—" I couldn't finish my question, because Stone had already rushed out the kitchen door. I worried Melly might own a gun, but Stone would know if that was the case and would presumably tread carefully.

Too weak to help him, I lurched across the kitchen, grabbing a long knife from the butcher block so I could watch for any movement from the pantry. I sank into a kitchen chair, my eyes unable to focus. My ears were ringing, too. I couldn't seem to breathe deeply enough.

Val rushed in the Dutch door, apologizing profusely. He'd taken a break to get some coffee from the gas station nearby, and he'd gotten to talking to the cashier, he said. That explained his absence in the Security booth when I'd run past.

"In the...pantry," I said, coughing out the last word. My voice seemed to be fading and I felt lightheaded.

Val's brow crinkled, then he strode over and glanced into the pantry. He turned, slamming the door behind him. "Jacques did this?" he asked, motioning to my neck.

Although Stone the fourth might have mentioned my near-strangulation experience to Val, from the way the security guard was gaping at me, I was sure the redness and bruising was now abundantly evident. I couldn't bring myself to answer, because the corners of my vision were going black.

Val caught me as I slipped from my chair to the floor, and then I was out.

Chapter 33

I woke to the regular beeps of a heart monitor. An IV was threaded into my hand, and someone hovered nearby.

I tried to turn to see who was there, but everything hurt from my chest up. "Who?" was all I could wheeze.

Someone's soft hand patted mine, and a woman soothed, "Save your breath. It's me, Ava. I came the moment I heard. Detective Watson called me. They've taken Melly in to the police station, and Jacques is in the hospital for now, but he's already under arrest."

"And Stone?" I asked.

Ava sounded slightly confused. "He's still at home, more sober than he's been for years. He can't believe Melly did this to him."

"Fifth," I clarified.

"Oh! Stone the fifth has gotten out of jail, I believe. He should be getting home soon. Don't worry about him. If I know Lani, she's already cooking him up a breakfast buffet that could feed an army. She's been so upset over his arrest."

I was reminded of Stone's own mother, who also seemed to be upset by his arrest, but mostly because her own plan to frame her husband had gone horribly awry. I wondered what kind of prison time an instigator like Melly would have to serve compared to Jacques, who had done the actual killings.

"Jacques?" I asked.

Ava gave my arm a light squeeze. I still couldn't turn to see her face, but I felt her tear hit my hand. "I hope he dies." Her voice grew stronger, charged by mother-fury. "He took my baby girl's life, and my grandchild's."

I saw a shadow in the doorway, and Adam Fenton walked directly in front of my hospital bed, where I could see him. "There's someone here to speak with you," he said, uncertain. Leaning in, he added, "If you want, I can tell him to leave. It's Stone the fifth."

* * * *

Stone must have come straight to the hospital, because his clothes and hair were rumpled. He looked pale as he approached the end of my bed. Ava had straightened my hospital gown, but it couldn't hide the hideous mess that was my neck. It felt like it had swollen to twice its normal size.

Probably sensing my hesitance, Ava stayed by my bedside. Although I finally knew beyond a doubt that Stone the fifth was innocent, I felt raw and exposed, unable to think clearly.

"It's been terrible for you," Stone started.

"And you," I said.

He frowned and leaned in closer, directly over my feet. Adam must've told him I couldn't look to the sides very well. "No one tried to strangle me."

"Not...your fault," I strained to say.

He winced. "In a way, it was. It happened in our house, and my own mother..." His voice trailed off, disbelieving.

We sat in silence until he finally spoke again. "Anyway, I came straight here because I had to see you. I know you can't talk now. Detective Watson has pieced things together fairly well at this point, given what Dad told him. I'm sure he'll be talking to you eventually, but right now, you need to take your time and get well. That was *way* too close a call."

I tried to offer a reassuring smile, but my lips were too cracked. "We caught him, though."

Stone moved up to my side, positioning his face squarely in front of me. He dropped his lips to my forehead and pressed it with a solemn kiss. "It wasn't worth the risk, Belinda."

It probably wasn't. But things had worked out. I was alive, Stone the fifth was out of jail, and the real murderer was heading to prison. I wondered if Melly would be going there, too. There were so many questions I needed to work through, and I was sure Stone did, too.

"What happened to Frannie?" I asked.

Stone's brow furrowed. "Detective Watson thinks she probably searched our house on Thanksgiving Day and saw something linking Mom to Margo's death. She must have approached Mom at some point and mentioned her hunch. Although Mom never left the house, she did call Jacques on that day to turn off the fountain and to check on your carriage house. It would've been easy enough for him to grab Frannie, strangle her, and dump her behind your place. No one else was around."

Lights blinked in my vision and I reached for Stone's hand. "Need... sleep," I said.

"Of course. This has been too much for you. I need to get home." His jaw clenched. "Dad and I have a lot to talk about."

I wondered if Stone the fifth would be giving his dad a well-timed push for sobriety. It was sad, but maybe watching his wife go off the rails was just the wake-up call Stone the fourth needed. Margo's death had certainly inspired the younger Stone to sober up.

After dropping a light kiss on my cheek, Stone the fifth wheeled around and strode out. Ava's comforting hand returned to my own. "I'm happy to stay as long as you like," she said. "But do you want me to call your parents?"

I hadn't even thought about that. Mom would be beyond horrified if she saw me in this state. She'd likely pack up my carriage house and move me home on the spot.

As I pictured my carriage house, I remembered Rasputin. What had Jacques said about the snake?

And today was Sunday! I had to get Rasputin into the city!

"Phone," I said, blinking to try to clear the spastic lights in my vision.

Ava leaned over. "You're white as a sheet. You're not well," she said. "I'm getting the nurse." She grabbed for the call button and I conked out again.

* * * *

The next time I roused, I felt much better. My neck was less stiff and I was more alert. I even felt hungry.

I tried to recall what I'd last been thinking about. It was something urgent, it seemed. Something to do with my carriage house...

Reginald!

A male voice said, "She's awake." It drew closer, and Detective Hugh Watson leaned in. "You okay?"

"I think so," I said. "I'm feeling better."

"Well, to be honest, you're looking far from bright eyed and bushy tailed, but hang in there. The doctors say you should get out tomorrow."

"I need to make a call today. I've been pet-sitting this snake and the owner will be getting back and he's—"

"Snake's okay," the detective said brusquely. "We checked over your house. I'll need your full story of what happened last night."

"But the snake?" I pressed.

"Right as rain. One of my men had experience with ball pythons—apparently he was quite the reptile enthusiast as a teen—so he slipped your snake back in its cage, slicker than a greased pig."

My stomach clenched. "What? The snake wasn't already in the cage?"

"Oh, no. It had broken out, I guess—the top wasn't fully closed."

I tried to remember the last time I'd messed with the cage. I'd woken in the middle of the night to turn up the heat, and I'd also turned up Rasputin's heat pad. Then the second time I'd woken, there'd been a crash of some kind.

I must've left the top lid slightly ajar, and maybe Jacques had bumped it on his way in? It wouldn't have taken Rasputin long to slide out, especially since he'd been more active lately.

"Where was the snake?" I asked.

"We found it in your bed, actually. The thing had been stunned."

I sucked in my breath. "But he's okay? The snake, I mean?"

"Yes, he started squirming the minute my officer picked him up. Jacques admitted the snake had blocked his path last night, like a fat log. He tripped on it on his way to grab you, which gave you the opportunity to jump out the window. Jacques said he grabbed the snake and tossed it against the wall before running after you."

I let that sink in. Rasputin had inadvertently saved my life. Then he'd been slammed into a wall, and left in state of shock all night.

Reginald would *die* when he heard this.

"I have to get home. I have to take care of the snake," I said.

"We have a veterinarian on the scene," Detective Watson said. "In fact, he wants to see you, too. It's your dad."

Chapter 34

In no time at all, my dad and mom descended on the hospital. It turned out that the last time I'd blacked out, Ava Fenton had told Detective Watson to call my parents. They'd made record time driving down.

Mom took one look at my neck, broke into sobs, then began to pull an arsenal of oils from her purse. She rubbed one on my neck, then demanded the nurses mix one in with hot water. As I tried to survive her ministrations, Dad leaned in, brushing curls from my forehead.

"The snake is going to be fine, sweetie. It was just stunned, that's all. Give me the owner's number and I'll explain everything to him."

Dad would be the best one to quell Reginald's fears, I had no doubt. He had a bedside manner that would make the most experienced doctors jealous. Detective Tucker had left my cell phone by my bed, so I was able to give Dad the number and leave things in his hands for now.

As expected, Mom had already formulated a plan. "Honey, I've talked with Mrs. Fenton, the nice friend who has been sitting with you. When I got here, she filled me in on things, then I asked her to go on home and get some rest. Anyway, she said she'd be more than happy to let you stay with her a little while, just to get your feet back under you. Then Dad and I could rent a truck and come down and move you." Her blue-green eyes urged me to take the path of least resistance, and it was hard not to.

Why *would* I want to stay in a place I'd hardly felt safe in? I could go stay with Adam and Ava for a while. Maybe they'd even have a room I could rent. I didn't have to stay at the Carringtons' estate one more day.

But I thought of Red, how kind he always was. And Val, who finally did show up in a pinch. And Stone the fourth, who had been surprisingly protective last night. And finally, Stone the fifth, who seemed so genuinely upset about the trauma I'd experienced.

"No, Mom. I've told you, I'm building my pet-sitting business, and carriage houses are hard to come by in Greenwich. I'll be safe now."

Mom nodded, although I know that wouldn't be the end of it. She'd probably rope Dad in and make one more attempt to cajole me to leave.

I'd be ready, though. I only had one life to live, and it had taken me years to realize that variety was the key to my happiness. Who knew what other exotic pets would cross my path in months to come? And at the end of a hard day's work, I would have my little carriage house cave to return to. All I had to do was unpack all my boxes, and I was sure it would feel as much like home as Larches Corner.

* * * *

Before I was released on Monday, Ava Fenton dropped off a box of expensive chocolates and made me promise to call her every week. Mom nodded her approval of the plan, then she and Ava chitchatted while I told Adam goodbye.

Dad drove us back to the carriage house, where he and Mom had hung up a "Welcome Home" banner and decorated with a few balloons. Mom had also unpacked the rest of my boxes, perfectly positioning all my favorite things throughout the house. She'd changed the blanket and sheets on my bed, no doubt knowing I'd be picturing poor, prone Rasputin lying on it.

Mom fixed me a cup of tea and spooned some of Jonas's honey into it as Dad settled on the couch with a local newspaper. "How's your throat doing? It looks like the swelling's gone down."

"I can swallow just fine, and I think my voice is back to normal. No more lightheadedness, either."

Dad shot me a quick look, aware I was glossing over things. But Mom gave a sigh of relief. "We were so worried. Your sister said she'd come down for a week, if you want."

I was thankful for my family, which never hesitated to jump to the rescue, but too many people had been hovering over me for too long. I needed time alone to wind down from my recent ordeal.

"I'll be fine," I said, taking a slow sip of tea. "She'll be using her vacation time for Christmas, anyway. I'll see her soon enough."

"Okay. When are you planning to come home?" Mom was obviously having a hard time letting go.

"I'm going to try to fit in a pet-sitting job or two first, but I'll shoot for a day or two before Christmas."

"That would be wonderful. Oh, and Jonas called, asking if you'd be in that Wednesday. Something about a book club breakfast? I figured you'd know what he was talking about."

I didn't. Maybe he was asking me to a book club meeting? But I hadn't even read the book. I made a mental note to give him a call.

As Mom bustled around, loading the dishwasher, my gaze fixated on the empty wall where Rasputin's cage had so recently sat. I felt a twinge of sadness that I hadn't gotten to say goodbye to the valiant snake, but Dad had assured me that there had been a joyous reunion when he'd dropped Rasputin off at Reginald's on Sunday.

"He's most unusual," Dad had declared, and I knew he hadn't been talking about the snake.

Yes, my entire snake-sitting experience had been one of a kind. I'd gone from loathing everything about the snake to owing it my life. I figured the least I could do was to swing by a pet store, pick up some frozen rats, and pay a little tribute to Rasputin someday this week.

* * * *

I stood on the porch as Dad and Mom pulled out. They drove slowly, as if tethered by some kind of magnetic force. I supposed it was the power of parental love.

I turned to go inside, and someone shouted my name. I whirled around and saw Stone the fifth, wearing his tennis gear and loping up to my house, just like he'd done the first time we met.

"Kind of cold to be playing tennis," I said.

"Burning off steam," he explained.

I could understand that. "How's your dad?"

Stone flipped his tennis racket around. "Good. He's actually surprisingly good. We went out to eat last night and he told me all kinds of stuff; really opened up. Apparently, he's known for years that Mom didn't love him. But he'd never strayed until just recently, when Margo came on to him in a big way."

He noted my raised eyebrows. "Yes, you heard me right. Margo came onto *Dad*. You know, the sad thing is that she was probably just like my mom—only interested in his money." He kicked at a pebble.

"How are you doing with all this?" I asked. "I mean, with your mom and everything."

"I don't know," he said. "I feel like I need to get away, you know? Do some soul-searching. I mean, who is Stone Carrington the fifth? I'm not my father. I'm not my mother. But I have to be *someone* in this life, and it can't be who I was before."

I knew what he was trying to say, but I didn't like where it was leading. Something told me Stone was ready to fly the nest, just when I'd begun to feather mine.

"I'm here for you," I said.

He looked at me, his beautiful eyes clouded by sadness and uncertainty. "I know you are, Belinda. Hey—Dietrich wanted to do billiards tonight, for old times' sakes. Get everyone caught up on things and sort of brush aside the shadow of death that's settled on us. We wanted you to come, if you could."

I appreciated his tacit acknowledgement that I might not want to ever step foot in the Carrington manor house again. But I was no coward.

"Sure. What time should I be up there?"

Chapter 35

I actually called Dietrich before attending the billiards party, unsure of what to wear. All too well, I could remember Margo's miniskirt and Louboutins.

Dietrich squealed when I said hello. "Darling! You're okay! Good heavens, what did they do to you? I heard Stone's mother went all crazy Baby Jane and the gardener turned out to be a homicidal Frenchman? And something about a boa constrictor on the lam in your house?"

I filled Dietrich in on all the details Stone must've skimmed over. He whistled. "You need a break like nobody's business. This billiards party is only the tip of the iceberg. I recommend you book a facial and a massage as soon as possible."

I laughed. "I'm feeling mostly recovered, thanks. I'm looking forward to kicking back tonight. But what should I wear?"

After I described my outfit choices, Dietrich agreed that boho-chic should be the look of the evening. I laid out my tiered skirt and ruffled blouse, then decided to putter the rest of the day away. I hit the library first, picking up a copy of *Tess of the d'Urbervilles* on a whim. After all, if Jonas Hawthorne, dairy farmer and all-around Renaissance man, could make time to read this classic, why couldn't I? Wasn't I just as worldly-wise?

I also stopped in at the Episcopal church. Father Jesse was adjusting a silk flower arrangement just inside the door. He barely managed to hide his irritation once he spotted me.

"Miss Blake, wasn't it?"

Sadly, he would probably remember my name for years to come. Stone was right. I had been a bit savage with the poor man.

"Father Jesse." I took a step forward, and he stepped back. "I dropped in to apologize for my rudeness the other day. It was utterly uncalled-for."

A hesitant smile crossed his lips. "I appreciate that. Now, if you don't mind, I need to—"

"Of course. I won't take any more of your time," I said, turning to leave. I hadn't so much as gotten down the first step when the church doors slammed behind me, and I could've sworn I heard them lock.

I knew he hadn't killed Margo, but there was still something I didn't quite trust about Father Jesse Woods.

* * * *

Stone's billiards room felt like a warm embrace. From the Italianesque color scheme—all terra-cottas and warm ochres—to the foods Lani had piled on the wet bar for us, I felt I'd snuggled into some kind of burrow. Greenwich didn't seem quite as foreign tonight.

Sophie and Jet looked exactly like what I'd imagined—both had long hair, multiple piercings, and seemed to exist on nothing but constant physical contact with each other. Only fifteen minutes into things, and Stone, Dietrich, and I decided to play cards and leave Sophie and Jet in their own restaurant-style booth in the corner.

As Stone cut the deck and dealt, I scanned the room. "She was here...the night she died." My voice was barely above a whisper.

"And Frannie too," Dietrich said. "Beautiful girls, gone too soon."

Stone sipped his soda, and I was thankful it wasn't alcohol tonight. "Have you remembered anything about that night?" I asked.

Stone shook his head. "I think I might have argued with Margo," he said. "Then maybe I followed her outside to apologize. I remember feeling cold."

Dietrich sighed, flipping over a Jack of Spades. "You're a buffoon, Stone. Of course you followed her."

We both stared at Dietrich. He took a long drag on his cigarette.

"What do you mean?" Stone asked.

"That night. I saw Frannie out, then I stayed in my car to take a quick smoke, just to calm myself down. I was still ripped about Margo's pregnancy. Anyway, Margo came out the front door. Stone, you were right behind her, trying to catch up, I think. I figured she'd told you about her pregnancy, too."

Stone groaned, smacking his palm to his forehead. "And I was too out of it to remember something as important as that. I *am* a buffoon! Why didn't you tell me this, Dietrich?"

"Because I saw what else happened." Dietrich flicked ashes into a vintage ˌseventies-era ashtray. "I knew you didn't kill her."

"And you didn't tell *me*?" I asked, upset. Dietrich had allowed me to question Stone's innocence.

"I couldn't say anything, because that might place me at the scene of the crime, wouldn't it? I didn't feel the need to tell anyone what I saw, because it didn't incriminate our friendly neighborhood buffoon. After Margo and Stone stopped to argue—right in front of the house, mind you—someone pulled out of the side parking lot. I think it was Mrs. Lewis. By the time her car moved out of the way, Stone was stomping into his front door, and Margo was stumbling off into the yard."

"And you let her go?" I demanded.

"No. I drove up and rolled down my window." Dietrich stopped short, running a hand through his hair. "I called her name and she wouldn't turn around. I figured she was heading toward the Security booth, or maybe she'd parked near the tennis courts. At that point, I didn't care. If she wanted to throw her life over for some jerk, that was her prerogative."

Silence fell over the green felt table. We each clenched a hand of cards like our lives depended on it.

Dietrich had been the last to see Margo alive, I was sure of it. Jacques must have strangled her soon after Dietrich drove off—maybe next to her car, or maybe in the dark lawn. My hand unintentionally flew to my neck, and I could almost feel Jacques's fingers squeezing.

Stone gave my back a comforting rub, and Dietrich grabbed my other hand. They didn't have to say sorry. Jacques had left his mark on all of us, forever.

Sophie and Jet danced our way, a welcome relief in our grief-stricken moment. Jet leaned over Stone's shoulder. "Dude, we don't want to interrupt your game, but Sophie wanted some more of those cheese puff things of Lani's. Can you call her up or something?"

Stone's eyes caught mine and he winked before standing. "Sure thing. Let me find Lani."

* * * *

The billiards party ended soon after Lani's snacks petered out. Dietrich reluctantly agreed to drive Jet and Sophie back to their apartment. Stone flipped on every light in the yard, then walked me back to my house.

I slipped the key into the lock, realizing how easy it had been for Jacques to get in. He'd simply borrowed Melly's copy of my key.

I whirled back to Stone. "Would you be okay if I had my locks changed and didn't give you a copy? I know you're my landlord—I mean, your dad is—but I just can't quite stomach letting someone else have the key right now."

"No problem," Stone said. "And would you hate it if I walked in with you tonight, just to check things over? I'll be fast."

I gave a short laugh. "Look at us. We're both paranoid now. Jacques isn't going anywhere, if Detective Watson has any say in it. Last I spoke to him, he was kicking himself for arresting you."

"He was just doing his job." He shoved his hands in his pockets, trying to fight the chilly wind. I needed to decide.

"You can come in," I said.

True to his word, Stone came in and made a quick check of all the rooms and windows. Before I could even heat water for hot chocolate, he was striding back to the front door.

"Wait," I said, walking to his side. I looked up into those azure eyes, but strangely, I didn't feel an urge to kiss him again.

He turned toward me fully, running his palms up my forearms. "Belinda, you're like no other woman I've ever met. Certainly not like Margo. Sure, she was easygoing like you, but she was using my dad. Maybe she even got pregnant on purpose, hoping he'd leave Mom and shower her with money. It was all a game to her."

I leaned into his chest. "We don't know that. Maybe she was just taken advantage of by an older, married man. Happens all the time."

"Dad's no angel; I know that. He has a fiery temper when he's drunk. But hopefully that won't happen again. He's agreed to join AA."

I drew back, looking up into his serious face. "That's wonderful! Things are working out."

Stone leaned down, but instead of kissing me, he simply took my face in his hands. "I love your enthusiasm for life," he said. "But sometimes there isn't a happy ending. My mom'll probably be in prison for years."

"I'm so sorry," I rushed to cover my insensitivity.

"She deserves it," he said. His tone was brutal and unyielding. Stone had closed the door on his mother, I realized. She was on the outside now, and he might never let her back in.

A tear slid down my cheek. Stone wiped it off and pulled his jacket tighter. "I need to get home," he said. "Get your locks changed, Belinda, and don't give the key to a single soul. You take care of yourself."

When he opened the door, a cold draft of air rushed in, carrying with it an unshakeable surety that Stone the fifth wouldn't be calling me again anytime soon.

Chapter 36

I actually landed three pet-sitting jobs before Christmas, which helped me keep my mind off Stone. Just as I'd feared, it seemed that our billiards party was some kind of last hurrah. Occasionally, I saw Stone's Lamborghini driving by, which was comforting to some degree. If the car was running, the installed Breathalyzer device had verified he wasn't drinking.

Stone the fourth surprised me by dropping off a Christmas gift before I left for my parents'. I was even more surprised by the thoughtfulness of the gift—a collection of expensive coffee syrups. I wondered if his son had told him what I liked. When I flipped the card over, both their names were on it. But Stone the fifth never showed up.

I visited Reginald and dropped off a few frozen rats for Rasputin. The snake looked like he was in perfect health as he slithered around on a new, fake tree. Catching a glimpse of his golden eyes, I leaned toward the cage. "Thanks, buddy. I owe you."

The ball python flicked his tongue, and that was enough for me.

* * * *

On the day I was supposed to drive home, Bluebell wouldn't start. I gave her a serious pep talk, then gave the key one final turn. She jumped to life.

Katrina must've relayed my car troubles to Tyler, who descended on the Volvo the moment I pulled into my parents' driveway. It took him all of five minutes to announce that I needed a new car battery.

Katrina looked thoughtful as she greeted me. Her baby bump was showing a tiny bit more, highlighted by her fitted red sweater.

"You look smashing in red," I said.

"As do you," she said, nodding at my own red coat.

I slipped it off, heading to the kitchen for some coffee. Dad stood to hug me, then stepped aside so Mom could have her turn.

"How's Stone?" Katrina asked, her eyes eager. There was only one Stone Carrington she was interested in—the one I'd kissed.

"He's good. They sent us some coffee syrups." I dug around in my luggage for the bottles I'd packed, handing them over to Mom.

Mom fingered a bottle of Creme de Menthe. "You need to call Jonas," she said abruptly. "He called again, about that book club thing. I didn't have my notepad nearby to write down the details. I think it's happening tomorrow morning?"

"I'll call him," I said, realizing I'd neglected to do that when I was in Greenwich. "How's his mom?"

"About the same, which is actually good," Mom said. "She's holding steady."

Katrina whisked me off to the living room, where she demanded I walk her through what happened in Greenwich. When I got to the part about Jacques trying to strangle me, I thought she was going to blow a gasket.

"How *dare* he!" she shouted.

Tyler moseyed into the living room and dropped into a nearby chair. Although his demeanor was relaxed, I knew he was ready to talk Kat down if she got too wound up. My sister could go from zero to Scales of Justice vengeance machine in about three seconds flat.

"I hope he's in prison, because I want to kill him," she bellowed.

"It's under control," I said. "He's in prison and he's going to be found guilty of murder. I'm fairly certain there's nothing you could do to make his life worse. But thanks, sis."

Tyler unobtrusively turned on the TV and flipped to an episode of *Psych*, one of Katrina's favorites.

The storm blew over fairly quickly, and I was thankful. I had never been so ready for Christmas.

* * * *

The next morning, I pulled on my favorite jeans, an old Ms. Pac-Man T-shirt, and my red coat. I was sure my mismatched attire would raise eyebrows in Greenwich, but I'd seen just about how far having the perfect outfit could get you, and I wasn't impressed.

I pulled up to the little coffee shop in town, cleverly titled "The Coffee Shoppe." I believe they thought adding the "e" at the end would give it a certain French flair.

I could see Jonas sitting on a barstool in front of the window. He jumped up and came out to greet me. We shared an awkward hug.

"Thanks for coming," he said. "Figured you might want to get a taste of our kaffeeklatsch. I thought I'd show you I don't just herd cattle all day or something like that."

"Hmm." I glanced at the small group of five that sipped at coffee in silence, books on their laps. "Herding cattle might actually be more exciting."

"Let me introduce you," Jonas said, leading me to a chair. I slipped my own copy of *Tess of the d'Urbervilles* from my oversized tote. I didn't have to let on that I'd read the Wikipedia summary, then skipped to the ending of the book. I planned to spend more time on the next read, because some ornery part of me wanted to keep up with Jonas.

After introductions were made, a woman swept into the shop, setting the bell ringing. Jonas's gaze shot her way. She was a bit taller than I was. She had an oval face and dark eyes that hinted at mystery and sadness. She reminded me of an Italian painting.

Jonas stood. "Delia, this is Belinda. Belinda, Delia."

So this was the elusive bakery owner. As she sat, Jonas asked, "You want the usual?"

She nodded, and a something broke loose inside me and rattled around. Jonas knew her usual.

He turned to me. "What would you like, Belinda?"

"Just a small caramel latte, please," I said. I didn't even have a "usual." In fact, I rarely ordered the same coffee twice.

When Jonas returned to his chair, bearing two cups of coffee, he handed Delia hers first. I was left with no doubt.

He liked her.

* * * *

The discussion turned out to be more rousing than I expected. One older woman argued that Angel Clare was the real villain in the book, sending Tess to her doom.

I thought about Melly and Jacques. About Stone the fourth's alcoholism, which he'd very nearly passed on to his son. About Margo, who might have been a moneygrubber just like Melly Carrington.

"Maybe they're all hopelessly flawed," I said.

Jonas's eyebrows raised, and I knew he wanted to talk. Right then. Instead, we had to sit through the rest of the discussion, which Delia somehow dominated with her occasional but utterly brilliant remarks.

After bidding the friendly crew goodbye, Delia, Jonas, and I remained. The lunch crowd was descending on The Coffee Shoppe.

Delia dropped her paper cup in the trash and walked to Jonas's side. "So nice to meet you, Belinda. Thanks for joining our discussion. I hope to see you again."

I found myself wishing she didn't seem so earnest, so I could dislike her more.

Delia adjusted her purse and gave Jonas a fleeting smile. "See you next week," she said.

The moment the door closed behind her, Jonas gave me a look. "Sit down."

As usual, I did what he asked without even questioning it. Why did I do that? I jumped back to my feet, giving him a challenging glare. "I feel like standing," I said.

He didn't buy it. If anything, he looked more concerned. "Something's wrong, Belinda. What happened?"

That was all it took.

He had tapped the dam, and it broke.

I raced outside, hoping to hide the tears that had already started falling. I unlocked Bluebell and climbed in, but Jonas caught the door before I could slam it.

"Let me in," he said.

And I couldn't stop myself. I did.

Jonas settled into my passenger seat as if he'd been in this car a thousand times before. My eyes traveled over his rugged jacket, his rough, strong hands, and finally I let them travel to his face.

He watched my every move, as if judging what to do next.

Because Jonas always knew what to do next.

"Tell me what happened to you," he said.

So I did. I told him everything.

And he didn't turn his back on me, like Stone had. Instead, as Jonas carefully traced the still-faint bruises on my neck, he gave me an intensely tender gaze.

"Don't let it change you," he said.

And I could feel my soul start to heal.

* * * *

When I got home, Katrina was waiting for the lowdown on the book club, so we cloistered ourselves once again in our old room.

But I didn't want to talk about the club. "Jonas Hawthorne," I said, and my voice was filled with wonder.

Katrina stared, then smiled. "I wondered when you were going to wake up," she said.

Please turn the page for an exciting sneak peek of

Heather Day Gilbert's next

Belinda Blake, Exotic Pet Sitter mystery

BELINDA BLAKE AND THE WOLF IN SHEEP'S CLOTHING

coming soon wherever e-books are sold!

Chapter 1

Rainy weather was an introvert's best friend.

At least that's the way I'd felt for years, but after four days of nonstop drizzle alternating with heavy deluges in Greenwich, Connecticut, I was about to change my mind. I needed to get out of my stone carriage house, needed to take in the rich smells of spring, needed to touch the velvety red tulip petals that had finally started to unfurl in my flowerbed out back.

I cozied up on my blue couch, setting my warm mug of Arabica coffee on the low table in front of me. Snagging one of my favorite Agatha Christie mysteries, *By the Pricking of My Thumbs*, off my shelf, I tried to pick up where I'd left off.

Instead, my gaze wandered to my wide front window, where I could see the shamrock-green lawn stretching up to the Carringtons' manor house. I tried not to think of my last encounter with Stone Carrington the fifth, but I couldn't help myself.

When Stone had broken a couple months' silence and shown up on my doorstep in early March, it was obvious something had changed. I could see it in his face—the way those turquoise eyes shone with expectation. I figured he'd tell me he'd found someone who'd made him forget all the stresses of his complicated family life.

Instead, he'd said something far worse.

He was heading to Bhutan.

Dietrich, our artist friend, had told Stone about a yoga retreat in the mountains of Bhutan that had revolutionized his perspective on just about everything. After researching the retreat, Stone had decided it might be just the thing to clear his head.

"I have to get strong enough to fight my own demons," he'd said.

"I think you already are," I'd responded.

He had smiled wistfully, then pulled me into a hug. His luxuriant leathery scent utterly wrecked my ability to concentrate, so I relaxed into his long arms.

"I'm glad you believe in me, Belinda." His lips had brushed my curls as he murmured into my hair. "And Dad's partner assures me that it's all systems go for me to take over the family hedge fund business. But I don't feel right stepping into that position until I'm sure that's what I want to do. I don't want to be locked into a life that sucks my soul out." He drew back and I met his serious gaze. "You understand what I mean. Look at you—you started a pet-sitting business in Manhattan, then you moved to Greenwich and grew your clientele even more. I love that you're so unafraid. That's how I want to live."

Several responses had run through my mind, but I was only able to articulate one.

"I do understand," I'd said.

And with that, I'd inadvertently given my blessing on Stone's big adventure, but I knew that was the way it should be. I would never hold someone back from finding their purpose in life.

Besides, my feelings for Stone were seriously conflicted. Since my visit home at Christmas, my parents' neighbor, dairy farmer Jonas Hawthorne, had given me weekly calls to discuss the classics I was reading along with his book club. Every time I hung up the phone with him, I found myself smiling like I'd won the sweepstakes. I hadn't analyzed our relationship yet, but I was pretty sure my psychologist sister, Katrina, would be more than happy to help me figure things out.

Life in the carriage house had seemed dreadfully boring since Stone hopped his plane for Bhutan. Doubtless, he'd had a full month of epiphanies while I'd stayed mostly housebound, playing video games and taking every pet-sitting job I could to pay the bills.

I turned back to *By the Pricking of My Thumbs.* I was reading the same sentence for the fourth time when my cell phone rang. I grabbed it from the coffee table and barked, "Hello," without even bothering to check who was calling first.

A woman's soft voice filled the line. "Is this Belinda Blake, the pet-sitter?"

"It is." I was ready to jump on any sitting job she offered, because it'd been two weeks since my last one.

"I'm Dahlia White. I have several large-breed animals I was wondering if you'd be available to help care for. You'd need to start in a couple of days and I'd need you for an eight-day stint. I'm sorry it's such late notice, but the other person I asked wasn't able to do it."

Dogs—my favorite. I responded enthusiastically. "Sure thing. I grew up with German Shepherds, so I'm no stranger to the larger breeds."

After a miniscule pause, Dahlia responded. "Well, that's the thing. They're not dogs—they're wolves."

I caught my breath as she rushed on.

"But my fluffy darlings are no trouble to care for, I promise. They're like my babies. You wouldn't have to do much, just help my primary feeder with his chores so he wouldn't have to stay overtime to get things done.

Since you'd advertised that you specialize in exotic pets, I assumed you would be quite comfortable with unusual jobs like this."

I hesitated. I'd never been to a wolf preserve—much less seen a wolf up-close—but the way Dahlia was talking, you'd think they were just like dogs.

"Umm." I floundered about for something to say, but nothing coherent sprang to mind.

"I'll tell you what, why don't you look up the preserve website online and check us out? It's the White Pine Wolf Preserve site. Many of our guests have left reviews of their tour experience, and they're all extremely positive about their interactions with the wolves."

"Okay. I'll do that and get back to you." I wanted to buy myself time.

"That sounds great. Actually, if it's not too much trouble, could you call me back in a couple of hours so I'll know if I need to find someone else?" She gave a brief pause. "Oh, and I forgot to mention that I'll pay top dollar for your services—I know you come highly qualified."

She must have read my endorsements from the Greenwich and Manhattan elite. I always tried to snag a quote when one of my wealthy clients praised my pet-sitting skills.

I had to admit, the top dollar payment Dahlia promised was more than a little tempting because it was sorely needed. I agreed to check out the preserve and touch base in an hour. As I hung up the phone, a book slid from my overstuffed bookshelf and hit the floor.

I walked over to pick it up and glanced at the title.

White Fang.

Was it a good sign, a bad sign, or just a coincidence?

At this point, it was impossible to guess.

* * * *

The White Pine Wolf Preserve website yielded minimal information. As I should have guessed, the featured reviews were completely positive. One guest bragged about how her autistic son had made an instant connection with a white wolf and had enjoyed his time petting it. A teen posted that during the tour, a timber wolf had begged for his piece of watermelon—and when he'd offered it through the fence, the wolf had gobbled it up and begged for more.

I clicked on Dahlia White's "About the Owner" section, and it certainly tugged at the heartstrings. Dahlia had rescued her animals from lives of fighting or even from imminent euthanization.

"Once I knew of the plight of these animals, it would have been heartless to walk away," Dahlia was quoted as saying in the local paper. "My animals have found healing here, and it's a joy to share their story with our visitors."

Everything sounded very professional, and the pictures showed people and wolves frolicking like it was the most normal thing in the world. The grounds looked spotless, and the wolves had clean teeth and coats, so it seemed they were well looked after.

I grabbed an umbrella, unable to sit around any longer. After pulling on my rubber boots, I sloshed out to the mailbox. My mom had mentioned that she'd sent me a care package, and I'd been anxiously awaiting it, even though I knew it would likely be filled with inedible cookies, healthy snacks, and vitamins the size of horse pills.

Creaking open the black mailbox door, I peered inside. There didn't seem to be a yellow package slip. Instead, I withdrew a handful of bills. I didn't even want to think about whether I had the money in my account to cover these, plus the rent, plus repairs on my car.

My older-model Volvo, which I fondly referred to as Bluebell, was temporarily out of commission. Bluebell had decided to shed her rusting tailpipe smack in the middle of I-95, and I was still waiting for the replacement to come in.

Sure, I could ask my parents for money, but it felt like giving up to have to do that. I had survived in Manhattan, scraping by on smaller pet-sitting jobs, so when I moved to Greenwich last year, I'd had high hopes that my business would take off.

Although Greenwich had widened my clientele, my income was still somewhat sporadic. And, truth be told, I needed an influx of money right now. My video game review checks wouldn't arrive until the end of April.

I shoved the mail into my jeans pocket and trudged back to my house. I knew what I had to do. Besides, it couldn't be that hard to work at a wolf preserve, could it? And the experience would look fantastic in the bio on my website. I mean, if I could handle pet-sitting wolves, what *couldn't* I handle?

Summoning my confidence, I dialed Dahlia's number and agreed to come in the next morning to sign the contract and tour the facility. She sounded understandably relieved. The number of people in Greenwich who would like to work with wolves could probably be counted on one hand—and I was betting those were the people who were already employed at the preserve.

Once I'd squared things away with Dahlia, my next call was to Red, the Carringtons' chauffeur. Once Stone the fourth had heard my car was in the shop, he'd volunteered Red's driving services so I could get where I needed to go. I wasn't sure if Stone the elder was being kind because I was a good tenant or because he felt he owed me something since I'd narrowly escaped a life-or-death situation in his house this past winter.

Red's gruff voice filled the line. "Yes?"

Red's ex-Army persona didn't throw me, even though his habit of carrying concealed weapons did make him seem more like a bodyguard than a proper chauffeur.

"Red, could you run me somewhere tomorrow morning? We can stop for Dunkin' Donuts." I knew Red had a sweet spot for their oversized bear claw pastries.

"You don't have to butter me up, Belinda." He chuckled. "I'll take you wherever you need to go. What time?"

"How about eight-thirty—that'll give us a little time to stop by Dunkin' D. And no, I'm not buttering you up—I promise. I like their coffee."

However, if the coffee and bear claw happened to loosen Red's lips as to any updates about Stone the fifth, it would be a happy bonus.

* * * *

Red pulled up ten minutes early, but I'd known this was his habit, so I was ready. I had donned jeans, my Doc Martens, and a light blue, paint-splattered Columbia University hoodie I'd swiped from my dad the last time I visited home. Normally, I wouldn't wear such casual gear for my first visit with a client, but the wolves were outside and though the rain had stopped, the ground had turned to mush.

I splashed through a couple of puddles to meet Red, who had walked around to open the door for me. He didn't bat an eye at my unusual attire, but instead tipped his chauffer's hat toward me in an old-fashioned gesture of respect that warmed my heart. Red always made me feel like I fit into Greenwich society, even though it was quite obvious I didn't.

Sharing Dahlia's address, I carefully omitted the fact that we were heading to a wolf preserve. If Red knew what I was stepping into, it was possible he'd balk at driving me there, and I didn't want to have to pay for a cab or car service.

On the way, Red stopped at the Dunkin' Donuts drive-through to pick up our goodies. He drove into a parking spot and distributed our food.

I took a slow sip of the deliciously strong coffee. Red pulled the tab back on his cup and positioned it in the holder, then started backing the car out.

I tried to sound casual. "So, has Stone called lately from Bhutan?"

The middle-aged chauffeur threw a quick glance at me in the rearview mirror. "Matter of fact, he did call, just yesterday. Wanted me to take his car in for inspection—he'd remembered it expires this month." His lips curled into a half-smile as he bit into his bear claw, bits of icing dropping all over the napkin in his lap.

I wasn't sure if he was smiling about the pastry, or about having the opportunity to get behind the wheel of Stone's yellow Lamborghini. I figured it was the Lamborghini.

An inadvertent sigh escaped my lips, which seemed to trigger Red's memory.

"He did ask about you," he added hastily.

"And?"

Red grinned. "He wondered if you'd been pet-sitting any more snakes."

I'd watched a ball python named Rasputin last year, and the experience was memorable, to say the least. "Ha. No more snakes of late."

I didn't add that I'd made a few trips into Manhattan just to see Rasputin. I kind of owed that snake, after all, and on some reptilian level, I was convinced he liked me.

Chartreuse-budded tree limbs arced alongside the road as we drove through a heavily wooded area. When Red slowed to turn off on Dahlia's road, I realized we'd gone a full three minutes without seeing one typical Greenwich McMansion—or any houses at all. Although I'd grown up in a rural area, the complete seclusion of Dahlia's wolf preserve felt a little sinister.

Halfway up the drive, a gate stood open, with a large sign affixed to it reading *White Pine Wolf Preserve*. My cover was blown. I slid down lower in the seat because I knew what was coming next.

Red pulled to an abrupt stop and turned to stare at me. "You sure this is the right place?"

I didn't meet his eyes. "Yes, it is. This is the address I gave you, right?"

He didn't even bother to answer my question. "Will you be working directly with wolves? This job sounds too risky."

"I don't know the details yet," I answered honestly. "And the owner said they're perfectly safe."

"Of course she would," Red muttered into his coffee cup.

Chapter 2

"Please keep driving," I said firmly.

Red finally gave a halfhearted nod and gently pressed the gas. As we neared the end of the long, paved drive, the White Pine Wolf Preserve began to resemble the tourist destination it was. An extended, renovated red barn bore a *Visitor's Center* sign. Behind the barn, I caught a glimpse of a white farmhouse with fresh new siding. Red pulled into a space in the good-sized parking lot adjacent to the barn.

He seemed to struggle for words, like he was hoping I'd back out of this, but his chauffeur decorum won out. "What time should I pick you up?" he asked briskly.

"I'll text you." I couldn't allow myself to chicken out, uneasy as I felt. Dahlia was counting on me and I knew she'd never find anyone else on such short notice.

Since no one had appeared to greet me, I gave a brief, hopefully confident nod to Red and stepped out of the car. I shouldered my purse and strode toward the barn. The outside bore a glossy coat of apple-red paint, and plum and lemon colored pansies had been painstakingly planted in the window boxes.

I pushed open the rustic wooden door. The inside of the visitor's center was just as carefully kept. The walnut plank floors and massive overhead beams emphasized the spaciousness of the barn. The shop was well organized, and I didn't find myself bumping into display tables like I usually did in places like this. Although there were the predictable wolf trinkets and T-shirts, it was the homemade items such as natural stone jewelry, handmade soaps, and unusual jellies that drew my eye. Burning wax melts and small twinkle-light grapevine trees lent the place a welcoming air.

"Good morning." A chic woman with a British accent stepped from behind the natural wood counter and made her way toward me. "How may I help you today? Were you interested in a tour?"

"Actually, I was looking for the owner, Dahlia White. I'm supposed to be helping with her animals."

The woman smiled, adjusting the silk scarf knotted around her slim neck. With her dark pixie haircut and flawless makeup, she looked like she belonged in an upscale art gallery, not working the cash register at a wolf preserve.

"You must be Belinda!" she said, extending a hand. "Dahlia had to motor into town before her trip, so I was instructed to have Shaun give you a tour around our facilities. I'm Evie Grady, by the way—Dahlia's administrative assistant."

Evie pulled a cell phone from her pocket, punching in a number to call Shaun, whoever he was. After a brief conversation, she returned her attention to me.

"He'll be here in a moment. Shaun Fowler has worked at White Pine since it opened three years ago, and he's one of the best tour guides out there. He puts the tourists at ease with his sense of humor, which is important for their first encounter with the wolves."

I still found it hard to believe I was gearing up for *my* first wolf encounter. "That's wonderful," I murmured.

Oblivious to my discomfort, Evie launched into a brief tour of the visitor's center, which boasted a cute kitchen area where employees could get coffee and take lunch breaks. She also pointed out a hand-drawn, framed map of the preserve that hung over the mantel of the stone fireplace.

"We have a thirty-acre fenced area for the packs," she said, gesturing to a thick green border line on the map.

There was more than one pack?

Evie rolled on with her monologue. "Shaun will be able to tell you more about each of the animals and how they came to us. I'm sure it won't take you long to acclimate to the routine, given that you specialize in exotic pets?"

"I should be able to pick things up quickly," I said. "I'm good with animals."

And not just any animals. The truth was that I'd built my business by watching the animals other sitters didn't want to touch. The wealthy tended to buy unusual pets, and they didn't like to leave them unattended when they went on trips. It was usually a win-win for me when the pets were easy to care for, like hermit crabs or turtles. Wolves had never factored into my consideration before, but I reassured myself that I would be well-compensated for whatever I was required to do on the preserve.

An oversized fellow bumbled into the door. He wore a neon green vest that had the preserve name emblazoned on it in white reflective lettering.

"Hi, I'm Shaun," he said, giving me a relaxed smile. "I take it you're Belinda Blake?" His eyes traveled over my hair, then slowed as they reached my face. His freckled cheeks flushed. "Say, you wouldn't happen to be *the* Belinda Blake who's a game reviewer, would you? You kind of look like her."

I was surprised, but flattered. I beamed at him. "I'm that Belinda, yes."

His eyes widened. "I read your reviews every month. You're one of the best."

"Thanks," I said. I couldn't help warming to a kindred gamer spirit.

I'd been reviewing video games in my free time for years, but since I'd landed a regular column at a bigger magazine early last year, I'd picked up substantially more followers. In fact, I was about to launch my own Twitch stream, where gamers could watch me live-play some of the newest releases.

"Let me get you a vest," he said, rushing into the kitchen and retrieving one. As he handed it over, I pretended to shield my eyes from the green glare.

"It's quite loud, but it keeps the employees visible," he explained, then gestured toward my right pocket. "There's a pepper spray in every vest, just in case of emergencies."

I patted at the canister in my pocket and raised my eyebrows.

"It's standard at wild animal preserves like this," he said. "Trust me, I've never used mine."

Shaun headed outside, so I followed him. It was a good thing I'd worn a hoodie, because the fickle April temperature had dropped since morning.

Shaun led me up a wide trail into the woods. A tall, chain-link fence came into view.

"It's eight feet high, just to be on the safe side," he explained. "We have to pay close attention after storms, because if a tree falls on the fence, those wolves can climb right up and out. They're very resourceful." He sounded like a doting father, proud of his child for doing something like punching the class bully.

"How'd you get interested in wolves?" I asked, my Doc Martens sinking into yet another puddle.

"I met Dahlia when she toured the nature center I used to work at in Stamford. She told me she was going to open a wolf preserve in Greenwich, and she said she was looking for outstanding tour guides, like me. I started working here the first day White Pine opened—about four months after we'd met."

I wanted to know more about my new employer. "So Dahlia already had experience with wolves?"

Shaun ground a sprouting blackberry vine underfoot. "Nope. Not a bit, actually. She was coming off a divorce, and she wanted to use this property in hopes of making a difference in the world. After reading up on wolf and wolf-dog breeding, she discovered that many of those animals wind up abandoned or euthanized because they're so uncontrollable—not surprising, because they're wild, right? Anyway, she dedicated herself to providing a shelter for them."

"That's admirable," I said, nearly running into Shaun's wide back as he paused to toss a rock from the path.

"Yeah, and Dahlia's also the one who puts in long hours to make sure each new wolf is integrated into a pack. We have two packs here, and at the moment, each pack has three wolves. Creating packs isn't easy—it can be brutal, like *The Hunger Games*. See, in the wild, packs form naturally around animals from the same bloodline. But in captivity, wolves can resort to serious infighting to establish dominance. I hate to say it, but omega wolves sometimes get killed in the process."

I slowed. So I'd signed up for an eight-day job, working with beasts who even killed their own kind? Maybe I should get out now, while the getting was good.

Shaun hiked past a double-gated entrance set into the fence line. A slight movement caught my eye, and I peered into the enclosed area. A gangly brown wolf with a black face was perched on a rock, her eyes fixed on me. It was quite mesmerizing. I actually started walking toward the fence, but Shaun didn't notice and kept plowing forward on the trail. I hurried to catch up and realized he was asking questions about my latest game review.

He finally stopped when we came to a second gated enclosure. After opening the first set of gates, Shaun led me toward the second. A large, white wolf loped our way, shoving its nose through the chain links. Shaun gave the animal's nose and part of its muzzle a thorough petting, and I could swear the wolf was smiling.

The wolf turned its butterscotch colored eyes to me. I wasn't sure how to mask my fear, but I knew enough not to stare right into its eyes. The wolf sniffed at the air, and I took a brief glance at its face.

It appeared that the animal was merely curious, not hostile.

"This one's named Njord," Shaun explained. "He's the only wolf that's been bred in captivity on the preserve, and he's the alpha of this pack." He reached out and the wolf approached his hand again. "And as you can see, he's about as tame as a wolf can be. He's my favorite to take into the crowd when I give a tour."

Njord licked his lips, and the sudden sharpness in his look made me antsy. "Is he hungry?" I asked.

"Might be. That's not my job—Rich O'Brien handles that end of things. We'll catch up with him today so he can show you what's what."

Leaving Njord lingering at the fence line, we headed out of the enclosure and back onto the trail. Shadowy forest branches filtered the sunlight, and we walked alongside a full, rippling creek that probably supplied water to the wolves. If Shaun wasn't with me, I'd be tempted to grab a book and a blanket and plop down on one of the rocky overhangs. The extensive grounds really seemed like the perfect place to be alone with nature and one's own thoughts.

A wolf's howl broke the silence, triggering a chorus of howling responses, but Shaun only grinned. "They talk to each other and sometimes to us. It tends to make the tourists nervous, but howling doesn't always mean wolves are on the prowl for food."

I was going to have to take his word for it, because to my ears, the howls sounded more than a little ominous.

The visitor's center eventually came into view, and I realized we'd made a complete loop around the property. A man emerged from the side door of the barn, loading something into a bucket in a wheelbarrow, and Shaun shouted to him. "Rich! I've got the new girl here."

Rich, a slim man in his mid-fifties, walked my way, but didn't extend a hand. "I have meat on my hands—loading it up for the wolves—but it's nice to meet you. Belinda, was it?"

"Yes, that's me. Belinda Blake."

Shaun gave me a quick grin. "It was great hanging with a gamer legend like yourself. Sorry if I geeked out a little. I'll catch you later."

My face colored a bit as Shaun lumbered off. Rich politely ignored my discomfort and went back to raiding the off-white refrigerator in the kitchen. I made a mental note to store my lunch in the other fridge that had a sign marked "Staff Use."

I held the side door open as Rich returned to deposit handfuls of raw meat into the bucket. Why didn't he didn't bother wearing gloves for this messy operation?

"I like to use the wheelbarrow because it's less disruptive than the golf cart," Rich explained as he continued his back and forth. "And I don't touch the meat with gloves, so it smells more natural to the wolves."

I was impressed with the way Rich seemed to put the wolves first in his caretaking. It was the same way I tried to operate as a pet-sitter. We'd probably get along fine as I helped him...although it was beyond me how I would feed raw meat to wolves without looking like an oversized, tasty morsel myself.

Evie strolled into the kitchen. Her garnet lipstick had been freshly reapplied, and the faint smell of spicy perfume drifted our way. Rich seemed oblivious to Evie's high-class beauty, his final load of meats in hand as he used his backside to slam the fridge door shut.

Evie's nose wrinkled at the sight of the raw, red mess stuffed into the buckets, and she quickly turned to me. "Belinda, would you mind sticking close to the visitor's center? Maybe Rich can show you how to feed the wolves tomorrow. Dahlia's on her way back and she'll arrive soon, and I think you should talk with her to nail down details before she leaves on her trip."

"Sure." I certainly didn't mind postponing my first feeding adventure.

We took our leave of Rich and headed back into the gift shop. Evie's cell phone gave a metallic ring, and when she picked up, her smile quickly faded and her tone turned serious. She strode out the main door, firmly closing it behind her.

Finding her secretive behavior strange, I absently started browsing the clothing racks. I was seriously contemplating picking up a snarling wolf T-shirt emblazoned with the words *Alpha Mom* for my pregnant sister Katrina, when a hipster dude with clear plastic glasses walked in.

He breezed past me and entered the kitchen area. I realized he probably thought I was a tourist, so I followed him into the kitchen to introduce myself.

He had just settled into a chair and was aimlessly thumbing through his phone as if boredom was his personal cross to bear. He didn't even look up as I lurked in the doorway. When he continued to look at his phone, I cleared my throat.

After what felt like five minutes but was probably only one, he finally glanced up and grunted.

"You new here?" he asked.

I nodded, curious as to what his story was. "I'm Belinda. Do you work here, too?"

The guy offered a smile that didn't reach his eyes, revealing small, straight teeth. "I'm Carson White. My mom runs the place."

"Oh! Nice to meet you. I haven't met your mom yet."

As if he couldn't care less, his eyes slid back to his phone screen. With his straight-leg blue chinos and plaid button-up shirt, he struck me as one of those preppy types who seemed endlessly restless and unhappy. As I turned to leave, a young woman with a long black ponytail walked in. Carson instantly snapped to attention the moment she spoke.

"Have you seen my vest?" she asked, but it sounded like a demand.

Carson jumped to his feet and began rummaging through the coat rack on the back wall. After he produced a lime green vest and handed it to the woman, she turned to speak to me.

"You're the new girl, Belinda, right? I'm Veronica—I'm one of the tour guides."

Carson injected himself into our conversation, probably in an attempt to get Veronica to turn her luminous brown eyes his way. "She's working on her Master's degree."

She shrugged her vest on over her fitted shirt. "I'm writing my thesis now. It's about the wolves, actually. I've titled it *Captive Wolves and Their Interactions with Humans: Pack or Prey?*"

The title seemed poorly worded to me, but it did seem like an interesting topic, and one Veronica would get plenty of fodder for while she worked at the preserve. I really hoped she'd conclude that captive wolves looked at humans like their pack, because the alternative was frightening.

Veronica swept out the side door, and Carson followed, hot on her heels. I was curious as to what Carson's relationship was with the lovely Veronica, if any. Had he been waiting here for her to show up?

I glanced out the window. Veronica was speed walking toward the woods, leaving Carson in her dust. Apparently, the attraction wasn't mutual.

I headed back into the gift shop. Evie hadn't returned, and I wondered how long I was going to have to wait to meet Dahlia. I considered calling Red and asking him to pick me up, but instead I decided to take a little jaunt outside and try to get my bearings at my new job.

Just as I opened the front door, a green Prius whipped into a spot in front of the visitor's center and a woman seemed to wrestle with her seat before getting out. Her frowsy dishwater-blonde hair and worn chambray shirt, half-tucked into her jeans, gave the impression of someone who didn't put much time into her appearance—an anomaly in this town. Gripping a plastic shopping bag, she bustled to my side. Her eyes darted to my face, then to the woods, adding to the impression that she was a woman constantly in motion.

"Good to see you—Belinda, right? I'm Dahlia, the one who called you. I'm *so* sorry I wasn't here—I had to pick up some last-minute pet supplies and the person ahead of me was buying out the store, it seemed!" She tried to shove her fluffy bangs to the side, but they curtained her eyes again. "Let's go inside, shall we? I need to talk with Evie briefly, then I'll explain your position to you."

"Actually, Evie's not in there right now," I said.

All her fidgeting stilled for a moment. "Really? That's not like her." She readjusted the bag in her hand, a bewildered look on her face. "Right. Well, let's go on in and we'll talk about what you'll be doing here."

I pushed the door open so Dahlia could walk in first. I glanced around, then immediately felt like a liar. Evie was sitting at the kitchen table, munching on a half-eaten croissant.

Dahlia turned back to me with a strange expression, and I felt like I'd failed some kind of test. "She wasn't here when I walked outside," I rushed to explain.

"Of course," Dahlia said, but there was a dubious note in her voice.

As she bustled into the kitchen, I trailed behind, trying to understand why Evie had felt the need to sneak into the side door after her phone call. It seemed the administrative assistant was hiding something, and I wondered what it was.

Made in the USA
San Bernardino, CA
02 June 2020

72649159R00119